AMBASSADOR 1A: THE SAHARA CONSPIRACY

PATTY JANSEN

CAPRICORNICA PUBLICATIONS

GET FREE EBOOKS

Visit pattyjansen.com
or scan the QR code below with your phone to sign up for Patty's
mailing list. You get four series starter ebooks for free!

1

THE CALL CAME late in the evening, a few hours after we had gone to bed. Exchange staff came to wake us, even though they knew we were on a flight before dawn, and I'd given instructions not to disturb us.

Dare I say the word *honeymoon*?

"It's very urgent," said the young girl who had been given the unenviable task to knock on our door and deal with my slightly rumpled appearance and even more rumpled temper.

I took the reader she held out to me. My eyes needed a few seconds to figure out if I was reading Coldi or Isla, never mind what was on the screen.

Words fought their way into the lingering fogginess of sleep.

Threat to security and Nations of Earth.

Immediately . . .

African . . .

Seriously, what the fuck.

Thayu had also gotten up and stood as a warm presence behind my back. She looked over my shoulder. She read some Isla, but wouldn't understand the nuances of the language, or, in this case, the lack of nuance.

Mr Wilson, you are to see me in my office immediately regarding an immediate threat to Nations of Earth security relating to the African plans.

It was signed *Simon Dekker,* who was one of Acting President Sigobert Danziger's henchmen.

As soon as I'd read it, the text vanished. I stared at the blank screen for a few dumb second before I realised that this was one of those untraceable high-security messages, keyed to a high-resolution scan of my retinas that every Nations of Earth employee with any level of clearance had to submit. I was surprised that the thing worked, because my eyes certainly weren't working too well.

I laughed. "See us in his office? It's in Rotterdam. We're in Athens."

The young woman said, "This device was brought to the gate by a courier. He's waiting there in a car. Apparently there is a hoverjet at the local airport."

I looked at Thayu. She frowned.

That urgent, huh? she said through the feeder.

A chill crept over me.

"Um, yeah." I scratched my head, feeling increasingly stupid. They would not come to wake us if it wasn't urgent.

The young woman was Coldi and a minor employee of the Exchange. She wouldn't have any more information than what she gave me. "Wait here. We'll be ready in a moment." I went back inside the apartment.

"Do you have any clue what this could be about?" I asked Thayu when the door had shut behind me.

Thayu was flicking through the news on her reader. "No."

"I thought Danziger was getting busy with his election campaign." And, being faced with some stiff opposition in the election, he had plenty of campaigning to do.

"Maybe it's *about* the election campaign."

"In Africa? He doesn't need to campaign in Africa. With all his humanitarian work, it's the only place where his vote is secure. It's the rest of the world he needs to worry about."

She gave me a blank look and I figured she knew little about Africa. I hadn't seen a reason to inform her. Lately we'd spent a lot of time discussing the point of *elections.*

"Africa is like . . ." I sought for words. "Like Beratha. It's hot. It's dry. Not many people live there because nothing grows there, and there are sand dunes and miles and miles of desert." Well, the northern and central parts at least.

She continued her blank look as if she wanted to say, *That sounds just like Asto, anything wrong with that?*

"Africa is where, many years ago, Mizha Palayi, Asto's Chief Coordinator at the time, planned a refugee camp." In the Sahara to be precise.

Her face cleared up. And then a frown. "I thought we established that this was no longer an issue. They're still going on about that?"

"I'd hope not, but I don't know. If he wants to see me urgently, and it's to do with Africa, I can't imagine that it would be anything else."

"I guess I better pack up, then." She went to do just that. And Thayu being Thayu, she was done in moments, because she always travelled light. I always joked that the weight of her little travel bag was less than that of her weaponry.

My preparations were much less organised. Hell, *I* was less organised, still grumpy from having been woken up. What the hell did one wear on a midnight meeting with the president when one had been on a holiday and only had worn, rumpled and dirty clothes? Would it be acceptable to appear in a full set of *gamra* blues?

Most of our possessions had already been delivered to the Exchange's freight counter for decontamination and packing for transport back to Barresh, with little chance of getting them back at such short notice.

I sniffed my dressiest but still decidedly non-dressy shirt that I'd worn on the flight from New Zealand to Athens. Urgh. I couldn't possibly wear that.

Gamra blues it was, then.

Damn, I better wake up Nicha, too.

I crossed the room and knocked on the door that connected our room to Nicha's.

He came to the door a moment later, just as rumpled as I had been. "What, time to go already?"

"Nope. We're going back to Rotterdam."

2

———

I GATHERED ALL MY electronic gear and stuffed it in my bag, hoping that whatever Danziger had to tell me wasn't going to divert us for too long, or I'd need to buy some clothes. I was sure that even if they didn't show it, Thayu and Nicha were similarly unprepared for a long delay.

And Nicha was none too happy with the situation.

"Danziger? Why the hell do you listen to that disloyal piece of crap?" Nicha asked me with his hand on the doorknob, about to go into the corridor. "You're independent now. You're Ezhya's. You don't have to listen to Danziger anymore."

"Yeah, I agree with him," Thayu said. She still sounded cranky from being woken up. Hell, we were *all* cranky. "Anyone who pulled on me what he did to you would get the big FU from me."

In my heart I agreed with them, but unfortunately that was not a feeling I could act on. If I was Coldi, oh yes, I could. By stalling on my salary payments and cutting off my communication with Nations of Earth, and by keeping Nicha under arrest for much longer than necessary, Danziger had broken his commitment to me big-time in their eyes. But this wasn't Asto, and Coldi style networks did not operate here. I had to contend with politics and democracy. Which in practice meant you could treat your subordinates like shit and still expect them to crawl for you, as long as most people still voted for you. Because you were the president. Welcome to Earth.

I told them, "You know how we discovered that Mizha paid for favours from some African countries? We only discovered that because some people in those countries were not careful with their data. Who knows which other countries were paid, where else money went and what was done with it?"

"That was all so long ago. Why does anyone get upset about it now?"

Another cultural issue reared its ugly head: Coldi lived much more in the present than people on Earth did.

"Because these are some of the poorest countries on Earth, because the people in those countries are susceptible to someone coming in and buying their way into their loyalty."

"You can't buy loyalty."

"No, on Asto, you can't." Loyalty networks were physiological. "On Earth, you can buy the support of people, especially if they're desperate. There are a lot of desperate people in Africa."

I thought of the scenes I'd seen when I was younger, of crammed refugee camps on the eastern shore, of people driven out of their homelands because of drought, and unable to enter any of the protected enclaves where the locals still had crops to harvest. Of refugees selling their children to pirates and slavers.

In places like Djibouti, where everyone came together in their plight to get out, there was no food, no water. Infrastructures had collapsed under the sheer weight of human despair. People just died, and everyone was too busy surviving to care. I'd never forgotten the images of the "skeleton fields" to the west of Djibouti: dusty remains of refugee campsites littered with bleached bones. There was a lot of scope for trouble in Africa. It only needed one crazy despot to light the fire.

I said, "If this is about some Coldi people trying to revive the colony plan, all of *gamra* is likely to be affected by this. If it is about Mizha and this money, Ezhya would want it solved. In this situation, I'm as much Ezhya's representative as Danziger's. I need to know what he has to say. If it's about something else, we'll listen and go home."

Nicha gave me a hard, grumpy look. "Do you even listen to your own bullshit? You're not Danziger's pawn."

"Actually, my contract with Nations of Earth doesn't expire until the end of the month."

"Ah." He pressed his lips together. "You could have told me that first."

Coldi: painfully blunt and honest.

The young woman had waited for us in the corridor. For some reason, it was quite busy in the residential part of the Exchange complex, and most of the apartment doors were shut because the apartments were occupied. The names of the occupants were listed on the doors. I read the clan names as we passed: Palayi, Lingui, Palayi, Azimi, Domiri—all the usual suspects. Those were the clans with money and power.

Our footsteps sounded loud on the lino floor. Many of these guests would fly out some time during the night, because the Exchange operated only at night, so there were soft sounds of people talking.

The woman accompanied us to the lift. Because the Exchange was in operation, the large hall on the ground floor was as busy as an airport terminal. People with cases and bags lined up at check-in counters and others used their passes to enter the departure and arrival part of the building.

Of course the vast majority of the passengers were Coldi, with their metallic-sheened, dark hair, and the destinations were not displayed anywhere except on people's readers, but they were all off-world.

The only wink to Earth was the giant television screen that hung at the back of the hall, and it displayed, as usual, the newscast from World Newspoint or something equally staid and boring, appropriate for the time of day. A man was reading financial news, I thought. The level of boredom from the announcer's voice was reassuring.

At least Danziger didn't want to see me because there had been some huge disaster.

That was good news, I hoped.

I wanted to go home. This morning I'd sat on the tiny balcony of the apartment at the Exchange, looking out over the hazy air that hung over Athens, thinking of the violent thunderstorms that would lash Barresh almost every night at this time of the year. The monsoon was about to start. From my balcony off the living room, you could see Ceren's twin suns set under the blanket of ominous clouds that rolled in from the land every afternoon. The sky would go green and wind whip at the trees, carrying clouds of pink petals. The air would be humid and sticky, but we'd go to the baths and sit there in the rain, then walk back cool and refreshed.

Damn it, I longed for those times.

The young woman led us out of the hall through the glass doors into the coolness of the night. There were a few Exchange-owned taxis outside the entrance and their drivers gave us strange looks when we started walking under the starlight. Nobody walked that way, certainly not at this time of day.

It was early December, and even in Athens the nights acquired an unpleasant bite that I had become unused to while living in Barresh. Not only that, but my *gamra* blues were made of thin fabric, and I'd been taking adaptation medication that increased my body temperature in preparation for going back to Barresh.

It was cold.

Some time in the twentieth century the building that housed the Exchange had been constructed as a private hospital. It had a long driveway lined with date palms that cut across the lawn—green because it was winter. The driveway led to a set of gates which the Exchange drivers operated from inside their vehicles. The headlights of a vehicle shone through the metalwork of the gate, making the dew on the grass glitter. Only a non-*gamra* vehicle would have to wait outside.

"There he is," the young woman said.

The car was a dark-coloured passenger vehicle, and the driver got out when he spotted us. He wore the grey uniform of the Nations of Earth general guard, and he was not a local. Not Coldi and not Greek.

The young woman tapped her pass to the gate. It rolled aside with some creaking and rumbling. We went through, into the glow of the car's headlights.

"Mr Wilson?" said a male voice in the dark.

"Yes, it's me."

"Come with me, sir. The plane is waiting." The driver took my bag, but gave Thayu and Nicha an odd look. "Um, Mr Wilson, sir? What about them?"

"They're with me. They're my *zhaymas*. I don't travel without them."

"Um, sir. Yes." He went to shut the back door, and then stopped. Clearly had no idea what *zhaymas* were. "Do they carry arms, sir?"

"Yes. For our protection. So do you." Why the hell did Nations of Earth insist on sending me these ignoramuses? It was almost as if they did it on purpose.

He fidgeted some more. "I'm not sure if . . ."

"I stand guarantee for them." Seriously, when were these people going to get over their *oh my god, it's an alien* hang-ups? "If it's not all right, I'm not coming. If you want to call Danziger about that, I'm happy to wait."

"Um. No, sir, it will be fine."

We got into the car. As per security protocol, I got in the back. Thayu came with me and Nicha sat on the front seat bench. I didn't think the driver was impressed with that situation. He must have been told to collect only me.

I didn't care. He should have been informed that I didn't travel alone, ever.

Nothing was said on the way to the regular airport where, ironically, I rarely came. I usually took the fast train to Rotterdam because it didn't take much longer, and the border guards weren't half as stupid as those at the airport.

Instead of dropping us at the main terminal, the driver went down a side road past the huge hangars. Bright flood lights spilled out of one hangar that faced the road, and maintenance personnel crawled over the solar suborbital plane inside, a giant delta shape with a top surface made of solar cells. We'd flown here from New Zealand in a similar craft.

Maintenance crew raised their heads and turned around at the approach of our car. They greeted the driver. The driver returned their greetings.

We plunged back into darkness past hangars where planes stood as dim silhouettes, waiting for daylight.

There was a spot of light on the tarmac to the left. By now we'd gone so far that we were almost on the other side of the airport.

The girl at the Exchange had been right. A hoverjet waited for us, lights already on, engine idling, ready for take-off.

3

———

THE PLANE WAS of the private jet type, unmarked and quite new, I thought. There was a Nations of Earth logo on the side. We climbed up the narrow ladder into the cabin, carpeted and lined with birch wood. A tinny voice that came from a hidden loudspeaker told us to strap into our seats. The seating consisted of a luxury couch and a couple of easy chairs with covers of cream-coloured leather, arranged around a low table. Works of art hung on the walls, and there were blue curtains over the windows, held aside with silver rope. Soft, cream-coloured carpet lined the floor. I checked my shoes so as not to make dirty footsteps on it. A short passage led to a kitchenette behind the front wall of the cabin, and sounds of clicking glass drifted from the open door.

The passage ended in a closed door with a panel next to it on which a green light burned. I presumed this led to the cockpit.

We sat and strapped into the chairs. Judging by the expressions on Thayu's and Nicha's faces, they felt just as out-of-place as I did. This was not a place for me or any of my team. This was a place for top diplomats and movers and shakers at Nations of Earth. I wondered if it was Danziger's private jet.

Some people clearly had far too much money.

Both Thayu and Nicha were looking around, dark eyes roving the ceiling—looking for bugs, of which I had no doubt there were plenty.

We did seem to have acquired a flight attendant. She came out of the kitchenette to ask if we wanted drinks. I asked for coffee—I was still trying to wake up—but Nicha and Thayu stuck with water. Before getting those drinks for us, the flight attendant pressed a button next to the door which set a mechanism in motion that pulled up the ladder and closed the door. Then, while the engine fired up, she brought our drinks, all smiles.

I spotted Thayu drop a little tablet in the water. It fizzed on the way down in a stream of yellowish bubbles. Some sort of red-coded supplement, likely with a high concentration of hydrofluoric acid—hence the bubbles? Something that was exceedingly poisonous to me for sure.

Nicha sat sideways on the couch, his eyes closed. Thayu was reading something. We didn't speak much. The message was clear: this was not our territory and we didn't know who would be listening.

Security-speak for this was "the weather forecast", since the weather was considered one of the safest subjects.

The plane took off and levelled out above the moonlit landscape.

I looked out the window, seeing patches of light scroll past. Cities and towns asleep, while I was up here, recalled urgently to attend to some disaster.

As usual, my mind mulled over the possibilities.

I'd recently discovered that way back in the time of Mizha Palayi, some time not too long after 1975, Asto had made payments to Libya for the use of their land to build a desert colony.

At the time, the murder of one of Mizha's seconds and the protracted subsequent troubles had left the whole of Asto's society in danger of collapse, and a good section of the Palayi clan had been looking for a way to safety.

I wasn't sure if the money was for a rental agreement or if land ownership had ever been transferred, but it had disturbed me. Ezhya had assured me that Asto had never considered the plan seriously, but the payment showed that it had been a good deal more serious than he made it out to be.

I'd learned that with Coldi, you needed to be careful with what they said about events in the past. They did not consider the past as important as most people on Earth did.

And now Danziger wanted to see me about this discovery, urgently, even? Had his main opponent in the election for the position of President of Nations of Earth gotten a whiff of the rumours surrounding the plan, and now wanted an explanation of what Libya had done with the money? That sounded like something Margarethe Ollund would do.

Last year, the murder of Sirkonen and subsequent stupidity by Danziger had almost brought the world to a war with Asto. I don't think anyone appreciated how close Asto had been to using military action to free their citizens trapped on Earth. Nations of Earth would have considered that an act of war and the situation would have spiralled out of control from there.

I knew little about Asto's armed forces. Heck, few people did, even Thayu and Nicha, and Thayu had worked for them, and their father was some kind of admiral. But what I knew about Asto's army was enough to realise that you did not, ever, want to provoke them.

It was still dark when the jet touched down on the runway in Rotterdam, and lights blazed in all the airport buildings. Smaller planes were waiting on the tarmac to take off, mostly private craft. It would be a couple of hours before daylight came and the big solar suborbitals could take off.

Another car waited for us outside the Members' Lounge entrance. It was a Nations of Earth service vehicle with a uniformed driver, who took our bags with barely a word spoken. The air was so cold that our breath steamed. Thayu clamped her arms around herself.

The car took us over the dyke that connected the airport to the rest of the city. Moonlight glittered on the water on both sides.

The streets were still quiet. The occasional tram trundled in the other direction, with the bleary light in the cabins wasted, but for the occasional passenger coming back from a night shift or going to work at this ungodly hour.

We arrived at the Nations of Earth complex, where the gates were closed, but the guards let us through with a simple wave. The only signs of life in the broad, tree-lined avenues were the guards that stood on the corners and a pair of squirrels chasing each other across the road in the headlights of the car. They brought a bout of laughter from Thayu who had spent many hours at my father's veranda feeding oranges to possums, and didn't want to believe him when he said that most people in New Zealand hated them because they were introduced pests.

She sat as a warm presence next to me, comforting in this very cold and bleary night.

We didn't stop in front of the building that held the president's office as I had expected, but turned into an alley that ran down the side. It gave access to an underground parking area, closed off by a steel gate that opened at the driver's command and rolled shut as soon as we had gone inside.

The car stopped in an underground car park in front of a set of double steel doors, gleaming, threatening and forbidding.

A reception committee of armed guards waited for us. The highest-ranking officer, with the emblem of the Special Services on his chest, came to me.

"Mr Wilson, come with me. The president's aide has been notified that you've arrived."

Another of the guards said, "Uh, sir, what about . . ."

He glanced at Thayu and Nicha.

I said through clenched teeth, "They're with me." Seriously, when was this nonsense going to stop?

"We need to check with our supervisor."

"They come with me. I am the *gamra* delegate and these are my *zhaymas*. They will come with me to the door of the meeting room. It's *gamra* protocol that they come inside with me, but we accept that the president may wish differently."

"Um, yes sir. I have to check, sir."

After a brief exchange of words with a supervisor, Thayu and Nicha were allowed in, to the door of the meeting room *only*. The guard clearly didn't like it.

The steel doors slid aside and let us into a dark corridor. I guessed this was the president's private entrance into the building, but why did we need to come in here?

I expected to be taken upstairs in the lift, but the Special Services officer took me along the corridor that was only illuminated by lights in little alcoves in the walls. There were a few doors to the left and right, but they were all closed, with security locks on the doors.

I'd heard people speak of this place. It looked like this meeting was going to take place in the safety bunker that was built for wartime purposes.

What the hell were we doing here?

4

TWO GUARDS TOOK US to the very end of the passage. It was a dank room, with minimal lighting, and the lush furniture did not dispel the feeling of darkness and disuse.

To my surprise, the man seated at the desk reading something on a screen was not the president, but Simon Dekker, aide to the Acting President Sigobert Danziger of Nations of Earth.

I'd met Dekker a few times and he always struck me as a perfect companion to Danziger: tall, thin, dark-skinned, perpetually dressed in grey, with a less well-developed sense of humour than a corpse.

His eyes met mine as I came in through the door. It was a cold, calculating look.

He pre-empted my question, *Where is the president?* by saying, "The president is indisposed."

"He's all right?" I felt compelled to ask, although I felt that if the president was *not* all right, everyone would have known already. The question of Danziger's advanced age—he was seventy-four—was a hot topic in the election campaign and the faintest whiff of physical weakness would send the media into a he-won't-last-the-term feeding frenzy.

"He's in bed. Campaigning is a never-ending grind." Said completely without humour.

I wasn't sure what he was telling me with this little exchange of words. Was it: *The president wants you to come urgently in the middle of the night, but it's not important enough to see you himself?* Or was he saying: *The president doesn't like you and is going to annoy you and let you wait until he gets up before he sees you?*

Those were the games that Danziger played and, yes, Thayu and Nicha were right. He would never get away with this in Coldi society. Our feeders didn't work in this bunker, but I didn't need them to know what Thayu would be saying to me. That I was weak, that Danziger didn't deserve my support, that I should tell him to get lost. Yes to all accounts, but there was that minor detail about my contract that had not expired yet. And I *did* feel weak. Like a jellyfish.

Dekker gestured me wordlessly to a chair, and I sat opposite him.

As soon as I sat down, he got up. He opened a cupboard behind the desk and took out a hessian bag the size of a decent bed pillow. By the way the muscles in his arm strained, it was quite heavy. He upended the bag and the content slid onto the table.

A gun.

More correctly, parts of a gun, made out of a light-coloured metal, with off-white ceramic trim. Dekker picked up a long piece —the barrel—slotted in the handgrip and attached a third piece that was—I thought—a sight and a control panel. A few spindly things went up on the top. I could only guess their function. The weapon looked impressive. The barrel gleamed, the handgrip looked new and solid. The whole contraption was a bit longer than his arm. I'd never seen anything like it before.

He lifted it and pointed it briefly at me. "How would you like to be at the wrong end of this thing, Mr Wilson?"

I looked at the discharge plate that would unleash a white-hot stream of plasma. "I guess that's why you brought me here—you're going to shoot me." Oo-er. Interacting with Coldi people brought out my bluntness. But I seriously didn't like to be woken up and flown through the night to face some humourless guy pointing a gun at my head.

He lowered the weapon. "Ha, ha, ha. The controls are disconnected." I had no doubt that he pointed the gun at me because he disliked me and probably dreamed of pulling the trigger. In fact, disliking me would have to be a prerequisite to get a job working for Danziger.

He put the weapon on the desk and pushed it across to me. "Have a look at this baby, Mr Wilson."

I picked up the gun, the metal cold in my hands. Oof—it was heavy.

He was right; the control panel was loose. It contained a few buttons and instructions in tiny letters, in Isla. Yet the main body of the gun was not a local product. Unless the Asto army had recently changed their models, this wasn't one of theirs. Then what? Locally made according to an offworld blueprint? With the tiny strip of Hedron steel that ran down the side of the barrel, that was unlikely. Made off-world to order? That thought gave me the chills.

"What is this? Where did it come from?"

"You tell me, Mr Wilson. I was advised that you know all about these things."

"These things" being *gamra* matters, administration and societal structures and customs, or politics. I was hardly a weapons expert. I turned the weapon over in my hands. "Can I show this to my *zhaymas*? They know a lot more about weapons than I do."

He moved his chin up which I took as a *yes*, so I rose, and went to the door. Thayu and Nicha stood in the corridor playing a staring game with the two guards on either side of the meeting room.

"Thay', Nich', can you quickly take a look at this?"

I'd spoken Coldi, but it seemed that Nations of Earth guards guessed the gist of it, and because both Thayu and Nicha went inside the room, they both came as well.

Thayu took one look at the gun on the desk and sucked in a breath through lips forming an O. She lifted the gun and turned it over.

"What is it?" I asked her.

"It's a type of plasma weapon. Very powerful. Most effective at distance. You can use it to do a lot of general damage to a building, or shoot down an aircraft at low altitude. Strangely enough, it's not much good at killing people at short distance."

"Does anyone own these legally?"

"Privately? No. You couldn't buy this thing. My permit doesn't even cover it. This is a military grade weapon, used by armies and militias. Not for use in civilian security. The plasma chamber is missing, though."

Dekker had been looking at us with an interested but suspicious expression on his face.

"She says there is a part missing," I translated for him.

"She's right." Maybe he'd left the plasma chamber off to test if we really knew what we were talking about.

"Where did you get it?"

"Before I tell you that, can you ask her where this type of weapon normally comes from?"

I was guessing he wanted Thayu out of the room as soon as possible. I translated his question.

Thayu said, "There are a few places where they use or make weapons like these. I would have to take it apart to know exactly where it was made. But Tamer or Indrahui is the most likely."

"Then what the hell is it doing here?" With text in Isla, no less.

"These are often custom-made to order," she said. "Not cheap."

Damn. I was starting to get a very bad feeling about this. As far as I knew neither of those worlds had much of a presence on Earth. Either the weapons manufacturers on those words were seeing business opportunities, this was part of an offensive by parties wrong-footed in the debacle surrounding Sirkonen's murder, or someone with a lot of money was getting involved in what had previously been the domain of poorly-organised militias. Or all of the above.

I translated for Dekker what Thayu had said, and then he put the gun back in the bag, looking pointedly at her.

This was as much as Dekker was going to share with Thayu and Nicha, so I made one of the security gestures I knew, the one that meant *I'm fine*. They left the room and the two guards followed them.

He waited until the door had shut with a click, the silence between us tense.

"This weapon, intact, was found in a container with similar *merchandise* in a crate in an airport hangar by an aid worker in a sea cargo terminal in Djibouti. The shipment was slated to go out to one of the refugee camps along the east coast of the Horn of Africa."

Of course, Djibouti. That had been a trouble area for years, with massive numbers of environmental refugees who had nowhere to go.

"Can I take a picture of it?" I wanted to show this to Amarru.

"You can have it. We got a whole crate of the damn things. I guess the only good point about that is that those weapons won't be used against us while they're sitting in our storage. The bad point is that we don't know how many more of these shipments there are and how they're coming in."

"I don't think customs is going to be impressed if I try to bring a whopping great big gun in my luggage."

He shrugged in a *suit yourself* way.

I put the gun in the middle of the table and took a couple of pictures of it from several angles, and several close-up shots of different parts of it.

I asked, "Why Djibouti? And why does that have anything to do with the Saharan plan? Djibouti is not in the Sahara."

"I was getting to that part next." Dekker sounded prim. He had put his reader on the table and flicked through images until he found the one he needed, and turned the reader around to face me. His fingers were unusually thin and long.

"When we got sent this weapon, we poked around a bit in the area, and discovered this, across the border in Ethiopia, not terribly far from Djibouti."

The screen displayed a satellite image showing a good chunk of the northeastern African coast. He zoomed in on the eastern tip, the bit where it looked like a chunk of Africa was about to break off.

He zoomed in and zoomed in, and different geological features flashed past: rocky outcrops, deep scars cut into the soil as if someone had taken to the planet with a knife. The land was red or various shades of pink, with barren hills and the multicoloured sores of hot springs and salt encrustations. I couldn't discern much in the way of vegetation or habitation. The landscape looked barren and alien. If someone asked me to guess where this was, I might have guessed Beratha on Asto.

Then the view scrolled past a thin line that resolved into a dirt road. A blue-green area in the top of the image turned out to be a body water, quite shallow, with bands of white and yellow salt encrustations that edged the shore like lace.

"What's the water?" I asked.

"That's the Afar inland sea."

I'd heard about Earth's newest sea. The region had always been well below sea level, and a combination of volcanic activity and rising sea levels had caused water to start seeping into the basin from the Red Sea. It had started about fifteen years ago, but had only been brought to the public attention in the last ten years. The basin was still filling up and had a long way yet to go.

Dekker said, "This is the Afar region of eastern Ethiopia. In case you're unfamiliar with this area, it's the hottest place on Earth. There used to be nomads trekking across this area, but the region is largely abandoned these days, because not many *humans* are happy at those temperatures, never mind their livestock."

His expression said, *but it's perfect for Coldi.* I was starting to get a Kazakhstan feeling about this, another episode we did not want to repeat.

"This area is wildland, pretty much abandoned by local government because there is nothing of value to protect, and it's too hot to enforce laws, and the local governments are too poor to supply services, if ever there were any in the first place."

He enlarged the image still further, so that I could detect individual hills and goat tracks through the sand. Several tracks joined into a dirt road where there was a small dark speck.

"Is that a car?"

"A truck," he said, and scrolled to another part of this huge, never-ending image. He pointed a slender finger. "Here is another one. And another one over here. As you can see, this area is a bit of a local highway." He flicked across to the next screen. "This is the place where they're all going."

I peered at the image, a pattern of geometric lines that were either dug in the sand or made from dark stone. It was hard to tell which. There were some clusters of heavy vehicles and a couple of sheds, which stood out because of their light-coloured roofs. "I'm not quite sure what I'm looking at. A building site?"

"Yes, a building site, and what they're building looks a hell of a lot like this, don't you think?"

The document that appeared on the screen over the top of the photo was more familiar to me than I cared to remember: the blueprints for large Coldi settlements in the Sahara. And yes, it did look that whatever was being built in the desert used the same building plan. The lines matched perfectly.

I met Dekker's eyes. I wondered if he'd been chosen to deal with this because he had a good deal of African heritage, or if he was just a part-African who happened to get this job.

"Mr Wilson, I assume you don't need my help to reach the same conclusion as we have. I do not need to spell it out. Last year, when you barged into the president's office with that dressed-up suit and your gorillas, you assured me that this settlement plan for offworlders in the Sahara, this colony, whatever you want to call it, was dead. Somehow, I don't think so."

"Well, this is truly the first I've seen of this project—"

"Mr Wilson, I'm not saying that *you* were lying, but obviously *someone* was lying. The aliens are here and they're building this settlement right now. They've even designed weapons especially for us so that, as is my guess, they can pass them to local officials and militias as bribes to make sure they keep their mouth shut about the presence of these aliens."

"Well . . . that's a bit far-fetched. I don't know how you come to that conclusion based simply on these images."

"What other conclusion can we draw? Is your memory capacity too small to have retained the name 'Kazakhstan'?"

I was now getting very annoyed. "Look, why don't you simply tell me what the problem is. I've just travelled for hours, and I'm not in the mood to be dicked about. I'm going home tomorrow, and I'm highly tempted to walk out that door." I could almost hear Thayu and Nicha cheering.

His expression closed. "I'm trying to."

"Without making false accusations based on nothing."

He pressed his lips together. A thick silence hung in the room. My contract had been brokered by Sirkonen, but ever since Danziger had 'inherited' me with the presidency, he'd made no secret of the fact that he never agreed with the appointment. I was almost at the point of hoping that Dekker would tell me that I was relieved of my duties.

He didn't.

I made an effort to get the discussion back on topic. "What do the local authorities have to say about this?"

"Nothing. They're up to their ears in trouble: refugees, over-crowding, lack of food, lack of money, disease, no water. They don't have any time to worry about this. It might be the reason why those people are in that spot. It's also likely to be a problem, if left to fester, that will eclipse everything else they're already facing."

I couldn't help but agree with him.

"We asked Lucius Brown about this development." That was the president of PanAf. "He said he was unaware of it, and would make investigations. A few days later he came back with the news that it was a tourist development to be the first on the shore of Earth's newest sea. A fucking *tourist development.*" Dekker's dark eyes met mine in a hard look. "Do you know how hot fifty degrees Celsius is, Mr Wilson? And why anyone would attract tourists to a place like that, unless you want to attract *alien* tourists? And I suspect that maybe someone in his chain of information got the words 'tourist' and 'terrorist' mixed up."

"I can assure you that from the point of view of *gamra,* the plan is dead."

He gestured at the screen. "This does not look like a dead plan to me. This looks pretty damn real."

I couldn't say anything to dispute that. It looked real to me, too.

"I want this investigated. I want this gone. I want these weapons out of that region. I want construction to stop and I want this trade of weapons—whoever they're trading with—to stop."

Everyone wanted it to stop, but since Nations of Earth wouldn't come to the table to talk about accepting *gamra* law, there were no legal mechanisms for anyone to do so. They were still getting hung up about the rumour that *gamra* prohibited religion, which was false, by the way. Welcome to the Wild West.

"I'm not sure there is all that much I can do. I will raise it with the assembly and Asto's Chief Coordinator—"

Dekker was shaking his head. "No, Mr Wilson."

What did he mean, no?

"You may raise it with the assembly, but any kind of action they will take is going to be too little, too late."

Unfortunately, I agreed with him. *Gamra* had very little interest in Earth because, you know, there were no laws.

I didn't know in how many languages they needed me to shout *Sign the fucking agreement* before they understood that they actually needed to, you know, sign the fucking agreement before *gamra* would be able to do anything about stuff like this. It was the standard agreement that no other *gamra* entities had any kind of trouble with. The one that said that no people should be systematically discriminated against and that original inhabitants should have the highest priority in people claiming use of a particular part of land. And if they signed it, people could get citizenship cards, and they could travel, the restriction on the Exchange could be lifted, and *gamra* laws regarding offworld citizens would apply on Earth, and any criminals that were caught could be formally extradited.

Dog, meet tail. "The longer we let this problem fester, the more it will start to look like Kazakhstan. Once these weapons are distributed all through the population, it will be virtually impossible to retrieve them all. We need to act swiftly and decisively."

"I agree. I'm sending you out there to investigate."

What? Like those guys were just going to invite me for a cup of tea and if I asked them to stop building, they'd smile at me and simply do it? "Sure, I can investigate, but there will need to be some formal structures in place before—"

"Good. The plane leaves in an hour."

What? "But—"

"You always complained that people who were familiar with Coldi customs were never involved in the Kazakhstan case, that they should have been consulted and that they could have prevented a lot of the trouble. I'm listening, and so I'm involving you now. Do your thing. Talk to all the important people. Here is your moment to shine. Prevent another Kazakhstan. You seem to know how this is done."

I could almost believe that I heard a joking tone in his voice. "Do I get any choice in the matter?"

"Yes. Chicken or fish?"

Ha, ha, ha. "How long is this for? I've got arrangements in Barresh—"

"I don't care, Mr Wilson. You are still in our employ until the end of the month and I've already got approval from the security council to extend it for whatever length of time it takes you to get these people out of there. If your new boss has any inkling of how we work, then he should respect that."

5

T HAT WAS ALL Dekker was going to say about it. He didn't mention where I was going, nor whom I was to meet or what he wanted me to talk about. My brief would be on the plane, he said, and it included all the details I was going to need.

He briefly discussed money. "You'll be paid a standard Nations of Earth stipend pro rata for the length of time you end up working on this problem. I trust that you're familiar with the rates and in case you want more, I'd like to inform you that I have zero flexibility in offering increased rates, including danger allowances, remote area allowances, overtime allowances, insurance, medical expenses and any other cushy nonsense."

That cushy nonsense was outlined in our work contracts, in case he'd forgotten.

"I will be your go-to person for any questions or problems you may encounter. The president is on the campaign trail and is not to be disturbed under any circumstances. Can I have a confirmation that you've understood this?"

"Any particular reason?" Not that I wanted to talk to Danziger anyway. The shrivelled old toad wasn't just blunt like this guy. He was vindictive as well.

"None that needs to be known."

"Any that *I* need to know?"

He gave me a *cocky bastard* look. "No, except that the press needs to be kept out of this."

"The press?"

"Yes, Mr Wilson. I know that you are an expert at turning the press against the president, but one word to them and you'll find yourself a persona non grata."

"I have to say that I'm really impressed by these threats."

"Good, because I'd hate to have to carry them out."

"I was joking."

"I was not." His face remained unemotional. He nodded stiffly. "You can go. The plane is waiting."

There were a thousand things I wanted to say. That I wasn't anyone's lackey. That I objected to being treated like this. That he could stick the last few weeks of my contract in an uncomfortable place, and that I didn't need the job.

But that would be ignoring the fact that I could see that this could become a very nasty problem indeed, and that I couldn't think of anyone else that Nations of Earth had access to who would handle this sensibly.

So I made some sort of lame greeting and left.

Outside the room, I caught up with Thayu and Nicha. They fell into step with me and said nothing while we were accompanied down the hallway by two Nations of Earth guards. I was glad that they were too cautious to speak, because they would surely scold me. I felt like a naughty boy being taken for rubbish pickup duty after a scolding by the headmaster.

"I've contacted the hotel," Nicha said. "Let's go and have breakfast." We usually stayed at the Central.

The steel doors to the underground entrance opened. The vehicle was still waiting in the concrete bunker. One of the guards rushed to open the door.

Nicha wanted to take the front seat, but a guard told him not to, so all three of us got into the back seat, the guard shut the door and got into the front seat. I shut the glass partition behind the front and back benches.

I said in a low voice, "We're not going to the hotel."

They both gave me sharp looks.

"We're going straight Africa." And when they said nothing, I added, "How much did you hear?"

"Not much. The door was shut most of the time. Feeders don't work in that bunker." Nicha had lived in London and understood Isla. "So I can't say that I understand the issue or why we should become involved."

The car started moving.

Nicha spread his hands. "I mean, this weapon-smuggling business has been going on for so long, Asto would have gotten the smugglers long ago if Nations of Earth had shown any interest in meeting them halfway about their conditions for entering member status."

That old chestnut again. I said, "Yes, it has gone on for so long, and you're right about the agreement, but it looks like we've got a new brand of arms smuggler active on Earth. That weapon he showed you was part of a haul that was intercepted accidentally in Djibouti."

"So. People are smuggling weapons. What's new?" He sounded seriously cranky. I guessed he'd been looking forward to a nice breakfast at the hotel.

"They don't want this to become another Kazakhstan." I explained in a few sentences what Dekker had told me.

Both of them listened but remained oddly quiet. No, I knew that they didn't want me to become involved. Heck, *I* didn't want to become involved, or at least not under the conditions—or lack of them—outlined by Dekker.

"We *have* to do something. What do you know about Coldi involvement in Kazakhstan?"

"That the whole rebellion was fed by the Zhori clan of Asto and that they sold weapons that outperformed anything the local rebel groups had," said Nicha. "And that this made the conflict particularly hard to contain. None of the troops sent to quash the rebellion were prepared for what they were fighting."

The doors to the bunker opened. The car went through and slowly moved down the side alley. Guards on either side of the entrance greeted the car's driver.

I thought of the reports that came out of Kazakhstan at the height of the trouble. I'd been studying on Mars so only the most important headlines made it through, but I remember the one that said, *Is this another world war?* It would have been fairly clear-cut if the Zhori hadn't decided that they weren't getting enough money and started selling arms to the troops who came to fight the rebellion as well. Except the rebels always seemed to have slightly better weapons. The conflict was endless, marked by regular raids by Nations of Earth troops to clean the area of alien armaments, which were always incomplete, and hurt the soldiers of whichever country had drawn the short straw in providing the peacekeeping troops. And some of those countries, in turn, decided to put an end to the conflict. And the Zhori sold weapons to all of them. Far too many countries got involved and burned their fingers.

"We don't want another Kazakhstan," I said in a low voice. "We don't want another block on the Exchange as happened after Sirkonen's murder. That's why we have to be involved."

He shrugged. "You're the diplomat." As if it was all my fault.

"Nich', I don't want to do this either, but if I don't help the current acting president, he will send his own clowns and that is sure to lead to fireworks."

Nicha blew out a breath. He leaned forward on his knees and shook his head. Then he reached out and squeezed my shoulder. "Just my luck, to be teamed with the most impressionable sook in all of *gamra*."

Coming from Nicha, that was a compliment. Coldi and most other *gamra* people were baffled and fascinated by Earth people and their propensity to do things for other people without obvious gain to themselves.

Nicha's remark dissolved the tension between us. I was an impressionable sook and, apparently, that was OK.

"Why did we have to see him in that shelter?" Thayu asked a bit later.

I shrugged. I wasn't sure myself. "Because Danziger was upstairs and was not to be disturbed? Or maybe a more mundane reason, such as that upstairs was being cleaned and was therefore not secure."

"Where was the president?" Nicha asked.

"In bed, Dekker said."

Nicha snorted. A Coldi leader would never let important things be done by assistants. Ezhya would have been there himself, bedtime or not. "Maybe Danziger is scared of us."

We chuckled at that, remembering when we'd barged into his office, with Ezhya posing as a security guard, to go through his files. That had been glorious. Stupid, but very satisfying.

Nicha asked further, "Does the *president* know about the meeting you just had with his aide?"

I was going to say *Of course he does* because that was protocol, wasn't it? "I presume he does. I can't see why he wouldn't." But damn it, did he know? Dekker had made me promise specifically that I wouldn't contact Danziger. I'd assumed that it was because he was busy with the election campaign, but it might be because he didn't know about this problem. That was a disturbing thought.

Thayu voiced my worry. "Why wouldn't he know about it? Because, as I understand this *election* thing, his job depends on how many people like him. Let's just say that he was a nice person and treated people fairly, which far too many people seem to believe that he does. Then he'd try to make sure that he continues to be seen as a nice person. That means he can't get involved with wars where people get killed and where, whatever he does, many people will always think that he's done the wrong thing. Well, I'm just judging by the mess that went on with this *Kazakhstan* place. If a conflict or scandal breaks out just before the *election*, he'll lose popularity and people won't vote for him. So his subordinates use you to fix up the mess behind his back. That means in case it all blows up in their faces, and in *your* face, your *president* knew nothing."

That was probably a pretty fair assessment.

"See, even my sister can understand why it's a bad idea to get involved. So close to the election, this is about *politics*." He used the Isla word because Coldi didn't do politics in the same way. "I don't understand why you didn't tell him to get lost. Yeah, you still have a contract until the end of the month, but nothing stops you walking away from it."

"Come on, Nich'. You saw that weapon. That was no ordinary charge gun. Ezhya would want to make sure that those kinds of weapons don't get too widely distributed on Earth."

"Ezhya doesn't care about Earth."

"I really don't believe that. OK, maybe he doesn't care about

Earth per se, but he definitely cares about the Coldi population on Earth. And he cares about not being seen trying to secretly annex Earth against *gamra* law. The assembly would go into a feeding frenzy."

They both nodded. Ezhya was very concerned about that. Asto and a couple of Coldi worlds held a very slim majority in the *gamra* assembly. Those entities that were perpetually looking for reasons to damage Asto's standing examined Asto's every move. I didn't doubt for one second that some of Asto's marginal supporters would readily switch allegiance if evidence of illegal annexation came to light.

Nicha sighed, admitting defeat. "So, then, what is the plan? What does this guy want you to do?"

"I don't know yet. The briefs are supposed to be on the plane, but I hate being totally dependent on them."

Thayu and Nicha nodded. I knew they hated it even more than I did.

"Since they kindly offered us transport, I'm thinking we might use it to drop into Athens on the way. We need to talk to Amarru about this. Once we're in the air, we tell the pilot that we have a change of plan and instead of going straight to Djibouti, we want to make a short stop in Athens."

"Yes," Thayu said. "Amarru needs to be informed. The Exchange may be able to help us."

The car went through the gates to the compound and entered the city streets. I stared at the back of the driver, suddenly feeling very tired. Damn, I wanted to go home.

Even though it was not so early anymore, the sky still had that "early" feel. While I had spoken with Dekker, the city had woken up, and we no longer had the entire street to ourselves. The sun had risen, but because it was December its shadows remained long and its golden light held little warmth.

It was busy at the airport, mainly with buses and taxis dropping off passengers going to work in different parts of Europe. I spotted another Nations of Earth vehicle in the throng.

Our car bypassed that crowd, following a sign that said, "Private transport."

When we drove past the terminal, Thayu turned around to

look out the back window. I recognised that sharp look, that subconscious twitch of her hand to her arm, where she held her gun in the arm bracket.

"Thay'?"

She didn't reply, but stared at the road behind us. Headlights from a car following us shone in her face, making her eyelashes show up brightly metallic. Damn, I loved that woman.

A few statements in code went through the feeder from her to Nicha. Thayu groped under her jacket for the gun. She took it out and lay it on her lap.

Meanwhile, the car continued on, the driver and the guard oblivious in their walled-off cabin.

The car stopped at the front of the VIP entrance of the building. The guard got out and went to get us our bags from the back. We got out.

An icy breeze cut straight through my clothes. A man and woman walking past gave me odd looks.

The guard slammed the back door of the car shut, slapped the roof as a sign that the driver was good to go. He accompanied us into the building. Thayu remained vigilant, even if she had put the gun back in its arm bracket so as not to alarm other people.

I wished I could ask her what was up, but she appeared to be listening to something, a frown on her face. My heart was hammering.

The guard was chatting away about nonsense as we crossed the hall. That we needed to check in, that they'd want to scan our baggage, that we'd need to hand in weapons, blah, blah, blah.

This part of the terminal catered for private flights and luxury airlines. The atmosphere was perhaps less chaotic than in the main terminal, but no less busy. We lined up at the self-serve customs counter, but the machine refused to take my pass. A press on a button brought a staff member from a door in the back wall. He entered my pass manually. My EXO-NZ designation came on the screen in red letters. He didn't know what the red colour meant, and managed to turn it back to its usual black after a couple of calls to a supervisor.

Thayu and Nicha didn't have these passes, but they produced the cards issued by the Exchange that showed only EXO. The man spent a ridiculous amount of time studying these passes. He asked questions: What were we doing in Rotterdam? Where were we going? How long were we here?

I felt vaguely uncomfortable with this level of scrutiny. For one, I had never been checked here in a similar fashion and, even though I preferred the train, I'd come through many times. But eventually, he appeared satisfied and let us through.

Our Nations of Earth guard was waiting in the luxurious departure lounge. He told us cheerfully that the jet was almost ready and then proceeded to talk about the weather. Yes, it was winter and maybe there could be some snow although it hadn't snowed this far south for at least fifty years. Bring the ice picks. We sat down. I took the tea he offered us, but it was so hot that I had to let it cool down. My hands felt like icicles.

Having run out of subjects to talk about, and lacking a response from our side—I really didn't feel like talking about the weather—the guard fell quiet. Thayu and Nicha watched the tarmac where the jet stood. It looked ready to me, the door open and light blazing inside. I had no idea what we were waiting for.

Finally the guard's receiver beeped. "Time to go."

I slung my bag over my shoulder, realising that I hadn't touched the tea yet. Oh, well. I looked at it, and the guard looked at it. He smiled uneasily.

Thayu met my eyes.

What? I asked through the feeder.

Something really odd going on. Can't quite determine what it is.

But it was all right, because the Nations of Earth jet would take us back to Athens within an hour. None of the Nations of Earth guards could get into the Exchange building. We could talk freely in there. Also, once I heard what I was supposed to do, I was going tell them that I'd arrange my own transport.

We left the lounge and followed the guard through the open doors into the cold air. The jet was the only craft on this side of the building being prepared for take-off. A couple of Nations of Earth guards hung around near the bottom of the stairs.

About halfway to the plane, Thayu stopped.

I had gone a little bit ahead before she called me. *Cory . . .*

What? She only used my name when there was something really wrong.

I can hear . . .

I could hear it, too, a low powerful hum.

Both Thayu and Nicha were looking at the sky over the top of the building that we had just left.

Something dark with a couple of floodlights rose low over the building's roof. Much too low to be legal. The bright glow from the floodlights travelled over the roof, over the tarmac—

Fuck it, that was a military gyrocopter.

The air was going *thud-thud-thud-thud-thud.* It was almost painful to my ears.

It whipped up a dust laden breeze that blew leaves and rubbish into whirlwinds. It was an unmarked, dark grey craft. The back door was open. A small light burned inside the cargo hold and when the craft banked, I spotted the silhouette of a man seated at a rocket launcher in the opening.

Thud-thud-thud-thud-thud.

Thayu took my arm and dragged me across the open space towards the cover of another private jet, locked-up and dark. She could run much faster than I could and all I managed to do was not trip. Nicha was behind us. The Special Services guards surrounding the jet had drawn weapons.

Thayu stuck her small gun in the belt bracket and got the big one. She wasn't even puffed out from having dragged me.

Shots rang out in the space between the buildings. It was one of the Special Services guards. Somewhere in a nearby building an alarm started wailing.

The gyrocopter slowed.

Thud-thud-thud-thud-thud.

"Shit, the guy in the back," Thayu yelled. She aimed her big gun. Her hand tensed. The gun discharged with the characteristic *floomp* sound. The discharge went over the top of the jet, into the cargo door of the gyrocopter. There was a flash when it hit. A small object fell out, followed by what was clearly a body.

Shit, that woman of mine was an ace shot.

Now the gyrocopter turned. First one and then the other rocket launcher went off. One hit the tarmac and the other slammed into the jet. Both exploded in a ball of flames. A few seconds later, the jet's fuel tank—fully filled and ready for take-off—exploded in an even bigger fire ball. The entire side of the building glowed with the flames.

Special Services guards ran towards the inferno, but even the heavy guns they carried would be no good against a military gyrocopter. It was turning again, coming back into our direction.

"Come on!" Thayu yelled. "Run!"

Nicha stood still, raising his gun. He aimed for the pilot's windscreen.

Fired.

The gyrocopter pulled up.

Thud-thud-thud-thud. The very air vibrated with it. A blast of hot air from the fire blew past.

And up.

The charge from Nicha's gun deflected off the armoured underside of the craft and dissipated harmlessly. He swore. The gyrocopter rapidly rose out of range. Elsewhere at the airport, a jet engine started up.

We ran.

A fire truck came towards us, and a whole bunch of security vehicles. But the jet was burning so fiercely that they couldn't even get close.

We ran across the tarmac.

Thayu didn't even have to drag me along with her. Either I was becoming used to running with Thayu or I was doubly keen to get out of there, too. Or Thayu was going slowly because she was speaking to someone on her earpiece. Amarru probably.

We ran back towards the terminal, but just before we got to the building, Nicha veered off to the right past the side of the building. There was a concrete-covered walkway with bushes on both sides. It led to another building which we bypassed across an area of lawn. Behind us, sirens wailed and engines roared. A hoverjet took to the air with screaming engines. The sky lit up with orange light.

We ran past the building to a concrete area where rubbish bins stood in neat rows. There was a gate on one end.

Nicha reached it first. He fired his charge gun at the lock from close range. It glowed bright orange and fell to the ground.

Thayu yanked the gate open. There was a service road at the back, where a car waited.

The doors opened automatically as we ran up to it. Thayu got in, and I followed her on the back seat. Nicha got in the front.

"Three of you?" asked the driver in Coldi. I didn't see his face, but he wore his hair, Coldi-style, in a tight ponytail at the back of his head.

Well, damn, this looked like the same driver who had rescued us from Eva's house months ago. Did Amarru have him shadow us or something?

How the hell did these people know where they were needed?

As soon as Nicha pulled the door shut, we set off.

"Who were those guys?" I asked, panting.

Nicha said, "We're still checking that. It seems our surveillance picked them up locally not long before the attack. The gyrocopter is a privately registered vehicle belonging to a company that hires it off locally for whale hunting."

"Urgh. Do people still do that?"

"Only the very rich," Nicha said.

Seriously. Use a high tech military vehicle to kill an animal? There were plenty of whales, they said. We need to keep the numbers in check or they are a hazard to shipping, they said, especially along the Arctic route.

We zoomed along the road into town. Emergency vehicles with screaming sirens were going the other way. Fire engines, police, ambulance, more fire engines, even more fire engines. When I looked out the car's rear window, I could just see all of them turning into the side road to the VIP customer lounge.

Our car left the dyke and arrived at the island.

"Where are we going?" I asked.

"To safety," Nicha said.

Dumb question. Mr Wilson. Leave it to the *zhaymas* and it will all be sorted.

Nicha was talking to someone in rapid code, and Thayu was reading something on her screen. I got the message. I was the diplomat so I should shut up. They provided communication and security.

6

―――――

"WHAT, EXACTLY, IS PANAF?" Thayu asked a little later, while the car had settled into a steady speed.

"What? Is anyone saying that they have something to do with the attack?"

"Not in as many words, but it's been mentioned enough times to make me wonder."

I glanced at her screen where she was flicking through pages that displayed lists.

"Where? What are you looking at?"

"I'm trying to trace the hire of the gyrocopter back to someone who would have a reason to kill you."

"And that had something to do with PanAf?"

"They get mentioned a few times."

I couldn't even get my head around that. "PanAf is like the equivalent of Nations of Earth, but for African states only."

"They have armed troops." It was not a question. She must have read it somewhere.

"They do. For peacekeeping missions."

"They use gyrocopters a lot."

"They do. Gyrocopters are faster than helicopters, have a much greater range, and a lot of the territory they cover has marginal services for air traffic at best. Like, landing fields. The fact that a gyrocopter was used in the attack doesn't mean that PanAf is responsible." PanAf was actually quite stable, if sluggish, not terribly rich and bureaucratic. Large political swings, point scoring of states against one another and perpetual skirmishes over resources and borders was the domain of the North American states.

Thayu nodded and continued to read. I didn't like her silence.

"Seriously, Thayu, why would PanAf have anything to do with this? If anything, they'd support us trying to find these illegal importers and smugglers."

Thayu gave me a pitying stare and said through the feeder, *People will do anything for money.*

I protested. "PanAf gets more money from Nations of Earth than it could possibly get from bribery, and its officials get secure, cushy jobs, too. If Asto was involved, yes, I could believe that PanAf could be bribed, but it's not, and no one else has deep enough pockets on Earth, or a strong enough interest to spend that much money to turn the entire organisation rotten."

"You're sure?"

I spread my hands and let them sink again. The bottom line was that we didn't know. We were stabbing in the dark.

I tried another angle. "It's well known that Danziger has quite good relationships with PanAf officials. Africa is one of the regions where he *doesn't* have to campaign much. As far as I know, the gun Dekker showed us was probably given to him by someone representing PanAf at Nations of Earth."

She nodded again and maintained her silence. What was she thinking with all her spy training? Why wasn't she saying anything?

"Anyway, how would PanAf know about my presence here? *We* don't even know what Dekker wanted me to do. The brief was supposed to have been on that plane. I don't see it. I don't see *one* reason why PanAf would take open, hostile, criminal action. On this world, shooting down aircraft is a major crime."

The latter part of that remark was a joke, but Thayu and Nicha didn't get it.

Thayu was now flicking through the news services. She said only, "We have to consider all the possibilities."

There was more to it, but she wouldn't mention a hunch to me unless it was a pretty solid one. That was one of the frustrating aspects of dealing with her.

I looked at her screen. Some news services already had articles up on the explosion. Flash Newspoint said, *Gamra Ambassador Wilson killed in Cowardly Attack.*

Well, that was—ah—interesting. Surely the Nations of Earth guards would have seen that I never got on the jet?

Thayu said, *They would have seen it, but those guards are not likely to have survived the blast.* She was talking about the ones who'd been standing next to the plane when it blew up.

"Then how can the news be certain that I'm dead?"

Nicha said, "Well, it's not likely they can check the wreckage for a long time yet, and it's Flash Newspoint after all. *Killed* sounds a lot more interesting than *missing.*"

True, but it was strange to read your own death notice.

Nicha continued. "That fire might have been so hot that they're unlikely to find bodies at all."

Also true, but services like Flash annoyed me with their lax approach to the truth. I was wondering if anyone saw an advantage in failing to correct them. Danziger perhaps? Because he wanted me out of the way?

"Here is a mention of PanAf again," Thayu said. She handed me the reader so that I could see what she was talking about. I flicked aside the frame that provided a Coldi version of the text. Those translations were often not the best.

The article said,

PanAf Secretary Lucius Brown stated that this was a cowardly attack and that the international community must stand together against this type of action. Mr Brown strongly denied that militant terror groups incorporated under the PanAf umbrella had carried out the attack.

"We vet all member organisations," Mr Brown said. "Any that do not meet the standards cannot join."

Yes, that was right. I had learned about that in the International Politics module I had taken at Mars University. Because parts of Africa were no longer under control of formal effective governments, PanAf included not only African states, but also major advocacy groups, like tribes that crossed borders and other ethnic groups. Some people at Nations of Earth—and especially people from non-African countries—said that this gave a voice to criminals, because some of those "advocacy groups" were rebel organisations, and the funding, ethics and legitimacy of those could be a bit grey, to say the least.

Most of the article was about Lucius Brown being on the defensive about these advocacy group members, but there were no real suggestions that any of those people had anything to do with the attack. I could understand why they were under such intense scrutiny. If anything, those were the people on the ground who would find Coldi money most beneficial. They would defend their income or supply of weapons. I was a major threat to it.

But yeah, this was really stabbing in the dark. So, no, I didn't believe PanAf had anything to do with the attack, but some of the advocacy groups might.

"Maybe I should try to speak to Lucius Brown," I said. I strongly suspected that this had been in the brief that had been blown up with the jet. "I'd like to know where he stands on these accusations and what he knows of involvement on off-Earth elements in Africa."

I tried to remember where he lived. This was truly Danziger's territory, because he had come to power through the ranks of the world's aid organisations. I would have expected him to be best mates with people like Lucius Brown. And I felt out of my depth because I knew little about the man.

I took out my reader. Of Lucius Brown, it said,

President of PanAf, 2110 to current. Born in Kenya in 2055 at the height of the first wave of oil wars and educated in Western Europe and Egypt, he rose to prominence as a political figure during his student years in Cairo as a member of the Return The Power movement.

Those, as I remembered, were a series of incidents of social unrest orchestrated online where the disenfranchised citizens of poor countries protested against the influence of the large international corporations over their governments: they had bought the politicians, had taken over the nation's debt or controlled the only source of income of those countries. Those countries rose or fell by the whims of a board of directors in another country.

After Lucius Brown went to university, he seemed certain to win an influential position. However, in his first year, both his parents died during the Nile Flu epidemic. The young Lucius Brown disappeared for a period of two years, and was rumoured to have spent the last year of this period with the Freedom Front.

This was the northern African rebel organisation that was formed out of militant interests from the desert tribes who had been displaced by the desertification of northern Africa. Homeless, violent, and full of very angry young men.

During that year, the Freedom Front was known for being highly organised, and carried out a number of successful attacks. Although Brown's influence was never officially documented, it is widely believed that their success, and the Freedom Front's subsequent absorption into the African Freedom Fighters at the time of Brown's return to public life, is no coincidence.

The African Freedom Fighters, of course, were one of those semi-legitimate organisations that had a lot of influence on PanAf's policies. They were not direct members, but their offshoot, the North African Alliance of Tribes, was.

Damn, I wished I had paid more attention in class about Earth political history. I'd grudgingly taken those classes at university. I remembered wondering why politics of Africa was of any importance to me, taking the classes on Mars, since colonial politics had nothing to do with Africa, because most of the continent was a basket case, right?

Well, I'd been a dumb, cocky, arrogant dick.

Everything was important. And sitting here in a car speeding away from a crime scene, not sure where we were going, all the things that I didn't know and I'd thought were unimportant, *local skirmishes*, pressed on my mind like a heavy weight.

Shit.

Shit, shit, shit.

Danziger, Africa, Lucius Brown, rebels, offworld weaponry, potentially Coldi interests. It had all the makings of a disaster.

Thayu still listened to the little voice in her earpiece.

I mouthed, *Are you talking to Amarru?*

She gestured, *Yes.*

Where are we going?

She made a gesture that I hadn't seen before and I wasn't sure what it meant. I didn't count myself an expert in signal code.

Nicha was talking to the driver in a low voice. We were now on the other side of town. No one had followed us yet and that could not be coincidence. It had to have something to do with Amarru. That woman knew *everything*.

Eventually, Thayu handed her earpiece to me. I affixed it to my ear. "Amarru?"

"I'm glad you're unharmed." Coldi women tended to have dark voices, but I always found her voice exceptionally warm, like a favourite auntie where you could always go for a hug and a pat on the shoulder. "I'm sorry that we didn't inform you earlier. This situation developed too fast and caught us unawares."

"Any idea who did this?"

"We can only speculate at this point in time. It's probably someone who is keen to show displeasure about your involvement with Danziger's mission to clear up the festering smuggling business."

"How do you know about that?" It never ceased to amaze me what Amarru knew about what people said and did.

She didn't answer the question. Maybe someone from Nations of Earth had spoken to her about the problem. Or maybe she had spoken to them. That was more likely, since I couldn't see anyone from Nations of Earth acknowledging her.

Maybe Lucius Brown had spoken to her.

"Whatever this new development is," she said, "we want it cleaned up, too. It looks bad for all of us."

"Hang on, it wasn't you who passed Nations of Earth that information and the weapon, was it?"

"Careful, Cory. This channel may not be secure. I'll talk to you when you get here. Stay undercover. We'll have to pretend that you were killed in the explosion."

"But . . ." I felt sick. Well, at least now I knew where Flash Newspoint had drawn that conclusion form. This news would go all over the world. My father would think that I was dead, and wouldn't even get a body to bury.

As I had suspected for a while now, the car took us to the train station. But rather than drop us off at the front of the building, we went around the back, where there was a loading dock for goods. It was now finally starting to get light, but clouds had rolled in, keeping the light level down.

When the car came into the dock, a man appeared from the building in the grey morning light. He had blond hair and a short beard, was dressed in dark clothing and wore a gun on his belt, a regular Asto guard-service charge weapon. That alone was strange, because he very obviously wasn't Coldi.

He came up to the back door of the car and opened it for us. He exchanged some code with Nicha.

Thayu and Nicha got out. I followed. More code signals were exchanged. I wished I understood more of it. I wished I knew his name.

The man led us wordlessly into the building, a large shed where goods stood on pallets, ready to be loaded onto trains.

He took us past a couple of plain concrete train platforms with cranes and loading lifts. The rails between the platforms were empty.

At a third platform stood a closed carriage with the logo of a German transport company. He went to this carriage and heaved a door open. Nicha stepped in after him. I glanced aside at Thayu. We were going to ride in a goods carriage? I didn't like this much, in addition to the fact that the man was an ordinary human and appeared to be well-versed in Coldi security sign language.

But Thayu's face was unperturbed, and if both she and Nicha couldn't see a reason to make a fuss then probably neither should I. After all what did I know?

The blond-haired man said, "Delegate, we apologise for the conditions, but your safety is of utmost concern." His Coldi was perfect. He made a subservient Coldi greeting, turned around and retreated from the carriage.

Well, what the fuck?

7

———

A LIGHT CAME ON inside the carriage and showed an awkwardly shaped but comfortable apartment. There was a little sitting room with a table and couch, two sets of bunk beds against the wall, a kitchenette and in the back, the door to what I presumed to be a small bathroom.

The blond man shut the back door behind us. Locks clicked. From the outside as well. I again checked with Thayu, but she seemed relaxed with this situation.

I still didn't like it, but then again, I'd drifted in space in a tin can that was under control of other people, so I could do a tin can that was on the ground.

"That was Klaus Messner," Thayu said.

"*The* Klaus Messner?"

"Is there more than one?"

"Well, no . . ." But it seemed overkill that such a top level spy for Asto would busy himself with this situation. Or—what did he know that we didn't?

Klaus Messner was, of course, someone I had often considered a brother-in-arms, despite never having talked to him in person. Like me, he was usually considered a traitor, working for "the other side" by the virtue of having been raised off-world in a mixed family and being in a mixed relationship. I'd gone the diplomatic route; he'd specialised in intelligence.

I now wished I'd said more to him.

We inspected our quarters. The bunk beds were firm. The couch seated only two, but one person could sit on the bed. The kitchenette held such wonders as a filter machine for making coffee and manazhu. There was even a half-opened jar of the stuff that looked and smelled fresh. I busied myself with making drinks. It was none too warm in this container.

"What sort of contraption is this?" I asked. "Does Amarru have these stationed all over the rail network?"

"A field station," Thayu said. "Klaus probably uses it a lot."

"Didn't he get his Earth designation revoked recently?" Nicha asked.

"Yeah. The case was really weak, though. As far as I understand, Danziger said, 'I don't like you,' and just deleted his GER designation." GER stood for Germany, as NZ stood for New Zealand on my ID.

Nicha said, "The case was a façade. He wasn't even there to defend himself."

"There was a lot more at stake than his designation, but I agree that it was not a blueprint for what you'd call a fair trial." To be honest, the case had given me the shivers. Sure, he'd been caught having some documents he shouldn't have had, but he was still legally a German citizen, and Germany had not been making a lot of noises that they didn't want him anymore. I suspected they probably *did* want him, because there was a strong Coldi presence in some of the southern German cities.

The action to revoke his citizenship had been taken solely by Nations of Earth. They had always had the power to revoke someone's nationality status, but had only started using it in seriousness recently. *In the interest of public safety,* they said. The fact that the harsher stance had happened at the time that Danziger took the lead was purely coincidence, of course, if the administrators had to be believed. If.

The percolator machine had produced a jug of dark green liquid. I took three cups from the cupboard and poured. Thayu took the steaming mug from me and clamped her hands around it. "I wonder if this place has a heater."

Nicha came to get his cup. He wore a blanket wrapped around him. They both felt the cold weather a lot more than I did.

Thayu rummaged in the cupboards under the kitchen bench.

"Ah." She found a heater in a cupboard. She unrolled the cord, dislodging several spiders as she did so.

The heater was an extremely simple device, with a cord and a glowing coil and a fan that blew hot air into the room.

"Wonder what century this thing dates from," she said.

Nicha said, "It still works, so probably mid twentieth. They don't make them like that anymore."

A cloud of dust blew out when Thayu turned the machine on. "Urgh, it probably hasn't been used for all that time either."

But whatever the age of the device, and the smell of burned dust it issued, it worked and soon the little cabin was comfortably warm and even grew so warm that I had to take off my jacket. Nicha fell asleep on the bottom bunk.

I sat on the couch and read the morning's news bulletins. There were a fair few articles about the explosion, most accompanied by an uneasy tone that seemed to hide the suspicion that extra-terrestrial interests were involved. An air of censorship hung over the tone of reporting. I checked if Flash Newspoint had any more news, because they were the network with the least scruples, but even they didn't mention those interests. That was Danziger's influence, clearly, or at least the influence of the men in grey suits behind Danziger. Because if you were in power, you could exert a degree of control on the media.

Thayu looked over my shoulder. She stood behind the couch in front of the heater.

"It's a strange thing," she said. "If they were people from PanAf, why would they have this attack in Rotterdam where everyone can see it? If we were going to Africa, why didn't they wait until we got there?"

I spread my hands.

A loud clang made the carriage shudder.

Nicha woke up with a gasp.

Thayu motioned him to be quiet. A man walked past the side of the carriage while talking remotely to someone. There were more clangs.

Then the carriage started moving, with a small jerk. This was followed by a lot of rumbling and jiggling over tracks and switches, maybe a turntable as well, and then thumps as we were hooked up to a larger train. That train then sat somewhere on the rails for an hour or so, at the station probably. I could hear other trains pass at low speed and the occasional voice and crunching of footsteps on gravel.

I'd decided to have a nap and lay dozing on the bottom bunk of the second set of beds when we again jerked into motion, and kept moving at increasing speed. The train settled into a gentle rocking rhythm. The goods trains moved slower than the passenger trains, but would still take us to Athens within a day. It was dark and really warm in the cabin. Nicha had taken up position on the couch next to Thayu, both with their readers.

I spent some time working on material I was preparing for Ezhya, but I felt distracted and kept checking the news every five minutes. That led to more distraction, since I hadn't read a lot of Earth news recently and I filled my quota of trivia about celebrities I didn't know and royal families—yes, they still existed—I barely remembered.

We inspected the cupboards for food and found the cabin well-stocked with various food types which we heated up and ate while sitting on the couch and the bed.

I climbed into the bottom bed of the bunk furthest from the door. I didn't know what the time was, but having been up most of the night, I was quite sleepy, and the stuffy warm air and the darkness inside the cabin didn't help.

———

The next thing I knew, the train had stopped. It was now pitch dark in the cabin and so warm that the side I'd been sleeping on was all sweaty. I sat up. The air blowing out of the heater made my sweaty skin feel cold.

Thayu went, "Hmmm." She turned on a small light that created a pool of gold on the couch, the table and surrounding floor. By its light, I could see her getting up off the couch and putting on her shoes. Her ponytail was all mussed up.

Nicha climbed down from the top bunk, muttering Coldi swear words.

I checked the time. It was almost six in the morning. Had we been asleep for that long?

People walked past the train, footsteps crunching on gravel. Locks clicked and someone opened the door at the front of our cabin. Through the open door I could see a few indistinct dark shapes silhouetted against the sky that was turning blue. I could see no buildings or lights. How long had we been in this tin can?

Someone out there carried a light, so that a second person could climb up the ladder. The silhouette was stocky. The person entered the cabin. "Ichumya ata."

I recognised the voice as Amarru's.

All three of us repeated the pledge of loyalty. It was that kind of occasion. She didn't often venture outside the Exchange. It must be serious for her to meet us herself. We stood in the dark at the entrance to the carriage. Amarru's hand was warm on my shoulder, but the air that came into the carriage had a strong bite to it.

"What's going on?" Nicha asked, yawning. His breath steamed in the light.

"This is where you have to get off."

We collected our things from the back of the carriage, put clothes and shoes back on, and followed her into the night. It was awkward to walk on the rails and gravel because it was still so dark on the ground that I couldn't see where the sleepers were. I imagined that Thayu and Nicha saw even less. A single light produced a weak glow on the veranda of a rickety building at the deserted siding. The Milky Way above had faded to a few of the brightest stars.

"Where the hell are we?"

"About two hours north of Athens. I thought it'd be safer to collect you here."

Outside the Exchange enclave? I glanced at Thayu, but it was too dark to see her expression.

Amarru led us across the tracks to the tiny station building. A barbed wire fence with clumps of sheep's wool hanging from the spikes separated the paddock and the yard, where a rusty motorbike leaned against a post. I imagined someone having come to work on the bike and having died in the little office years ago, while no one noticed, and trains went by and his motorbike stood in the rain.

It was that kind of place.

On the other side of the building stood an unmarked minibus. I'd seen the vehicle before, usually when Nicha and I lived at the Exchange and it had been used to transport VIPs. The bus had bulletproof glass and sides. The last time I saw it, it had no valid registration that allowed it to leave the enclave.

It still didn't.

We climbed in. The driver sat behind the wheel, his face lit from below by the dashboard lights. He was Indrahui, the man I'd come to recognise as Amarru's regular security guard. She seemed to like Indrahui guards, because my own Evi and Telaris had also come to me through her.

We sat down, strapped in, and the bus started moving. Nicha yawned, covering his mouth with the back of his hand.

After exchanging a few words with the driver, Amarru came to sit between us. She wore tight-fitting trousers and a fur-lined, waist-length jacket zipped up under her chin. Both garments were Earth style. Her hair was more grey than black these days and she usually only tied back the top half. The glasses made her "Chinese matron" look complete. I'd never found out whether she actually needed them.

Her somewhat frumpy look belied the hardness underneath. Amarru Palayi was the highest-ranking Coldi person on Earth.

"Danziger is trying to shut us down," she said.

I said, "He's been trying for years. Now he got sent that plan, and has been trying to find some illegal activity that stems from it as an excuse to crack down on the Exchange."

"This is different." Her voice sounded serious.

I frowned at her. "Does the Exchange have any knowledge of this business in Africa? I mean, knowledge that Nations of Earth doesn't have?"

The short silence that followed worried the heck out of me. Amarru was uncharacteristically diplomatic for a Coldi person, which was why she was such an excellent candidate to head the

Exchange's Public Relations department, but sometimes I wished she was a little more blunt.

She said, "You would normally think that getting the smuggling under control is a good thing. And it is, and we should get it under control."

That didn't answer my question at all. "But there are complications?"

"We don't know who any of them are."

"And I'm guessing you normally do when something like this pops up?"

"We usually have a pretty good idea."

"My guess: some of the Zhori clan?" On Asto, the Zhori clan specialised in running and stocking the giant warehouses and food distribution chains. When they left Asto, many ended up doing the same thing, except not legally, especially in places where legal import and export was forbidden.

She shrugged. "Maybe, but we have a Zhori representative at the Exchange. He knows nothing about it. He says there are no Zhori in Djibouti or Ethiopia."

Here a normal person would question if her contact spoke the truth, but if this person was in Amarru's loyalty network—and he would be in order to work for her—he *would* tell her the truth. Then, in a twist that Earth people found bizarre, he would tell his clan leader that he had told Amarru this. An Earth person also would never employ someone who so clearly worked for the enemy, but that juxtaposition, balance, *rimoyu*, was the essence of Coldi society.

That was why the loyalty system worked and led to fewer armed skirmishes.

I asked Amarru, "So what do you think?"

She blew out a breath. "Maybe part of the Zhori clan has splintered off. I think there may be a link to Lucius Brown."

"What? Is he responsible?" With the best will in the world, I couldn't imagine that. He wouldn't be so stupid.

"Not immediately, and how much he really knows remains to be seen, but he's a pompous idiot who is susceptible to smooth talkers peddling criminal schemes. He's pretty much crawling at the feet of people who want to invest or relocate to northern Africa."

"That's understandable."

She shrugged. To a Coldi person, large-scale desertification would not be much of a threat, but successive politicians had called the entire northern half of Africa *the eyesore of the world.* Climate scientists had called the region a barometer for the health of Earth's ecosystem, and it had been pointing at *tempest* setting for the last seventy-odd years. The Saharan countries, and all the countries around them, and even the countries around those countries had been hit very, very hard.

Amarru continued, "If you go digging around in Lucius Brown's biography, you'll find that he disappeared for two years."

I nodded, not sure that I liked where this was going.

"It was after the outbreak of the Nile Flu, which killed both his parents. He was nineteen years old and fled across the Mediterranean to Greece."

Nope. I definitely didn't like where this was going. "Let me guess: it was during the time that the Zhori clan had their headquarters in Crete."

"You got it."

Damn it.

Matriarch Dyiizhu Zhori had been one of the main criminal elements in the Kazakhstan weapons smuggling case and that had never been dealt with satisfactorily. Oh yes, the Kazakh rebels had been dealt with, but apart from Dyiizhu Zhori, who had been killed by a sniper, the Zhori smugglers had dispersed, gone back to Asto, or assumed false identities and continued plying their trade.

While the bus travelled over bumpy back roads, she explained to me how the situation stood, to the best of her knowledge.

Apparently, the hard core of the Zhori had moved to Africa following the suggestion by Lucius Brown. It was, in a way, ideal territory for them. Hot and dry like the lowland desert of Asto, vast swathes of land were pretty much abandoned by anyone except some hardened tribes and rebels, and people who still operated some of the old oil rigs, small scale refineries and drove vehicles that ran on petrol. How quaint. To them, it meant independence, even if what they did was illegal. The Zhori clan's trade was technology that allowed similar rebel groups, and other odd bods and communes, to operate independently of governments.

Lucius Brown had connected the Zhori clan with these African outcasts and rebel groups. Since he came from a rich family, had held a pilot's licence since the age of fourteen and had a plane, he had travelled extensively throughout the region and knew it well. He would have known which country or ex-country was amenable to overlooking the fact that one of the most influential organised crime groups—and Amarru did actually use the word "mafia"—established in their country, and would be happy to take bribes from them.

But instead of choosing one locality, the Zhori mafia had spread out over a variety of locations including the north and east coast of Africa, especially towns that were suffering because of drought, infiltrating towns and setting up businesses. Coldi did heat and drought very well, of course.

This sort of thing had been going on for many years. The presence of the Zhori clan kept the locals happy. They had money and gave the locals jobs. And the vast majority of their activities were legal, so they blended in with the local population.

I said, "So, they went straight and led mostly honest lives. Maybe they helped some of the rebel groups organise themselves better. What changed? Why did they start importing weapons?"

"A few things happened recently. Because of the election, and because Lucius Brown controls a vital part of the vote for the assembly, people at Nations of Earth—non-African people—started digging into his past. That's what journalists do."

I nodded. I'd experienced some of that myself.

"The journalists found this connection with the Zhori clan and didn't like it. Questions were asked. He's busily trying to cover up the damage, claiming that he was idealistic and naïve and had no idea who these 'Chinese-looking' people were."

"A classic case of a politician covering his arse."

"Pretty much. But it is because of these investigations by these journalists that these weapons were found. We don't know how long it's been going on. Secondly, the part of the continent where those weapons were found is in the grip of a particularly power-hungry warlord, and it is this man whose name was on the crates that contained the guns, and this man who claims ownership of the land where the mysterious building site is. The man is Robert Kray, of whom we have no information other than a few grainy pictures that may or may not be of him. He heads a band of rogues called the krayfish, who apparently can be recognised because, as a bizarre initiation ritual, they have their front teeth knocked out."

Ouch.

"For some reason that we don't know, they were given—or bought or offered to build—the plans of this Asto desert settlement that was slated for Libya in 1975, but never got off the ground. These krayfish, who appear to be local youths from the refugee camps, are the people doing most of the building, and protecting this planned settlement."

"All right. Now I'm officially lost. What does this have to do with Lucius Brown or the Zhori mafia?"

"The Zhori are everywhere in northern and eastern Africa, and I suspect that part of the clan has broken with the clan leader and is operating their businesses in the lawless refugee camps and the bases of sea pirates along the shore. And judging by the size of that haul, they must be planning something major. The region is particularly sensitive and volatile. We have hundreds of thousands, maybe even millions, of refugees in camps along the coastal towns of Djibouti and further south. We have a warlord planning projects in what's considered an uninhabited or uninhabitable area. We have a warlord recruiting these desperate people, and we have someone, possibly Zhori, supplying these people with weapons."

"Why would they import non-Asto weapons? They're harder to get if you have to go through official weapons Traders, and they have to keep records and keep it all above board."

"Have you seen these guns?"

"I have. Impressive."

"There is your answer. They're impressive. In Kazakhstan, plain second-hand service guns were impressive for the rebels who used them. These days, everyone knows those guns, and every self-respecting rebel group has them, so something more advanced was needed."

"Where did the weapons come from? Tamer or Indrahui?"

"That's another disturbing thing: we can't tell."

"Can't tell?"

"No. We haven't seen this type before. They contain no foreign air bubbles that we can clearly identify as Indrahui or Tamerian. Someone is being very careful."

She further explained that the Exchange had already secured the cooperation of the Trader Guild to see if they could unearth how the weapons could have made it to a shed in the area normally used for foreign aid in Djibouti. A couple of Traders were facing intense questioning, but the most obvious candidates had already been cleared.

"So that attack on me—those were krayfish?"

"Most likely, since they have the strongest motive to stop your investigation. These are not people to be toyed with, which is why you have to stay dead for the time being."

"So that was you feeding bullshit to the media? I thought it could be Danziger because he wants to keep me quiet and avoid another 'ALIEN ATTACK!' news storm."

"Yeah, that was me. We have Melissa now." Journalist for Flash Newspoint, in training to take over my old position as Earth observer to *gamra* at the end of the month. I guessed it was probably always a better idea to have a media person in that role.

"Danziger knows very little of what's going on, thankfully," Amarru went on. "He's edgy because of the election. He's prided himself on his *being tough on these terrible chans* position, and he's not going to be happy if a second Kazakhstan breaks out."

It was weird hearing her refer to herself with this derogatory term, but Danziger would use it. He was one of the few politicians who got away with it.

I said, "So, someone brings him this weapon, and he thinks 'Aha. We still have this upstart Cory Wilson at our disposal until the end of the month. Let's get him out of harm's way and send him to Africa to solve a problem.'"

"Pretty much."

There was also a persistent rumour that I controlled the vote of much of the colonials, that I lobbied them and sent them secret messages.

"He's trying to remove as many obstacles to his re-election as he can. 'If the hands are busy, the mouth cannot work overtime.'"

Amarru said, "Your knowledge of proverbs has improved a lot recently."

"It's a necessity." Ezhya used a lot of them. "But getting back to the problem, this is much bigger than I can solve by myself. What am I supposed to do? Danziger had something lined up for me, but thanks to Mr Kray's thugs, I never got to see the brief."

"From all information we have, he was going to send you to Lucius Brown."

"I did suspect that, although there would have been little point if he fell out with our friend Mr Kray. So I wonder why Dekker would send me to Lucius Brown."

She shrugged. "To send you down a political boghole? To show to his opponents that 'Look, this is what we are doing about the problem'? I don't know."

"What do you want me to do? Go in hiding until after the election?"

"No. We *do* want this solved. A group of small entities at *gamra* filed a complaint against Asto that we are trying to annex Earth despite years' worth of warnings. If this material becomes publicly available, the complaint may well stand. These are smart people. They know about the Zhori clan and their history. They don't care that the Zhori may not actually be involved in this case themselves."

"But what can I do by myself?"

She nodded. "You can't do much alone. But I have a contact lined up for you. We're going to meet this contact now."

I looked outside. The sky had turned pale blue and the sun was about to come up. Through the heavy, bulletproof glass, I could only see rows and rows of leafless grapevines and the occasional old farmhouse surrounded by pines or cypress trees.

"I guess that's why you're taking me to some remote rustic place?"

She grinned. "Secure locality, Cory."

"Yeah, whatever."

8

———

NOT MUCH LATER, the bus turned off the main road, as much of a goat track as it was, and went up the drive of what looked like an ordinary farmhouse.

The sun had risen about a hand's width above the horizon. The sky was a bit dusty but otherwise cloudless and the low light edged rows of grape vines in a golden glow. The plants had no leaves because it was winter, and the soil in between the rows was stony, dry and fallow. I had suspected that we were close to the Exchange enclave, which included Athens and its immediate surroundings, but it now became clear how close. Between the hills I spotted a small section of a fence. It was at least three metres tall, made from wire mesh with barbed wire on top. This was likely why the house had been abandoned: none of the locals liked living close to the Exchange enclave. Once, before the fence went up, Athens would have been their main market. After the fence went up, they would have to travel a long distance to sell their products.

The farmhouse itself was made from natural stone, with red terracotta roof tiles. It had to be at least three hundred years old, but seemed to be in reasonably good condition.

In the back yard, surrounded by olive trees, the bus came to a halt next to two solar vehicles. There was also a rickety shed, the door half open. I spotted a glimpse of metal inside. Some sort of vehicle bigger than a car. I glanced at Nicha to check if he'd seen it, but he was looking at the farmhouse.

Now the bus had moved and I couldn't see it anymore.

Certainly, they wouldn't bring offworld aircraft here, would they? All Exchange traffic was supposed to stay at the Exchange. And if they brought an aircraft here, would they so carelessly leave the door open so that I could see it?

The driver opened the door to the bus and I got out, feeling stiff from the long journey. I really hoped there would be some opportunity for a proper rest and, while I was at it, how about I contacted Barresh to let them know there had been a snag and I was meant to solve an impending implosion on Earth before I returned home. Oh, and Ezhya, too. He'd be impatient about my sudden disappearance.

The farmhouse's door opened as soon as the bus had stopped. In the doorway stood a Coldi person, gender unspecified, whom Amarru appeared to know.

We followed her across the yard. Thayu looked cranky and Nicha wondered aloud whether the farm's hospitality was likely to include breakfast.

It did.

We entered an old-fashioned kitchen with a wood fire stove. Around a rustic wooden table sat at least ten people, all of them Coldi and dressed in silver temperature retaining suits, wearing armour and carrying weapons on both arms as well as their waist belt. Inner Circle guards.

In the middle of the table stood a whole bunch of food containers and wrappers such as the Exchange kitchens used. A couple of old frying pans on the stove indicated that they had been heating up the meals, and the air smelled of mushrooms.

Great.

Red-coded food. Would there be anything I could eat?

A couple of the guards rose to make room for us at the table.

It was probably planned like this, but I ended up across the table from the only person in the room who did not wear a uniform. He had been sitting with his back to the door and talking to others when we came in, but now he studied me with an intense look.

For such a dusty and rural location, he was exceptionally well-groomed. He looked clean and fresh. His dark, security-guard type of clothing was remarkably free of smudges or wear. Not someone, I guessed, who regularly wore this type of attire, because, I made a further guess, he usually wore a uniform. He wore his hair, Coldi-style, pulled back from his face and tied into a tight ponytail at the back of his head.

Thayu and Nicha went around the table to greet him in the traditional subservient way: with their arms by their side and head bent. He touched both of them on the shoulder. There was a certain fondness in that gesture that made me think I knew who this was.

To me, he said, "Delegate, I see you come well prepared."

Well prepared? What for? Did he mean Thayu and Nicha? Did he mean because I had Coldi people with me?

Coldi didn't *do* introductions. You were meant to know the identities of the people you met, especially when they were highly ranked. With his Inner Circle guards, he would be very highly ranked. Unless I was mistaken, this was Asha Domiri, admiral of some part of the Asto army. He was also Thayu and Nicha's father. If I was correct. I hadn't seen him for a long time, and had only ever seen him from a distance or on a screen.

He turned around and asked the guards, "Do bring the Delegate's food."

One of the guards, a man with broad and muscular shoulders, brought a parcel on a plate. Thayu and Nicha were already at the table and eating.

For a while, the talk was all about the journey. A few of the guards appeared to be familiar with Amarru's "field stations". Amarru asked if there was anything wrong with them, and some jokes were being thrown across the table about heating and the quality of the beds.

I unwrapped the thin paper of my meal parcel. Inside I found one cardboard container with rice and another with some kind of sauce that contained little round things that looked like meatballs, but were probably a vegetarian thing. Not only did Coldi not eat the meat of higher animals, they thought it was dirty to cook it, too. The food was all right, if not really the right kind for breakfast, but it wasn't as if I cared.

In the middle of that chatter the man across the table met my eyes squarely. "I understand that you're the man who is signing a contract with my daughter."

Asha Domiri indeed.

"I am indeed." The man was technically my father-in-law, but Coldi didn't care much for such things, since their partnership contracts were usually for short periods only. "You will be welcome at the official ceremony in Barresh." We'd already had a partnership ceremony for my family in Auckland.

"Why?" He gave me a bemused look.

"Because I like her."

"But you can sleep with her all you want and don't need a contract for that. It's not like you need to have a contract with her to get an heir." Trust Coldi to be blunt.

Business talk tended to be off-limits during meals, but deeply personal talk was not. I'd run into this several times.

"We simply like each other," I said.

"What about Taysha?" The man who had already arranged a contract with Thayu for a second child.

A couple of the guards had stopped their conversations and were looking at me.

"I'm going to buy him out."

Asha took in an audible breath. "Do you know what you're letting yourself in for?"

"I think so."

"All just because you like her?"

"Yes." Also because I didn't want her to lose her last opportunity to have a child in a relationship where the child would be living with her.

"Well." He shrugged and eyed his daughter. She returned his stare. "Well," he said again. "It's your choice."

Clearly, he thought we were nuts.

By now most people had finished eating. A couple of the guards got up and left the kitchen through a door that led into a dark hallway. Amarru had also disappeared. I'd felt so flustered with the deeply personal questions that I hadn't even noticed her leave. Thayu and Nicha had ended up at the far ends of the table, and it was clear that they were here only as observers.

Asha set his cup down with a kind of finality that made it clear that the time for banter was over.

"This building site is a problem," he said. "It's a problem for you, and a problem for us."

I nodded. "Amarru explained."

"No, I don't think she has explained everything. I'm giving you some information that no one else has, not even Amarru. It's not a simple problem."

"I never thought it would be."

He pulled out a reader, turned it on and brought a picture up on the screen. "This is Robert Kray."

He turned the screen to face me.

The grainy image showed a man looking to be in late middle age, a photo taken at some function where he held a glass and was talking to another man. He was tall compared to the people standing next to him, and his white suit made his very dark skin stand out. He had a strangely flat forehead from which his nose jutted out at the same angle. He wore sunglasses, but they did not hide his heavy brow.

He was dark enough to pass as a full-blood African, but his nose was narrow and flat, not broad. His hair was curled in ringlets, not in an African frizz. He'd died it black, but I was guessing its natural colour would be bronze, and the sunglasses would hide moss-green eyes.

Robert Kray was Indrahui.

And that opened a whole host of nasty possibilities. Not only was Indrahui the most violent, war-torn of worlds, it also wasn't a full *gamra* member for this reason.

"That is . . . interesting." Were I not faced with this man I needed to impress, I might have said a few choice words. At the *gamra* assembly we had countless problems with the never-ending civil war at Indrahui.

"*Interesting* would not be my preferred word choice. This has potential to become a full-fledged crisis. I guess you don't recognise him from the picture, but this man is Romi Tanaqan, one of the most wanted criminals of all the settled worlds."

I had heard that name before. "Isn't that the guy who was caught smuggling weapons into Indrahui?"

"Caught, but never convicted. Smuggling small arms, smuggling large arms, recruiting children, recruiting off-world, the list goes on. The scale of the business was astonishing. The rebel stronghold at Deverra collapsed when he could no longer supply them. This man was responsible for keeping that entire region on a war footing. He supplied to both sides of the conflict. Thousands died. He managed to give everyone the slip before we got to the stage of bringing him to court. Now he's trying the same thing here, with a different supply source. Different conflicts. This situation is absolutely unacceptable. At the *gamra* assembly, Asto was blamed for 'allowing' him to escape, because they said that we would be afraid that an investigation into his dealings would uncover things about the Outer Circle and the *zeyshi* desert pirates that we wouldn't want to be widely known." He snorted. "As if there is any story from the Outer Circle that hasn't been turned over three times already. We absolutely need to stop this, because, much as Asto is not supposed to interfere with this world, you will see that we will be the first to receive the blame if it gets out that a major criminal offworld figure has taken up residence. Mr Kray—Romi Tanaqan—is a warlord of the worst order. If we give him no resistance, he'll work himself into a situation where far too many people are dependent on him and will support him either through dependence or fear. What is worse, there are no laws that allow us to take him to court, either locally or through *gamra*. He does not hold *gamra* citizenship. This is not a *gamra* world."

"Then what do you want me to do?" This was much bigger than anything I could handle.

"We're in the early stages of handling this crisis. We need information. I'm told that you are one of the few people who can freely travel in the region without arousing much suspicion."

"I am?" *Have you seen what Africans look like?*

"Amarru has a cover identity for you that would explain your presence in the area."

"This man will have scores of people on the lookout for visitors. I kind of . . . stick out."

"Yes, but the cover is good. Sticking out is not bad. It stops you being killed easily."

Gee, thanks.

"We need information about his activities. If you need to find out about a person, it's no good trying to stay hidden from him, because in the desert, there is nowhere to hide." Another proverb that was chillingly apt. "Because if you have to stay hidden, you will never get close. Better to walk up to him and start asking him questions that are so innocent that he would never think that you were dishonest about asking them. In the process, you can see if you can find anything that we can pin on him. If not, where to hit him hardest."

I restrained a gasp. "You're not going to take . . . military action, are you?"

"Of course not." His voice was dry, almost bemused. "We have a treaty and all that."

Why didn't I believe him for one moment? Oh boy, the sweat was running down my back under my shirt.

"Gather information. Take your assistants. Look around. Report back."

"If we're undercover, we won't be able to take much equipment." Hell, I was never too fussed about the gun, but I wanted to take it if I went to a place like that.

"True, but I have something that will help you." He dug in the pocket of his jacket and put a feeder on the table. Since it was not attached to someone's skin, the thing looking like a daddy longlegs was inert. The legs activated through body heat.

"I already use one," I said.

"Yes, but this one is different. Try it."

I moved to take my regular feeder out of my hair, but he said, "You wear both."

"Is that all right?" Ezhya was said to have three, but that would kill a mere mortal by freezing up the vital brain functions.

"I have two in addition to this one."

But he would also be one of those exceptional Coldi with very high brain functionality.

He kept looking at me, and I figured that for a short period it probably wouldn't do any harm, and if it did, Thayu was there to remove the thing; so I put the second device in my hair, where it sought out my skin. After the characteristic burst of heat, my vision blurred. I was about to say something about it when I realised that I was looking at a satellite image of the Earth as evidenced by the curve of the horizon. I was seeing part of the Atlantic Ocean and South America probably from about a thousand kilometres above the surface. The land was about to go into night, but I could see the outlines of the continent through a rim of city lights. Also, the dusky landscape underneath me *moved,* very slowly, but it did. "What's this?"

"A live feed, from our ship. It bypasses the Exchange, so you don't need to book a slot in advance. We'll come a bit closer once you're in position. You can see *exactly* what happens at the surface."

From a *military* ship? Out there in orbit? Spying on Earth? And no one knew about it? It really shouldn't surprise me, but surely Nations of Earth would know that this ship was this close? Surely?

"I'll return up there to monitor the feed. We can zoom in quite a bit. Once we know where to look, we can even read people's tags. You tell us what you want to see and we give you the image and then you can ask further. We can also deliver precise fire that targets exactly the building or person you want to hit."

Hell, no! "I think it would be better if, when we discover illegal activities, we let Nations of Earth or a local government deal with it."

"If the dealing is sufficient." His eyebrows flicked up.

"It will be. Arms smuggling carries long jail terms in all countries."

He gave me a look with the typical Coldi dead fish expression. Clearly he didn't think that sort of dealing was anywhere near sufficient. He wasn't even thinking writs and retaliatory action stemming from them. That was civilian law on Asto. He was thinking . . . however the Asto military dealt with problems. I had a feeling I didn't want to know.

I was grasping at straws. "Asto or its representatives," like, the armed forces, "should not get involved in this. That will make a bad situation worse." Especially if they shot at settlements of Earth from a giant military ship in orbit.

Oh shit, oh shit, oh shit.

He still stared at me, and gave me a tiny nod. He repeated,

"There is an exclusion zone, and a treaty. We won't violate either. If the dealing is sufficient."

And that was all the promise I was going to get. I would certainly mention my concerns about this ship's presence so close to Earth to Amarru, but I had no illusion that either she could tell him to go away—he'd be much higher up in the Asto pecking order than she was—or that, in case someone else told him to go away, he would actually do it. And I didn't really know how close those ships had ventured before. There was a minimum distance of five hundred kilometres—which was the distance that the Exchange core relay orbited at—but as far as I knew, Asto had not officially recognised that unilateral demarcation. I had a feeling they just laughed at it.

Asha Domiri got up from the table. "Keep the feeder on you when we take you there tonight. Have a look around. Report what you see. You'll be hearing from me soon. Oh, and one more thing: don't tell anyone that you know who Mr Kray is."

"Not even Amarru?"

"Not even her. Even if she knows already—and she may—it's best not mentioned again. One never knows who is listening."

"I understand."

"Then I'll leave you to it."

And then he was gone, without even saying goodbye to his children.

Well, crap. If she'd asked, I would have asked Amarru for a few people to accompany us with special security clearance so that they could keep track of where we were and whether any danger was approaching. I hadn't asked for a full-scale nanny with a whopping great big gun.

A voice at the door said, "Are you free now?"

I said that I was, and Amarru came in, followed by two achingly familiar faces: my trusted guards Evi and Telaris.

I greeted them. "Mashara."

"Delegate."

I didn't ask them how they had gotten here when they were supposed to have been in Barresh, and who had told them that they needed to return here and why, but they looked just as relieved to see me as I felt to see them.

9

THE CRAFT I'D SEEN in the shed, of course, was Asha Domiri's, and he was bold enough to leave during the daytime. Even the regular Exchange wasn't in operation then, because the entry point to the anpar lines lay just outside the atmosphere, and the intense vortices of energy that the Exchange core produced when it connected to the anpar network interfered with regular air traffic.

Also, Nations of Earth tolerated the Exchange under the condition that they knew who came in. This craft in the shed violated all the rules, which clearly didn't apply to people high up in the hierarchy. Then again, he'd only be going up into orbit and wouldn't be using the Exchange. Even that gave me the chills. Just where was this home ship of his and why, with all the monitoring of the sky, had no one on the ground noticed it?

We watched the shuttle leave while standing in front of the kitchen window. It was a plain Asto-produced model, without markings of ownership. Apparently this was typical of the Asto army. They wore no uniforms and did not advertise their presence.

One of the guards piloted the craft and it glided over the vineyards in plain daylight until without notice, it disappeared from view. The pilot had turned on the current that ran through the craft's surface that rendered it virtually invisible.

As I looked up where I thought it would be, I wondered: should

I tell someone at Nations of Earth that some sort of huge war ship was hanging around in orbit?

That was another uncomfortable thought. I could just about imagine the furore in the assembly if that bit of information made it into the hands of the media. And the fact that I had a direct link to it made me a traitor, no matter how many times I had to tell them, *Look, people, we're on the same side!*

Then again, that ship or ships might have been there for a long time. Someone, somewhere would already know about it. Observing was not the same as fighting. I'd never seen any evidence that Asto's military was trigger-happy.

And rest assured, if I had anything to do with it, the dealing with these warlords *would* be sufficient.

Since we were not going to leave until dark, Amarru told us to get some rest. My reader beeped. Before I could look at it, she said, "Your documentation for this project has now been made accessible for you."

One of the guards showed us into the dark corridor and a room off the side. Evi told me that they were not tired and they would talk to Amarru's security about their brief and other issues they needed to know about.

We followed the guard into a room at the right hand side of the corridor.

"Wow," Thayu said.

The windows and glass door on the far side of the room offered a view over hilly terrain with vineyards. The sunlight turned every-thing golden. The sky was light blue.

The room was the size of a ballroom, and had a high sloping ceiling with exposed beams. A fire roared in the hearth.

"You can rest in here," the guard said before leaving the room.

We put our measly packs down near the door. After the kitchen with its fire and roaring stove, it was none too warm in this room.

Thayu first headed towards the window. No doubt a matter of habit to check out the windowsill for listening devices, since I couldn't believe she would worry that her father or any of these people spied on her. As she approached, a very large black and brown dog outside rose to its haunches from a lying position outside the glass door and barked a deep *Woof!*

"Whoa!" She froze.

"It's all right, it's only a dog." I had to use the Isla word, because Coldi knew no dogs.

"But . . . look at the size of it. It's nothing like your father's dog."

"They come in a lot of different sizes." My father and Erith had a kelpie that loved to run on the beach and catch sticks and get so filthy wet and covered in sand that you'd have to hose him—which he loved. Since Asto had only invertebrate animals, most of which hid during the day, it had taken Thayu a fair bit of courage to get over her fear of the dog. But Fred was the ultimate people's friend. We often joked that he would probably wag his tail if a burglar came to the house. This animal, almost waist high, ears pricked, tail still and growling softly, was quite a different kettle of fish.

"That is a mean guard dog." I wondered who this house belonged to, because I couldn't see any Coldi handling an animal like that.

We took off our jackets and sat on the couches surrounding the fire. The dog slid back down to the ground, resting its head on its paws. It looked like a giant cat watching a mouse hole.

Thayu sat on the couch, studying the ceiling. She'd want to know how much listening equipment there was in the room, but she also didn't want to go back to the window and upset that dog again. She clamped her arms around herself. Not happy at all. I wanted to ask her about specific concerns, but not knowing where the listening devices were and who they belonged to, she probably wouldn't reply.

Nicha was looking at his reader. He showed it to his sister. "This is where they want us to go."

She took it from him, still with a glowering expression on her face, and read aloud, "Ethiopia is one of those African countries that these days exists only in name. While the rich and relatively cool highlands where the capital Addis Abeba is located are a safe haven and closed off to outside visitors, the northern lowlands, including the Afar region, have largely been abandoned, with the exception of the main road and railway which link the landlocked Addis Ababa region to the port city of Djibouti. The Afar region is known as the hottest region on Earth and over the past fifty years, has seen a slow depletion of its population due to conflicts, unbearable heat and the rising of the water table which rendered the region's main industry—salt mining—unviable by dissolving years worth of salt deposits. Being barred from going up the mountains to the capital, the local population mostly fled to Djibouti. The mining companies which were said to have been responsible for the nuclear tests that caused the 2097 earthquake have since collapsed, leaving the area with the ruined, rusty remains of their activities and a new ocean that is rising at a rate of one metre per year. The area is more than a hundred metres under sea level and the earthquakes have opened underground aquifers to the Red Sea. Because of the area's volcanic history, the water is highly acidic, poisonous and devoid of any life." She pursed her lips. "Sounds riveting."

Nicha said, "Are you sure you're not talking about the Circular Sea?" This was the shallow and poisonous body of water between the two main continents of Asto.

Thayu continued reading. "As a consequence of people leaving, huge swathes of the Afar region are effectively lawless wildlands. Any people who still live there are required to pay dues to militias to protect them, but 'ownership' of settlements changes so quickly that often families can't pay all of their dues. Payment is then made in the one currency of which those people have plenty: children. The boys are cannon fodder, sent out to fight pointless disputes with the next warlord. Most of those never get to fight. They die of heat stress in the desert. The girls fare a little better. They spend most of their lives indoors as domestic slaves or greenhouse workers and, if they are deemed healthy enough, they are forced to remove their IUD and have children." She glared at me, as if this was all my fault. "Militias, cannon fodder? Reminds me of Indrahui. No wonder this guy Tanaqan feels at home."

She showed me a couple of pictures of people: there were young men and boys brandishing guns. A picture that disturbed me was one of a boy barely twelve posing with one foot on his kill: an older man in a faded army vest. There were picture of smiling women, many barely out of their teens, with many children. One picture showed a girl in a filthy hospital room holding a baby with waxy grey, blood-streaked skin, the umbilical cord still attached and disappearing somewhere between her legs.

Death and birth by the time they were twenty.

There was a wide range in types of faces and skin colours. Some people looked very African, some people had dark skin but more of an Indian face shape, some had the lighter skin of the Arabic people who had fled to the region from across the Red Sea in the first of the oil wars.

I scoured the pictures for Coldi faces, as had been prevalent in the Kazakhstan conflict. I found none. Either they were being careful not to show themselves, or they simply used locals. These locals would be grateful to them for providing work and more safety than they might have known in their entire lives.

"In what sort of area is this construction site supposed to be?" I went to sit next to her so I could see the screen.

"This area." She pointed and flicked through a couple of different maps.

The most prominent feature about the maps was that they showed little: a few dots, an occasional dotted line that marked a trail, and one uninterrupted line that said *Afar Development Road* —but in brackets it said *(defunct)*; a few settlements that said *abandoned*; and tentatively drawn in a dotted blue line was the shoreline of the rising sea.

A dot said Dallol Volcanic Research Station and a little info window popped up with the climate. December happened to be the coldest time of the year—an average of a mere forty-five degrees. In summer, the temperature went well over fifty.

Holy, holy crap.

Even more ideal for Coldi than Libya.

A separate document was a report from some sort of aid agency that had worked in the area to the west, but the information was at least ten years old, at which time, according to the report, workers had left because of repeated threats by the krayfish who controlled the camps, camel routes and towns. The krayfish worked in a large area. They held up convoys of trucks on the main road from Djibouti to Addis Ababa. They controlled the camel trains that went to the north. They owned aircraft that flew into Djibouti.

They owned warehouses and shops in coastal towns, including Djibouti.

It was said that Robert Kray had an estimated thirty thousand followers—which was huge in an isolated region like this.

Nothing was said about any offworlders being part of the group.

The rest of the report concerned food supplies to refugee camps, embezzlement of aid funds by administrators in the towns and smuggling of such supplies to war zones. While the situation was sad, and this sort of stuff always made me glad that I'd been born in a safe part of the world, nothing in the rest of the report caught my eye.

10

I HEARD A SOUND behind me. It was Amarru coming into the room. She carried a tray with four steaming cups which she set on the table. The smell of manazhu drifted on the air.

She sat down on the couch next to Nicha and clamped her arms around herself. "It's cold in here."

There were some nods of agreement.

The leafless grapevines bathed in golden sunlight, but under the house's overhanging eaves, it was bitterly cold. Outside the window, the dog went *woof* at something.

Amarru glanced briefly at the fields, but the dog went back to snoozing.

I asked, "A *rabbit?*" Coldi, of course, had no word for "rabbit".

"Maybe. Or a neighbour stepping out his front door. The dog is used to the smell of us and doesn't make a single sound if any of us go outside." Coldi smelled like hot stone. I didn't need to be a dog to notice the scent. "Your *zhaymas* could step outside and he wouldn't do a single thing. For you, it's another matter."

"I won't go out there," Thayu said. "No matter what you say."

"That's smart. The people who are most likely to be attacked by the dogs are the ones who don't know how to handle dogs, but think they do." She nodded at the screen of the reader of the table. "You looked at the information?"

"We did. I'm not sure I like the sound of this," I said. "It disturbs me."

"This disturbs everyone. If we handle this wrong, it will be worse than Kazakhstan." I noticed how tired she looked. Had she slept at all last night?

"I'm puzzled that there don't seem to be any Coldi or any *gamra* people in any images I can find of people in this area. If Mr Kray had brought in a lot of workers from outside, then people would have noticed."

"I don't know that he uses a lot of non-locals."

"Then where does the Zhori clan come in?"

"If they're present, they're being very careful in where they are seen."

"False identities?" It used to be that anyone who left the Exchange enclave was given a valid Earth identity. Many people still had them.

"We usually know where the holders of those passes are."

True.

The door opened and Evi and Telaris came in as silent black figures.

Amarru gestured them to the couch. *"Mashara,* do sit down."

They did, looking uneasy as they always did when they were asked to join us. They were truly most happy when standing outside guarding the door.

She now touched the underside of the tabletop. It lit up like a screen.

On it was a more detailed satellite image of the area. "This is what we're looking at. This was taken this morning."

I stared at the lines in the grey-brown landscape. There was a lot of activity at the site if the little specks in the sand were anything to go by. A lot of dust, too. She flicked across to a nearby area, where a sprawling building with a white roof stood on a hilltop close to the encroaching new ocean shore.

The water was shallow and a sickly green colour. You could see the bottom for the most part. It reminded me of seeing the images of the Aral Sea drying up: little salty waterholes surrounded by a salt-encrusted landscape.

"This image shows Mr Kray's house. You can see the pipes running down to draw water from the shore."

I could see the pipes going even underwater.

"When the sea is full, the house will be right on the beach. As you can see, he's got palms in his yard already. We'd love to know what goes on in these buildings, what is being built at the main site and why, who he is using to build it and how they're being paid."

"They won't be paid," Telaris said, his voice dark. He spoke seldom enough that the sound of his voice shut everyone up.

Amarru gave a *go ahead* sign. "This is why you're here, because you are familiar with his customs."

"All the Indrahui warlords have obtained their power through the life debt system."

"You're talking about the thing called *pahemin?*"

"Yes. People who are very poor pass their debts onto a leader in exchange for their capacity to work. The leader effectively owns this person."

Amarru nodded. "And the leaders frequently abuse this power. The poor people have nowhere else to go, because they have no money to buy out the debt, and what is worse, they pass it onto their children. It's a very abusive situation."

Telaris nodded, his expression distant.

Amarru put a grey folder on the table and pushed it across to me. "Here is your documentation and your cover."

I picked the folder up and opened it.

It contained ID cards, a couple of scientific articles and a list of numbers. A thin flexi-screen with an ID page had my photo, but the name was Martin Spencer. Designation EN, no EXO. Geology researcher—the articles in the folder were all in his name. Married, two little kids. Well, I guessed this was the only way I'd ever be a father.

"There is a small research station in the region that used to belong to the Geology Department of Reading University in England. The research staff pulled out about ten years ago. It's now about to go underwater as a result of the filling up of the Afar basin. You're going to be visiting this area to check up on the Department's prior work. You will be an academic with no further knowledge of what's going on in the region."

"I presume I'm not going alone. What about my assistants?" All of whom were decidedly from off-world.

"The university employs a lot of Coldi people. Everyone who has them can use their local names. I've created a new one for Thayu." Back in the days that the Exchange was hidden, it used to issue Earth passports and other ID under assumed names. It still produced a new identity for every *gamra* person who did any work outside the Exchange enclave. I guessed Thayu was overdue to receive one. I glanced in the folder.

"Gracie Chan? Could you at least have given her a tough name?"

"Let me see." Thayu snatched the card out of my hands and goggled at it. "I can't even read that."

Nicha glanced over her shoulder. "That doesn't look like you. Here, it says that you live in Rome."

"Where even is that?"

Amarru waited until the two stopped clowning with the card. She was also one of the people with the least-developed sense of humour I knew. Well, outside Danziger's office at least. She continued, "If you manage to get onto Mr Kray's land, you will simply ask if it's all right if you take a few measurements on his land— which isn't really his, but let's keep it polite. On one of the datasticks, there is a huge dossier of papers that you can show him to prove that you're the real deal. You might read them because some of them are quite interesting. Did you know that the Afar basin started filling up after the 2097 earthquake, which was triggered by testing of fusion bombs in the area?"

Seriously, was there anything she didn't know? "What if Mr Kray tells us to fuck off?"

"I'm assuming there is a chance that might happen. Then you'll tell him in a very old-style British way that it's your right to work on parts of the shoreline that are not private land. According to the records—you'll find them on the datasticks, too—he simply annexed the land and doesn't own any of it. If you can, try to avoid his patrols. Do use Asha's excellent satellite images. You'll find them very helpful."

"By the look of things, Mr Kray might have lots of people with guns. That will stop us."

"Still, tell him you'll complain to the authorities and that it's your right to visit the station. It's on a piece of land that *does* belong to the university."

I blew a breath out through my nostrils. "I don't like this. You're sending me out to provoke. I might as well take a writ and staple it to his front door."

She grinned. "You are getting very clued up on Coldi habits. No, we'll do no writs. We're sending you out to investigate with a couple of people who should know the man's customs." That was what Evi and Telaris were for. "Nations of Earth was going to send you on a diplomatic tour where people who know nothing would have confirmed that it was all fine and taken care of. They know it's not, but like Kazakhstan, they were going to ignore it. You can't ignore Romi Tanaqan and not suffer for it."

"What do you actually want done about him?"

She formed her hand into the shape of a gun and made a sound like a gunshot.

I felt chilled. "That's what Asha is here for, right?"

"He is monitoring the site from orbit. The ship has ultrahigh-resolution cameras. I'm sure you've already seen the quality of the images."

Why didn't I believe her? And worse, what was I supposed to do about it? If Mr Kray was caught for some transgression, he could never be brought to trial, because he didn't fall under any laws. To speak with Asha, the dealing could never be adequate if we had to keep it legal. But if we allowed Asha or some other assassin types to interfere, we'd have to deal with the fallout of breaking the Nations of Earth imposed "treaty", which determined that Asto's military had to stay outside the 500 km exclusion zone. And Danziger would use that as a vehicle to close the Exchange.

If we *didn't* "deal" with these people in this illegal way, Asto would face serious allegations at the *gamra* assembly.

There was no winning this issue.

"You're leaving tonight," Amarru said. "We've got everything organised. Take everything you've got with you except documentation that identifies you by your real name. You're supposed to be dead."

"Can I at least let my father know that I'm not dead?" I asked.

She shook her head. I'd known that. "We'll drop him some hints. Give me your ID. I'll look after it."

She held up her hand and I deposited my *gamra* card in it. She was good. I trusted that the news that I was very much alive would reach my father in some way, because he was sufficiently clued up on *gamra* communication to pick up on it.

I was going to ask her about Ezhya, but stopped myself before I made a fool of myself. Of course he'd know I wasn't dead. He didn't read Flash Newspoint. Sometimes even I needed to be reminded that Earth media were not the main source of all information.

———

Amarru told us to rest, and we slept a good part of the afternoon, Thayu and I in the bed and Nicha on the couch. The room was so large that it refused to warm up despite the fire. At least the down blankets were warm.

When the day faded into night, we gathered in the kitchen for an evening meal. It was just on the tail end of getting dark, and a pale glow remained on the horizon, visible from the kitchen window, although I wondered if those were the lights of Athens rather than the setting sun.

While we were asleep, Amarru had returned to the exclusion zone, and we were left in the house with a few guards who said little beyond the necessary. A few times one or two got up from the table and went into the hallway. We'd hear their voices, but whatever they spoke about wasn't important enough to mention to me.

Likewise, Thayu and Nicha said little because they didn't know which association the guards belonged to and Evi and Telaris said nothing at all because they rarely did anyway. I spotted one of the men leaving the kitchen with a bowl of dog food.

It was not the most amicable meal I'd ever shared.

When we were done, we were told to pack and wait outside.

We did, not that "packing" was the right word for collecting our bags from the room, which took all of a minute.

The night was without clouds. The Moon had yet to rise, but an ice-cold wind had come up. I shivered in my hot-weather clothes. I hated to think what Thayu and Nicha felt. In fact, I hated the entire mission already.

I should have told Dekker to get lost. But I also knew that I couldn't have, and he knew it, too. In the ramp up to the election campaign, Danziger sought to bring me under his influence so that I couldn't be too outspoken against him. If I'd refused the job, he would have attempted to discredit me and the people I represented. He would find plenty of ammunition to do so.

All of a sudden there was a whoosh of air that was a good deal stronger than the icy breeze.

If I hadn't known what to look for, I wouldn't have seen the aircraft that landed in front of us. With the current through the surface, the craft was never rendered entirely invisible, but it was close enough not to be noticed.

Holy crap, did the Exchange regularly break its own rules about no craft landing anywhere other than at the Exchange?

And of course Thayu knew what I was thinking. "They have security reasons why they sometimes do it."

A door opened in the side of the craft and the ramp extended. We clambered in, getting covered in dust that blew up from the downward jets. It was dark in the cabin, with only bluish light coming from the controls. There were three rows of seats behind the pilot. We found a seat each. I sat next to Thayu with Nicha on the other side of the aisle. Evi and Telaris went in the back. We passed our bags to them, and Evi stacked them on an empty seat.

Apart from the pilot and communicator, there were no other crew on board.

To my surprise, the pilot was not Coldi, but Indrahui. That was . . . unusual. One of the guards outside shut the door and banged his hand on the metal surface. The craft was off with a sudden jerk and when I next looked out the window, we were high above the land. The glow of the city beckoned on the horizon, not as close as I had suspected.

The craft climbed and climbed. We left the land behind. The moonlit ocean glittered below us. It never ceased to amaze me how powerful these engines were. I also wondered about flight routes and air traffic control and if the Exchange had anything to do with this highly illegal flight. The communicator was doing all kinds of things on his screen, but nothing that looked like normal air traffic control stuff from the Exchange. Of all things, he was looking at satellite images.

Soon, the outside view turned dark, except for the occasional light from a tanker on the tranquil waters of the Mediterranean.

Neither the pilot nor the communicator spoke to us. I wanted to ask exactly where we were going, but that wasn't a thing delegates did. Your staff was meant to be responsible for that, never mind that they wouldn't have a clue either.

Evi and Telaris were discussing something in Indrahui. Their voices were soft and barely rose over the rushing sound of the engine and the air under the wings of the craft.

Nicha used the time to catch up on some sleep, but Thayu was studying something on her reader. She was normally the first to sleep, but I could tell that she wasn't happy with the situation of being in an unfamiliar world without knowing where we were going.

Well, that made two of us.

11

I MUST HAVE DOZED a bit, because all of a sudden there was a lot of noise around me, and I woke up feeling sweaty with a crick in my neck.

It was still dark outside. Judging by the tilt in the floor and the low hum of the downward jets, we were landing somewhere, apparently. Already?

"Where are we?" I asked, my tongue still rubbery with sleep.

But Thayu must have decided that it was safe after all, because she was fast asleep in the seat next to me.

Nicha sat up, wiping sleep out of his eyes. "I have no idea. You're the expert on this world."

I tried to look out of the window, but all I saw were a few lights in the darkness. A vehicle, I thought. It was hard to see because the air was hazy.

The craft settled on the ground. The shuddering of the floor caused by the downward jets stopped. Dust drifted past the windows.

Evi and Telaris were peering out the window. Their night vision was better than mine. Thayu had now woken up with an unhappy moan.

"Is this where we get out?" I asked.

"It seems so," Nicha said. He didn't sound particularly happy either.

The communicator opened the door. Sharp and crisp dry desert air came into the cabin, laced with the smell of hot stone— the result of the downward jets roasting the sand.

I rose, feeling sick and stiff from sleeping in an uncomfortable position. Ow, my neck.

Outside in the dust stood a battered old minibus. The head-lights lit a patch of pebble-strewn sand, dust swirling in the beams. The driver wore some kind of loose-fitting kaftan, with cloth wound around his head. A pair of brown eyes studied us through a slit in the fabric. The surrounding skin was dark and wrinkled.

We got into the bus. The seat directly behind the driver was taken up by haphazardly stacked boxes.

Evi and Telaris took the seat immediately behind that, Thayu, Nicha and I behind them. Our bags remained on the floor in the aisle because the very back seat was also buried under what looked like the local parcel deliveries.

The driver exchanged a few words with the aircraft's communicator before the door to the craft shut again. I had no idea what language they spoke.

The driver came to the bus, jumped up the steps, dropped in the seat and took off. Never mind talking to us about where we were going. Never mind closing the door.

The road was bumpy, full of dustpans and potholes. Whatever little of the countryside was revealed in the beams of the headlights didn't look particularly interesting: sand and rocks and more sand. Most of it was brown and dusty. The terrain was rough and hilly. Sometimes we went down a gully where there might or might not be water when or if it rained. Sometimes a few clumps of dead grass or the occasional dead bush or tree trunk that had long since lost its smaller branches.

Too hot even for termites.

It was December, I had to remind myself when I thought that it wasn't particularly hot today.

After an hour or so, the sky started to lighten in the east and, because the sky was cloudless, the sun rose soon after. The first of morning light revealed a desolate landscape that looked disturbingly like Mars. The terrain was rough, with deep gullies and sharp ridges. The truck had to pick its way over a goat track that wound up and down the rough and rocky hillsides. The parched soil was yellow or brown, with rocky outcrops. The only vegetation consisted of small clumps of grass between the rocks, and the occasional grey bush.

For a long time, we saw no people, but the path we followed was marked with many tyre tracks. Then again, with the little amount of rain this region received, who knew how old they were?

Later on, there was a little more vegetation, mostly greyish grass. A few camels roamed the hills, although there didn't seem to be anywhere near enough vegetation to sustain them.

Around this time, probably about eight in the morning local time, my feeder sprang into life with a crackle that made jump.

A voice in my head said, *I see you've arrived.* It was the dry voice of Asha Domiri, sounding like he sat in the bus with us.

I breathed deeply to calm my racing heart. It was just me hearing this, right?

Thayu and Nicha were both dozing, Nicha leaning against the window, Thayu lying curled up on the bench on the other side of the aisle from me.

Can you hear me? the dry voice came again.

Yes I can. My excuses. I wasn't expecting this.

You have arrived at your destination.

I don't think so. We're in a vehicle. I'm not sure how long we still have to travel. We seem to have been given a ride with the local postman.

You're in the area. We can see you.

Great.

We'll be doing some scans of the region with this pass. At our current orbit, we will be overhead twice a day for you, and we won't have reception the rest of the time. You'll also find that your local feeder will move in and out of action as we pass overhead and disappear out of range. The area where you are has zero Exchange coverage.

I had not expected any different. The feeders generally only worked in some parts of Europe. When we visited my father in New Zealand, they didn't work either. And of course that information now went to him.

I could feel his mirth when he chuckled. *You are truly a curious fellow.*

Curious and a subject of Coldi interest, maybe, but I was going to make sure that this whole project, and Asto's obsession with not being seen to be involved in activities that would get them in trouble with the *gamra* assembly over their involvement on Earth, was not going to lead to anything that would lead to *my* getting in trouble with Nations of Earth. Not to mention cost any lives on Earth.

I want to make it clear that I'll use the images you obtain, but if you want to come any closer, like, to get involved in a conflict, I have to abide by Nations of Earth rulings and will have to notify the assembly. In the current climate, I don't think they will take too kindly to that.

I understand completely.

Why did I get the feeling he was laughing at me? Why, every time I dealt with a high-ranking Asto figure, did I see that article at Flash Newspoint, written by Melissa Hayworth when she still worked there: *They Toy With Us.*

Because they did, and one day, something was going to blow up in someone's face, and that someone was likely to be me.

We kept driving. Gradually, we came to areas with more vegetation, some green vegetation even, although the latter was mostly in fenced-off farm fields. Camels made way for goats and donkeys. We met a small truck coming the other way, and then a second one. We occasionally came through little villages where people lived in huts made from rough stones, where kids ran after the bus and the occasional other vehicle honked at us.

This was also where I saw the first petrol-driven vehicle I'd ever seen outside of a museum or some historic parade. It was a little truck with an open tray at the back that had once been red, but was now a faded shade of pink dotted with spots of rust. It was being driven by an old wrinkled man whose hair was much lighter than his skin, and the tray held a cage made out of concrete mesh, which contained two goats. Likely, the age of the vehicle was more than twice that of all its occupants combined.

It turned into the road in front of us, blowing a cloud of black smoke from the exhaust. Urgh.

Thayu had woken up and was watching the scenery with wide

eyes. To be honest, she looked a little alarmed, especially when we passed someone with a camel that had a giant net full of cardboard boxes strapped to its back.

Nicha had also woken up, but Evi and Telaris were both asleep.

"Look," Nicha said.

Before us the land sloped down to a jumbled shantytown. I checked my map. We had arrived on the outskirts of Djibouti. According to my documentation, this had been a refugee camp after the second wave of oil wars.

Both sides of the road were taken up with a messy jumble of flimsy constructions. Tents, cardboard, plyboard and many things that would collapse into a soggy heap when they got wet. Rain must be non-existent, because the street, dirt, guarded and closed off on both sides by a forbidding fence, was dry. Clouds of dust followed each vehicle. Children combed through rubbish thrown out by the side of the road. People sold melons and other produce in little stalls.

At intervals there were taps with, concrete washbasins, where long lines of mainly women waited to get water or do their washing.

As in the images I'd seen, there were many different types of people. Dark-skinned women in colourful robes, some with their heads shaven, others with their hair in little plaits; men in white kaftans, wearing head coverings like our driver; some men wearing modern clothes, shorts and shirts and sports shoes. There were children everywhere.

It was now midmorning, and the bright sunlight had washed out the colours. A haze of brown dust hung over the city.

Seen from our air-conditioned comfort, the scene was surreal.

"Just like the Outer Circle," Nicha said.

"Nah," Thayu said. I understood that she had spent a fair bit of time in the Outer Circle, although she never spoke about it much. "This society has no structure. Everyone works for themselves." Coldi had an infallible sense for societal structure. Nicha had once explained that the first thing they'd look for in any group of people was its leader. They would determine in a glance if the leader was of higher or lower status than themselves, and if higher, they'd find the next level and work their way down until they found someone of the same status as themselves. To my question how they knew this, I got a blank look. It was *sheya*, the instinct. You knew. There was no explaining this.

Our bus got some odd and suspicious looks either from other drivers or people across the fence. The vehicle had been clapped out and old by my standards, but compared to local traffic, it was brand new.

Sometimes little children ran after us on the other side of the fence.

"What are they shouting?"

"Probably they want money or jobs," Nicha said. His voice sounded dark. Over the four years I'd lived with him, I'd learned that he appreciated his comforts.

Gradually, the buildings became more solid, even if that wasn't saying an awful lot. Row after row of three or four storey apartment blocks stood crammed together. Exposed raw concrete was eroded and stained with rust. Most of the windows no longer contained glass. Some of the walls bore bullet holes from past conflicts. Were those from struggles between warlords or was this damage from longer ago?

There were people everywhere. On the balconies, on the streets, leaning on the windowsills, in the alleys between the buildings. Many of them were black, wearing long robes. Some were weathered desert people wearing white, grey or blue robes and fabric wound around their heads. Some were lighter-skinned, Arabic types.

The road was no longer fenced off and the chaos of vehicles, bikes, pushcarts, pedestrians and animals was complete.

For some reason, Thayu and Nicha went to sit on the floor between the seats. Both were intently listening to some security instructions that I wasn't privy to.

The way Thayu frowned usually meant trouble.

I tried to get her attention so that she could tell me what was going on when the earpiece stopped talking to her, but it didn't. She motioned for me to sit down on the floor, too.

They woke up Evi and Telaris, but they remained seated.

The floor of the bus was extremely dusty. It was also hard and the road bumpy. Either that or my backside was too skinny.

From my position in the aisle with my arms looped around my pulled-up knees I could see Evi's face. His moss-green eyes roved but the rest of him was perfectly still. The gun rested on his upper leg, so that the barrel protruded in front of the window, where everyone could see it.

Then the bus stopped.

Another traffic jam?

People shouted outside. Cars honked their horns.

What's going on? I mouthed to Thayu.

She listened and shook her head. Nicha was listening, too. A man outside was yelling, but I couldn't make out what he said.

My vision wavered for a moment. I gasped, steadying myself on the seats on either side of me.

A voice in my head said, *Leave the vehicle.*

What? They were going to give me instructions up there, too?

For your own safety. Leave the vehicle now. A bunch of armed people are coming in your direction.

Thayu was already on her feet, walking to the back of the bus.

Evi said to the driver, "Can you open the door?"

"We're not at the place yet." This was the first word I'd heard the driver speak.

"What's going on?" I asked Thayu.

"A militia road block."

"Are they looking for us? Are they krayfish?"

From his seat, Nicha said, "Likely. We don't want to find out. We don't want any of them to register our presence here."

Thayu pushed the rear window. In most buses, it came out easily, but not this one.

The driver said, "You want to leave? Wait, I'll open the back do—"

With the butt of her gun, Thayu smashed in the rear window.

The driver protested. "Hey! Who's going to pay for that?" He'd gotten out of his seat, but was being held back by Telaris.

A blast of hot air came in.

Thayu kicked the remaining glass out of the frame. Evi jumped through the hole onto the street. Nicha handed him the packs, then he more or less manhandled me out of the window and jumped down himself. Then Thayu. The driver tried to hold her back, but she simply pushed him aside. Telaris was the last to leave the bus. He handed the driver a small object—I suspected either a bundle of grubby bank notes or a credit chip, and vaulted through the opening.

A small crowd of people who had left their vehicles or pushed their bikes or carts closer to see what was going on had gathered around the bus.

"Follow me," Evi said. He lifted his gun so that everyone could see it. Onlookers pushed out of his way. We followed him in single file through the traffic chaos. Around cars, behind trucks. Curious folk had gathered everywhere.

It was so hot that the heat radiated through the soles of my shoes. The light reflecting off car windows was so bright that it was hard to see where we were going.

I tried to look to the side to see if anyone was following us, but sweat was running into my eyes.

"They're following," Nicha called out. "There are three, no, four of them."

He didn't say who, and there was no time to explain. I had trouble just keeping up with my team.

We reached the side of the street, where even more people had gathered. A woman yelled at us, waving her hands. What did she want?

Evi led us into a side alley crowded with onlookers and street vendors and beggars and graceful women carrying jugs of water on their heads, and men in kaftans sitting at tiny little tables smoking.

At the sight of us, a good number of people started down the alley, more than the narrow passage could cope with.

Evi called, "Out of the way. Out of the way." In Coldi because no one here would understand Isla anyway.

Women yelled, staring at his gun. Within seconds, a crowd of people had closed in behind us and I could no longer see the road behind us where we had left the bus. Neither could I see anyone following.

Evi was still calling out, "Out of the way. Let us through!"

We moved forward following a narrow path through the crowd. First Nicha and then me and then Thayu with Telaris bringing up the rear. In that maddening throng, I concentrated on Nicha's back.

We turned left and right a few times. It didn't take very long before I'd lost completely where we were going. I fixated on Nicha's back. If we became separated, I would be seriously screwed.

And then—whoa—the street opened up. We entered an open square surrounded by a ring road of traffic. On the other side were a few glittering high-rise buildings. We crossed the stream of traffic —which wasn't moving very fast.

In the middle of the square was an attempt at a park, but the grass was dry and trampled by hundreds of street sellers and beggars, many of whom watched us. A few came up to us. Some got scared by Evi's gun, but a few yelled out, presumably to me, "You wanna buy pills, mista?"

Some were even blatant enough to wave said pills in little plastic bags.

Nope, I did not want to buy their drugs.

I had enough trouble keeping up with the pace that Evi and Nicha set.

We crossed the stream of congested traffic on the other side of the square. Here we entered an upmarket shopping area, where guards in uniform shooed the street sellers and beggars away. Girls in western style clothes got out of black chauffeur-driven cars. Many were accompanied by some poor maid or male servant, walking a few paces behind them to carry their shopping. Western-style music blasted out of air-conditioned shops. Beautiful, groomed—and rich—people sat in cafes and sipped their drinks through fancy straws. A woman carried a handbag that contained a baby cheetah. The poor thing was looking around at the strange surroundings with bewilderment.

There were only a few streets of this clean, rich and surreal haven before we passed another line of security guards and were back in the dark backstreets with the beggars and street sellers.

By now I was so hot that all my clothes were wet.

Thayu gave me a concerned look. "It's not far from here," she said.

"I don't even know where we're going."

"Just somewhere to stay while we organise ourselves."

Not much later, Evi led us into a building that was no different from the dreary bullet-hole-ridden concrete apartment blocks that surrounded it.

It was not until we arrived in the foyer—a low-ceilinged job with a worn and dirt-stained tiled floor where it smelled of spicy cooking—that I saw the "Hotel" neon sign on the back wall of the foyer. Guess it would have been easier to see had the sign been on, but it wasn't, and it was so dark inside that I wondered if there was a power outage.

A single man sat behind a rickety desk that served as check-in counter. He was one of the Arabic type people, with fairly light skin, curly hair and a beard streaked through with grey. He took one look at us, rose without a word and disappeared through the door at his back.

"So much for service," I muttered, staring at the empty desk.

A moment later, he came back in the company of a woman. A Coldi woman.

Ah, now I understood. This was a place from the *gamra* register. Stupid me. I should have realised that they were everywhere.

12

———

THE WOMAN'S EYES widened at the look of Nicha's Palayi earrings. She took up a subservient position and he had to lightly touch her shoulder and lift her chin up before she could meet his eyes. She turned her attention to the counter, leafing through a grubby book, flicking pages forward and back again.

The man said something to her and put his hand on her arm as if to calm her. I couldn't hear what he said and probably wouldn't have understood but I guessed that he didn't like it when she did this. He was not alone in this sentiment. This superior and inferior ranking business made even me uncomfortable, and I'd lived with it for years.

"I'm Tamu," the woman said in Coldi, her voice timid. Omi clan, judging by her earrings. "How can I help you?"

"We need a place to stay for a few days," Thayu said.

"Yes, yes." She leafed through the book, running her index finger along the lines. "I can't fit all of you in one room. Our best rooms have only three beds. Or a double and a single."

"You don't have any apartments?" We'd become used to that luxury.

She almost flinched. "We have nothing as fancy as that. This is not a very good area. If that is what you want, you will need to go downtown."

"That's fine, we'll have two rooms. Adjacent ones if possible."

That was possible, she said.

She took a long time writing our names, mine as Martin Spencer in Isla, Thayu and Nicha's in Coldi in the awkward hand of someone who hadn't written Coldi for a long time. She grew even more flustered when trying to enter Evi's and Telaris' names in the book. She claimed she "didn't know their language" and asked them to accept her apologies. Was I correct in thinking that she recognised them as Indrahui and that this Robert Kray/Romi Tanaqan guy had really made a name for himself even in this town?

Thayu and I would share with Telaris and Nicha with Evi.

She accompanied us up a set of rickety stairs. The upstairs corridor was dark, with a bare floor, and a few lights that could be nowhere near bright enough for her Coldi eyes.

She babbled on. "You're lucky. We were very busy just a few days ago. Lots of visitors from all over. They're gone now. Here are your keys. Rooms 34 and 35 are yours." She gave another subservient greeting and then she turned around to go back downstairs.

Nicha snorted when she was out of earshot. "I must have been living here too long, but I hate that simpering and cowering."

Yes, I disliked it, too.

"Room" was a misnomer for the hole in the wall on the other side of the first door. Both rooms were on the street side, now in the shade, but the windows would receive full sunlight in the morning. It had a narrow double bed under the window and a single bed against the side wall, leaving enough space to walk around, but barely enough for bags. The walls had once been painted in a strange kind of ochre coating, but roof leakage—did it even rain in this place?—and substances I did not want to know about left dark stains on the walls.

Nicha and Evi definitely got the better deal. Their room had two single beds in the same space where ours had a single and a double.

I opened our window but the air that came in was neither cool nor fresh. In fact, it smelled like the curious combination of hot cooking oil and garbage.

"Urgh," Thayu said.

Coldi noses were more sensitive than mine and even I found the smell too much to put up with. I shut the window again, annoyed at the stuffiness in the room. Even in Barresh the air wasn't as breathless as this, or maybe it *felt* better because it didn't smell so bad in the places I frequented.

"Well," Thayu said, dropping onto the bed. The bottom was exceptionally springy, like a trampoline. "Let's look at this from the bright side. It looks like we've managed to shake all minders, body-guards, guides and spies. Unless the woman downstairs at the desk is someone's plant, but I'll get that checked out." She fiddled with her reader. "I need to wait until the ship comes over, though. No reception." She leaned back, folding her hands behind her head.

I sat on my side of the bed. It creaked and wobbled ominously. "I'm a bit more worried about how we are going to get to this research station without running into any unexpected nasties. It's quite a distance from here, and the krayfish patrol the roads." I wiped my face. Damn, it was so hot and stuffy in this room.

"We're getting there our way. We got coordinates, we got some help up there." She looked at the ceiling. It was also water-damaged with big brown patches.

"Thay', we can't let your father have his way with his guns. Just can't. He jokes about the exclusion zone, but it's serious. If Danziger even knew about all the spying that they're already doing that's outside the agreement, the fallout would be huge. I don't know how to make him understand."

"My father is one of Ezhya's direct thirds. No one makes him understand anything."

"Why did Amarru get him involved? *She* understands."

"Amarru did not *get* him involved."

I stared at her, finally realising who was calling the shots here, quite literally. There was infallible logic in that realisation. If he was the highest-ranking person involved in this project, he would be in the lead.

Except I didn't have to adhere to Coldi structures. I often did out of respect, but I didn't have to. *That* was why I was involved. As a safeguard. As subordinate to him, Amarru could not tell him "You can't do this." There was only one person who could. I was that person.

Damn.

———

We waited until dark before Evi and Telaris went out to get something to eat. I wasn't hungry. In fact I was starting to feel ill. My stomach was grumbling a lot and that usually didn't bode well. I administered some adaptation medicine in the hope that it would clear it up, but this kind of rumbling rarely ever vanished without first getting worse.

Evi and Telaris came back. Clean water was expensive, they said, and most of the food was of dubious quality. They'd bought some packaged stuff which was also not cheap. Most of the shops didn't accept credits and the hole in the wall where they went to get local currency charged them way too much. They tried to barter it down, but it had been clear that they were giving a hefty commission to the local police because apparently they were not allowed to change any money for "chans".

Evi and Telaris weren't chans even, but when I said that sort of treatment set the tone for the kind of reception they were going to get here, they said that they'd had to beat off a few people who'd come up to them asking for jobs.

The pre-packaged things they had bought were mostly dry biscuits. I forced myself to eat some, because we'd be unlikely to get anything of better quality.

While we were eating in our room, my vision suddenly went dark. For a moment I thought I was going to faint, but then I realised: I was getting an image sent from the ship. I focused on it the same way you could get a reader to work with your mind. An image resolved from the fog. It was a city from above. There was a mass of cars and people standing around doing nothing while a couple of cars with an emblem on the roof blocked the traffic. It looked like the jam where we had escaped the bus. On closer inspection, the emblem on the roof was the PanAf symbol.

A male voice said, "We processed this and enhanced the resolution. It's a test run."

This would be a lackey appointed by Asha to communicate with us.

"I'm receiving it clearly."

I streamed it through to Thayu, who was busily putting through all her requests while we had connection. She looked at me and nodded. "I thought they were responsible."

"You don't know that they were trying to stop us in particular. No one came after us when we ran into the alley. It might have been just a random road block."

"It might." Clearly she didn't think so.

"Come on, Thay', just tell us what you're thinking, because this is kind of frustrating. Also, if we know, we can help you keep an eye out for whatever you want us to look for."

"There's the thing: I don't want you to look for anything. I don't even want you to know *that* any of us are looking for anything. You are a scientist and we are workers."

"But I only want to help you. Two pairs of eyes miss less than one."

"Honestly. You know how Amarru said that the people most likely to get bitten by a dog are those who don't know how to treat a dog? So I stay away from dogs, because I don't understand them. You stay away from trying to be an amateur spy. Because I want you to go home with me when we're done in this horrible place."

An intensity in her eyes stopped me from making a joke. She wasn't joking, and the situation was not to be joked about.

"OK, then. But what sort of cover do we have? Everyone knows we're here. It's kind of obvious with me being pale and taller than many. Evi and Telaris are being recognised as the same, perhaps related, to Robert Kray. The place isn't exactly a tourist destination."

"Well, last week it was."

I frowned at her. Then remembered that Tamu at the front desk had also mentioned that it had been very busy.

"I asked my father and he got into some images from around here." She took out her reader and showed me an image, much enlarged, of a bunch of vehicles travelling down a dusty road. They were accompanied by a gyrocopter.

"It's flying really low," Nicha said, looking over his sister's shoulder. He mentioned just how low, which he calculated from how far the shadow was from the vehicle, the angle of the sun, the coordinates of the location and the orbit of the ship. Yeah, just like that. Maybe I could do it after spending half a day struggling with formulas and calculators.

Thayu enlarged the image even further but even at the highest resolution, we couldn't see any demarcations on the gyrocopter. Just like the one that had attacked us in Rotterdam.

"PanAf, again," Thayu said.

"I don't understand why you think that."

"They use gyrocopters."

"And alone that makes PanAf a suspect?"

"They always were suspect."

"Well then you know more than I do. PanAf is part of Nations of Earth."

"PanAf are probably doing very well out of the krayfish. They administrate an area that was previously lawless and useless and make it orderly and give locals jobs. They don't want anyone to poke about in their business, because they know the president won't like it, but people are happy and they have food, so what's the alternative?"

I spread my hands and was going to say something self-righteous about laws and international responsibilities, but the only time people would care about such things was when they had enough to eat and had a safe roof over their heads.

———

We went to bed, but I had trouble sleeping. Even if I'd taken some adaptation medicine, it was too hot and stuffy in the room. I tried opening the window again, but the owner of the shop downstairs was having a protracted argument with his wife that involved a lot of yelling. And although he was no longer cooking, the smell of it lingered and annoyed me.

The double bed was like a hammock and Thayu's body temperature was running at higher than normal. I couldn't avoid touching her and lay sweating most of the night. My stomach was still making strange noises. When it started getting light, I felt like I'd been awake all night. My back was sore from trying to stop myself sliding against Thayu.

I must have slept some, because I woke up sweating with morning light streaming into the window, and Thayu and Telaris making rustling noises with paper.

They had bought breakfast: some kind of doughy bread rolls pre-wrapped in plastic.

Telaris complained again how all the food was really expensive.

I suspected it was only expensive because of what they bought: western, packaged food. However, being Indrahui who ate yellow-coded food, there were certain ingredients they needed to be careful with, and normal street food didn't come with ingredient lists. They were weary, might have been burned before, or might be intensely aware that being sick precluded them from doing their jobs. They took their jobs very seriously.

Hence bland pre-packaged food.

There was a knock on the door and Nicha and Evi joined us in the already cramped room.

"Thought I could smell food," Nicha joked. The all-pervasive smell of oil mixed with garbage was so strong that even he couldn't possibly smell anything over that.

There was little room, so Evi sat on the bed where Telaris had slept and Nicha on the big bed. This made the mattress sag even more.

"Whoa." He had to stop himself sliding towards the middle. He looked at me. "Did you sleep well?"

"Ha, ha, ha."

"I slept well. I'm ready to start work." He held a reader and a projection attachment under his arm.

But first, we ate the odd breakfast of bread with some sweet drink from a bottle. The fluid was cold. Magic!

"Someone obviously has a working fridge somewhere," I said.

"No idea how. The power is off half the time," Nicha complained.

"Well, obviously, this is not the Exchange," Thayu said.

He glared at her and her implication that he was soft and unused to such hardships caused by computer failure.

I was not in the mood for their good-natured underhanded stabs at each other. Thayu was exaggerating her tough girl stance as much as Nicha professed to liking luxury. My stomach started growling again after that strange meal. This was not good.

After we finished eating, Evi set up the reader and projector in the middle of the double bed.

He looked at me for a sign to start talking and began when I nodded. "We need to plan how we are going to do this, how we'll travel there without being noticed, what we will be looking for once we're there, and what plans we have if things go wrong."

Everyone fell silent and listened. I guessed this was a security type briefing that I wasn't normally privy to. I felt strangely honoured to be included but would have been a lot happier if my bowels would stop gurgling like a sewer.

"This is the area where we're going."

The projector sprang into life with a three-dimensional map. It showed Mr Kray's mansion and the abandoned research station. Evi took us through the distances between those places. The research station was barely two kilometres from Mr Kray's mansion, but it was on an island in the middle of an area that was about to go underwater and Mr Kray's mansion was on the shore. The building site was also on the shore but about five kilometres north of the house.

The elevation of the research station was sixty metres below sea level. The temperature was forty-three degrees Celsius. It was seven in the morning.

It sounded like fun.

13

———

THE FIRST QUESTION was how we were going to get there. For a settlement that was supposed to be built as a "tourist destination" it sure knew how to make sure no one ever visited the place.

The only sign of civilisation in the area was the mining town that had seen bursts of activity followed by long periods of abandonment. There had once been a train line, but it hadn't been used for well over a hundred years. A road project that linked the mining developments up with the main road from Djibouti to the Ethiopian highlands had been abandoned before it had been completed.

There was a goat track of a road to the research station but it probably hadn't been maintained since the researchers left and was so badly eroded and covered in sand that it would need desert trucks with large wheels to get through the sand drifts. We might have to travel at night, Evi said, but also added that there was not much in the way of cover and that however we travelled, anyone keeping an eye out for intruders would easily find us.

"What about by air?" Thayu asked.

To which Evi replied that he had seen no airfields in an extensive study of Asha's images.

"Aren't the locals fond of gyrocopters?" Nicha asked.

"Too noisy," Telaris said.

They all agreed with that.

"Maybe we could hire a water plane," I said. "We want something light that doesn't make a lot of noise, doesn't need an airfield and doesn't show up on radars."

"I thought you supported the ban on *gamra* vehicles outside the Exchange enclave."

Yes, any of the lighter Asto-built craft would do very well.

Still, they agreed that to hire a private pilot might be the best alternative.

Then we needed to buy some supplies for a trip.

Thayu said, "We are meant to be a research team and they would be well-prepared, having travelled there before. This is extremely hostile and remote country. They would have to know what they're doing."

I agreed. The information Amarru had given me about this Martin Spencer indicated that he had travelled extensively in all sorts of remote areas.

I suggested that we ask Tamu for the best places to get what we needed.

Thayu said, "I agree, but I've submitted a background check of her to the Exchange. I don't want to say anything sensitive to her until that comes back clear." Sensitive information obviously also included the fact that we were going into the desert.

"She's Omi, not Zhori."

"I know, but I still want to be sure."

Nothing was ever sure in the eyes of security. In an unknown place, every person on a corner could be a spy.

Next, Thayu insisted that we got clothes that would make us less easily recognisable. She went out with Evi and Telaris' quickly diminishing pile of grubby bank notes, and returned with a bunch of kaftans wide enough to wear armour underneath. Thayu was adamant that I should disguise my hair, so she had bought me a headscarf of the type that many of the local men wore.

Evi and Telaris got a pair of colourful African gowns. She carried black hair dye in her gear—given to her by Amarru in case she needed to disguise as an Asian, and spent a good deal of the morning in the rather disgusting bathroom at the end of the corridor dying their hair.

By that time, my insides had completed their noisy deliberation about the food I'd eaten and had decided that they didn't like it, so I spent a good amount of time there as well, while said foodstuffs were being expelled from both ends. But enough said about that.

We went into the afternoon sunlight while it was turning golden. We wore our disguises. The kaftan was cooler than the suit and it looked like my adaptation was starting to kick in. All good things to make me feel better. I still felt a bit shaky but Thayu informed me that she thought I looked better, and also that adaptation medicine at higher doses messed around with my digestion as much as the natural adaptation did with hers.

Thanks very much for that bit of detail.

She grinned at me.

Wandering around the surrounding city blocks didn't provide us with any information about transport. We did find a place that rented out old, open-cabin vehicles and got one to make it easier for us to move around town. The traffic was chaotic but we were fairly close to the edge of town and went out into the hills on badly-maintained bumpy roads. There were young boys with goats and camels going in and out of town and here and there a couple of fields where a bunch of old women were hoeing in the dust waiting for the rains.

It was a dusty, desperate, desolate landscape.

While we stood on a hill overlooking the countryside in the lowering sun, Thayu's request on Tamu's background came in. The Exchange judged her to be safe and clear.

She read off the screen. "Born in Athens. Never been to Asto. Too poor, probably. The guy who runs the hotel is her partner."

This was another side of the equation that people like Danziger often forgot: so many of these Coldi had lived here for generations, no longer had connections with Asto, or even with the Exchange.

Tamu was by all measures an Earth citizen. Apparently, she had lived in this area for about four years.

Thayu was not entirely happy. "The Exchange register is not always right or up-to-date."

Nicha said, "No. But it's the best we've got. If she's lived here for that length of time, any illegal activities that she'd been involved in would have come out."

"I'm not worried about legality. I'm worried about possible connections with Mr Kray. They can't know everything. So yeah, I asked. I got a reply. There is nothing obvious, but I'm still going to be careful."

We'd walked up the hill and when we came back to the vehicle, we found it surrounded by a mass of curious children and a few adult women. The children ran as soon as we approached, but a few of the women lingered when we got into the vehicle. Evi was about to put the car into gear when I had an idea.

"Wait."

I opened the door again and went up to the group. One of the women was clearly the boldest and maintained her position whereas the others retreated a bit.

"Can I help you?" I asked in the clearest Isla I could manage.

She held out her hands in a pleading manner. She was quite young, in her early twenties, and her face still had the pretty roundness of youth. "My husband. My brother. Where are they?" She was looking not at me but at Evi in the car.

"I'm sorry. I don't think I can answer that question for you. What happened to them?"

"The big man, he comes in a big truck and he takes all the men away. They like to work for him because he promises good money. He turns them into krayfish. And then they leave and we never see them back. You are going to see krayfish, right?"

A chill crept over me.

Here I was standing talking to a victim of the warlord while highly visible in the countryside. Anyone could tell that we didn't belong here, that I was poking my head in places where it was likely to be chopped off.

I said, "I'm very sorry. I don't know anything about missing people. I'm just a scientist studying geology." I gestured at the fields. "I study soils, so that you can continue to grow things." I smiled, feeling like the biggest coward on the planet.

While I walked back to the vehicle, I realised that the majority of the people we'd seen working in the fields had been older, women or children. The majority of people on the streets in town were older, women or children.

Either the men were fighting, or they were dead, or they were working for Mr Kray.

We drove back in the fast-developing dusk. The dust in the air rendered the sky in fiery reds and oranges. It was very pretty and too tranquil to be real. I felt uneasy. Someone in that chaotic jumble of traffic, dilapidated houses and messy markets had to be spying on us.

Tamu sat at the desk watching something on a screen when we came in. The suburb's power was on, but the only light in the foyer was a feeble tube light without a cover. She looked up, her face lit from underneath by the screen. "Oh, there you are. I thought you might have been caught in the traffic jams in town."

"Isn't that the normal state of affairs?" I said. I realised immediately that I wasn't supposed to have said anything in Coldi, and her eyes widened in such a way that I guessed she rarely heard a non-Coldi person speak it.

"You're very good."

"Yes. Apparently I have an aptitude for languages." Like, fifteen years' worth of study kind of aptitude. Dumb move, Mr. Wilson.

"No, the traffic is not usually like this. The army has set up roadblocks and is combing through whole blocks house by house."

Thayu gave me a sharp look. *Searching for us.*

I nodded. Highly likely. PanAf was looking for us because PanAf didn't want us here? Because they meant to orchestrate my visit and now they had lost sight of me, thought I'd been killed and realised that I had made it here without being chaperoned to "approved" places by some government official.

"We didn't see any army people or road blocks," Nicha said. "Where was this happening?"

She mentioned a part of town. I didn't catch the name and it didn't mean anything to me.

Thayu said, "We're interested in travelling to the Afar Sea, and have been trying to find out what is the best way to get there."

Her eyes widened. "Why do you want to go out there?"

I was highly tempted to say, *It's supposed to be the next hottest tourist destination,* just to check her reaction, but stuck to a more professional approach. "We have a research station out there. Our institute abandoned the station five years ago, and we were always going to check how the area was coping with the rising water levels. I'm a geologist." One who speaks perfect Coldi. I was still hitting myself in the head for that stupid move, but the damage was done so I might as well continue.

"But it's dangerous out that way." Clearly she knew little about rising water levels. "Some of the gangs have their base out there and you don't want to interfere with them."

"We're fine. We're armed."

Thayu showed her a glimpse under her jacket.

She looked at us with wide eyes. "Well, if you really want to go, people normally fly out to places like that."

"I thought so. Where can we find a pilot?"

14

———

ONE OF THE LESSONS of life: white material in a plastic bag spells trouble, especially when slapped onto the counter of a dark shop in the outskirts of Djibouti by a man missing his front teeth and with a look that said, "Here's the stuff, now give me the money."

Trouble was, I had no idea what was in that bag, and neither did I have any money of the type that he would accept. I'd walked into his shop because Tamu at the hotel had told me this was where I could hire a pilot and I wasn't going to become an accomplice in someone's drug ring. With his teeth gone, the man could be a krayfish, the first we'd seen. Could be. Or he might just have bad teeth. I was starting to distrust everyone in this crowded, stinking town.

I eyed the white stuff, which looked like a bar of soap crushed under an elephant's foot, and decided to ignore it.

"Actually, I'm looking to hire a reliable pilot. Can you help me?"

He squinted at me. Sounds of people talking drifted in from outside, as well as wafts of hot desert air. "I help people with eperything, mista. Where do you want to go?"

"I'll tell the pilot that."

"Oh, there are no secrets here, mista. You leave and ask permission and then eperyone will know where you go."

"Do you or don't you have a pilot?"

"I hap the best pilots in the world." I had to admit that the lack of front teeth did interesting things to one's ability to say the letter v.

"Then get me onto one those pilots." I pushed the bag with the white stuff back to him.

"Don't you want—"

"No, I don't."

"You go out there, you die, mista."

"I think we'll be fine." I had my adaptation medicine. I'd take an extra dose. My body temperature would go up and I could stand the heat.

He put the bag back under the counter with a kind of *suit your-self* look on his face. No, I did not want his drugs. I really didn't.

"A pilot," I reminded him, hoping that my refusal to buy his drugs was not going to create ripples. We could handle small-time crooks, but really wanted to stay out of the way of the big guys on top of everything else.

"Yes, yes." He pulled an earpiece out of his pocket. Earth-made, so that was all above water. He didn't seem to like how I watched, so he turned his back to the counter. He spoke to someone in local dialect, with a lot of hand gestures.

I waited.

Lights blinked in the far corner of the shop, where I guessed he had some sort of hub setup.

I waited, eyeing the various wares for sale on rows of plastic sheets on the dirt floor and tables for the smaller items. There were engine parts, bits of agricultural equipment such as ploughs, battered-up tools, control panels of machinery, a plane propeller. Many of the parts dated from the fossil fuel era.

Thayu studied a giant jet engine that sat just inside the door, and Nicha walked around a big scoop that might have come from some sort of mining vehicle. How had this guy even obtained all this stuff?

Everything was very dusty, so maybe it had sat here all that time.

Primitive as the shop looked, I'd noticed that the roof was made of solar panels when I came in. There was a bank of batteries in the corner and I'd noticed a charging station with a couple of differently shaped docks, currently empty. Was that for charging weapons or equipment? It made me vaguely uncomfortable that I didn't recognise the make.

The shop owner finished his conversation.

He turned around. "There ya go, mista." He shoved a reader across the counter. "Pilot." He pointed at the screen with a dirty, yellow-nailed hand. It showed a map of the area, the same as I'd been given by Tamu with directions on how to come here. He dragged it across to where a small local airport was marked on the map. A box popped up on the screen with details of an ID with the CF designation, whatever that might mean. The man's name was Henri Dubois. CF stood for what? The shop owner pointed. "Pilot."

I copied the ID to my reader and sent Mr Dubois a message: *Are you available for hire?*

He must have been bored, because he replied almost straight away. *I'm free right now.*

Good. I'm coming over.

I gave the shop owner the thumbs up. "Thank you for the help."

"Hey, what about money?"

"What money?"

"You give me money for getting you pilot."

"According to my contact, you get money from the people we hire." Tamu had warned me about this guy's double-dipping. Seemed she was not quite as dumb as Thayu would have her.

He glowered, but didn't protest.

Ha. Mr Wilson: one, corrupt officials: zero.

I walked out of the shop, collecting Thayu and Nicha near the door.

It was almost midday and the light was so bright that my eyes needed a bit of time to get used to the glare.

The vehicle we'd hired sat in the blazing sun. Evi sat in the driver's seat and Telaris perched on top of the curious-looking frame that I presumed was for attaching a bank of solar cells.

Surrounding the vehicle was a sea of kids and teenagers holding out their hands to them, going *ferengi, ferengi!*

One of them shouted. A number of the youths turned around, and they took off. All the others followed.

Well, what the hell.

I walked across the cracked pavement and climbed into the car. It had been sitting in the sun, and the seats were like hotplates. Ouch, my butt.

"*Mashara,* what was all that about?" I asked Evi and Telaris.

"That was what I said earlier," Evi said. "They came out as soon as you were gone."

"Any idea what they wanted?"

"*Mashara* couldn't begin to guess."

Money, probably.

"I got the name of a pilot," I told them. "Henri Dubois. Usually hangs around the airport." I felt like a real bright spark when I said that. Where else would we find pilots anyway? I could imagine Thayu rolling her eyes. Thankfully, she didn't. I wasn't in the mood for smart remarks.

"All right, let's go there, then."

Telaris let himself slide off the frame and dropped into the back seat. Thayu got in next to me. The gun in her arm bracket made her jacket bulge. Just looking at her made me sweat. It was much too hot for a jacket.

But I was glad for the car, primitive and noisy as it was. With the dry desert wind in my sweaty face, life almost became bearable.

15

DESPITE HIS EUROPEAN name, the pilot was a local. Not as old as the fellow in the shop—in fact, I could have believed him to be still a teenager—and quite a bit lighter-skinned, with curly, rather than frizzy, hair and in possession of his front teeth.

He smiled and held his hand out to me. "Henri Dubois. I got your message."

His Isla was perfect. Canadian, I thought. That surprised me. "I'm Martin Spencer and these are my assistants." Time to pull out the fake ID. "I'm a geologist for Nations of Earth. We need to go to the Afar Rift Research station. Can you take us there?"

His eyes widened briefly. "The station is dead, mister. Abandoned. No one there. About to go under water."

"I know. We'll be making climate measurements."

"We have only one climate, Mister, and that is fucking hot. It's dangerous out there. I take you to the coast. It's much nicer."

"Nice try, but why don't you let me decide that? You can either do the job or you don't and then I'll go and find someone else to do it."

He digested that for a moment. Then he asked, "You pay creds or trade?"

"Creds. Three hundred a day, in return for the hire of your time, the plane and fuel. Oh, and your silence."

His eyes lit up briefly. I could see the greed flash behind his eyes. But he didn't agree straight away as he would have if there'd been no objections or risks to circumnavigate. Which, obviously, there were.

"Interested?"

"I might be."

"We'll be gone for a few days at the very least. You'll provide our transport. You get paid on arrival back here."

"You kidding, sir? Most likely, you don't return. That's not a safe place where you're going, and I like to have my bases covered."

"I think you don't understand. You're coming with us all the way. You'll get to see what we're doing and get to explain it to the locals. That's my deal, take it or leave it."

He snorted. "You play hardball."

"I need you when we're there, too. While we're there, we'll want you to fly some survey trips around the shores of the sea."

Another double take. "It's dangerous, Mister. Because of rogues."

"You tell me where it's dangerous, and we'll avoid those areas."

He thought for a little while. Nodded. "It will be extra."

"We can talk about that."

"Are there any other trips you want to take when you're there?"

Good. He was weighing up his chances of seeing his money.

"It depends on what we find when we get there. There is an area of hot springs I may wish to visit if it's still here, and I want to survey the surrounding countryside. Do you want to do it? Because I'd like to get there today. If you don't want to do it, I'll find someone else."

"No, no, I'll do it. When do you want to go?"

"We're ready when you are."

Still another double take. "In a hurry? That will be ex——"

"Take it or leave it."

He scowled. "Come with me."

He preceded us over the cracked and dusty concrete. I guessed he needed the job after all.

There was a lot of activity at the airport, with heavy long-range aircraft probably coming in from the north, from Europe. They were big fat things constructed of the lightest carbon-fibre with double-walled, helium-filled frames and huge solar wing areas including expandable sections that would unfold like an umbrella once in the air.

I glanced inside the cargo hold of one of those giant planes. It was filled with crates wrapped in yellow plastic. The black lettering across the side was too small for me to read. Foreign aid? Also, was this where those guns had been found?

"It's food and things," Henri said when he noticed me looking at the crates. "Especially because of the election, the rich countries give us lots of things. The president wants to make sure that he has a job after the election."

I expected Henri's plane to be some old thing dating from last century. A single propeller six-seater or something like that. The other small planes at the airport were all standard, battered-up models, some of which had to be almost two hundred years old—patched up, hand-painted old rattlers.

It was worse. He had a bloody power glider.

I stared at the flimsy structure thinking, *There's just no way I'm going in that thing*, and he was already loading the bags in a shopping basket like contraption attached under the main wing structure. The wing-sails were paper-thin, dirty, but on closer inspection turned out to be a complete solar sail on carbon-fibre movable struts. The cabin was made from a metallic-looking material I recognised as some sort of carbon, with brackets of a light brown alloy I had never seen.

Well, what the hell. This place continued to throw curve balls at me.

We climbed into the cabin. Evi and Telaris behind the pilot's seat, then me, and Nicha and Thayu elected to sit at the very back.

Nicha, sitting across from me gave me a suspicious look. I guessed he wanted to ask me if I thought that was going to be safe or make a comment on the origin of this plane, but we had agreed not to speak Coldi, because we shouldn't be advertising ourselves too much.

Henri climbed in, making the whole construction wobble ominously.

The glider hooked up to the launcher, which propelled us to a less-than-impressive speed and I was convinced, glad almost, that the bird wasn't going to fly. But then there was a soft click and solar sails unfolded from underneath the wings. Dark film soaked up sunlight. Thin material billowed full of hot air. Hot air collected under the wings. I could see it shimmer. The upper surface of the fabric became silvery as the photovoltaic cells activated. Holy shit; it had a nanofilm. The vehicle picked up speed of its own. The single jet engine fired, smooth. This thing was designed for stealth.

Nicha was staring out the window. I could see that look on his face that said that he was trying to figure out some technical detail. He was surprised, impressed. Nicha wasn't often impressed.

The plane levelled out, giving us a view of the entire city in its dusty, jumbled-up glory. To the right in the hazy distance, I could see the azure blue waters of the ocean. A long pier jutted out towards the horizon, with a couple of behemoth freight ships moored on either side. This was the main importance of this town. This was why everyone tried to control this little speck of land and why everyone was trying to buy up land and warehouses.

We soon left the city behind and flew over a rural area with little green fields and mud brick houses.

Soon after that we encountered the rugged terrain that we had crossed while coming here in the bus.

I stared out the window. The country that glided below us looked alien. Jagged pink-brown hills strewn with rocks. The slopes were steep and sometimes the strata exposed by erosion were so clear that it looked like someone had hewn steps in the hillsides. It was basalt, according to Martin Spencer's notes, volcanic country, and the area where we were headed contained many active volcanic features.

The only vegetation were little bits of grass in the valleys or the occasional bush. Occasionally, too, there would be a faint dusting of green over the landscape, where some rain had fallen recently. There might be a badly-eroded road, a few abandoned shacks or the remnants of a few fields. The endlessness of it was depressing.

The plane was quite fast but Henri informed us that it would be almost dark before we arrived.

I tried to sleep, but I could never sleep well on flights, so I watched the landscape change underneath us, not in a good way. If anything, the surface became more like the pictures I'd seen from

Asto. More hostile, with jagged rocky outcrops poking through sand dunes, with dried up lakebeds having deeply cracked soil, with clouds of dust blowing across the land.

Then the landscape became more alien still. Sharp columns of stone poked to the sky. The valleys were scarred and pitted, marred with vast tracts of saltpans of different colours: bright yellow, green, orange, pink. Quite a lot of water for the fact that we were in a desert.

The earth's crust was at its thinnest in this region of the world and it was being ripped apart at amazing rates. The Earth's tectonic plates moved under each other in the Pacific. That was why we always did earthquake drills in New Zealand when I was young. But here was the spot where plates were being ripped apart and new earth formed and cooled. Apparently, geological features moved apart as much as a couple of metres per year. Yellow pools, pink pools, green pools, vents spouting poisonous gas. This was the arse's end of the world, and the world had been eating beans.

"Interesting," Thayu remarked. "It's got the colours of Asto and the steam vents of Barresh. I wonder if it smells as bad."

"I bet it does."

I gave her the quick rundown of what I'd read in my notes. The deepest point of the Afar Rift was a good deal below sea level. In 2097, a combinations of the earthquakes that might have been caused by the underground testing of fusion weapons by an Indian company and rising sea levels in the Red Sea was thought to have allowed seawater to seep into the area through underground aquifers. It currently filled an area half the size of England, and was up to twenty-five metres deep and salty as old boots.

Land and the new ocean bled into each other with areas of salt pools and mud flats. We flew over this area when sunlight was starting to turn golden.

The water below us was pink-brown, with pools of green and yellow to the side. The sand dunes that surrounded the water were orange, pierced by jagged pinnacles of rock that pointed at the sky like deathly fingers.

There were several islands in the new sea, and the research centre lay on one of those: a couple of dusty and forlorn buildings surrounded by rocky ground that sloped to the water. It was kind of strange when it came into view. A desolate landscape with a rim of encrusted salt at the water's edge that had grown over everything on the ground: rocks, a discarded tyre and an oil drum. There was no vegetation at all.

The plane circled over the island a few times and put down on the flat next to the lake. When Henri opened the door to the cabin, a blast of heat came in that was so strong that at first I expected it to be a hot stream from the engine. Except the plane didn't have much of an engine to speak of, and it was at the top of the cabin, nowhere near the door. I'd expected the water to have a cooling influence, but it didn't. Holy crap. The heat radiated through the soles of my shoes. I'd have to dial up the adaptation a notch.

We took out our luggage and walked over the sand flat to the buildings that looked even more forlorn on the ground. People had come past in the five years it had lain abandoned and scrawled slogans over the walls. There were remains of a fire on the doorstep, and a couple of empty bottles.

The soil around it was cracked and dry. While walking across it, the crust broke and my foot sank into a layer of soft mud that covered the top of my boot.

"Holy shit, we have to watch this stuff."

I pulled my foot out. The soft goo was bright yellow.

THE RESEARCH STATION'S box-like residential building was so hot that it almost hurt to breathe the air inside. We opened the doors and windows, and the breeze that came through was a little cooler, if extremely dry. It stank of sulphur. Everything around here did.

The research station's air-conditioning was fried. Thayu spent some time trying to get it going, but too much of the insides of the machine had been fused together by an electrical fault, and rusted over because of the salt-laden air.

We inspected the living quarters. Sweat was running down my back, and Henri's face was shining with it. Evi and Telaris remained on the veranda with the excuse that we needed a lookout.

Thayu and Nicha didn't care about the heat. I didn't care too much because I could take an extra dose of adaptation, but I worried about Henri. The station had closed years ago because people had died from heat stress after the electrical meltdown. Henri was our only way of getting out of the place. Yet when I asked him about coping with the heat, he said he was fine, albeit in a slightly nervous way.

We allocated rooms: one for me and Thayu and one for Nicha and Henri and one for Evi and Telaris, although they hadn't yet come inside. We unpacked our food supplies. Henri looked suspiciously at the packets of red-coded sauce.

He didn't say much, watching with wide eyes. He seemed too innocent for the type of job he did. I asked him some questions. Yes, he had grown up in Canada, but had left during the North American crisis. There were no jobs, he said, no nothing if you came from the wrong part of town. People were just being shot in the street and their only crime was to be poor. Was it any wonder that unrest had broken out and that people with extremist views on both sides had gone to battle?

He was black because his mother came from Ethiopia so he had gone to stay with his family. He had learned to fly locally. To the questions where he had gotten the money for such an advanced plane, he merely smiled. Crime, I suspected. Smuggling of something or rather. I still wondered what the CF on his pass stood for, but I didn't ask because I could look it up.

We ate from our rations around the rickety table in the single kitchen-living room. At least us four did. Evi and Telaris seemed to prefer to stay outside. Both the heat and the tense conversation were pressing.

I explained to Henri what we wanted to do tomorrow: survey as much of the shoreline as was feasible and take photographs of the soil and geological features.

He asked if we knew that we would need permission from the local ruler to fly over the shore to the north. I said we did. We planned to get that permission.

He laughed, uneasily.

He still had all his teeth.

"Don't you think he'll give it to us?" I asked, innocently.

"Well, um . . . he'll want to know who you are." He glanced at Thayu.

"You can explain that for us."

"Me?" It came out as a strangled squeak.

"Yes. That's part of the reason we wanted a local guide: so that he could communicate with the locals and explain the situation to them. You speak their language."

"Um. Yes." He was looking at his hands. He wiped his face, leaned forward on his knees and wiped his face again. "That will be . . . more." He mumbled something else.

"More what?"

"More money. For talking to the warlord. Up front."

"When we come back. We don't have any money that we can give you here."

"You have connection. I saw it. You can put it in my account."

"Why can't you wait until we're back? That's what we agreed."

"Because I have to live, mister! If you die then what am I supposed to do?"

"You'll grab all our stuff and sell it. That's what. I stand by my offer and our agreement. You'll get all your money when we come back."

He nodded, but didn't meet my eyes.

Soon after, he got up from the table. "I'll be going to my room, then. To contact the warlord."

"Let us know when there's a reply."

He nodded, but as he went into the corridor, I realised that he hadn't even asked for our full names, so there was not a chance that he was actually going to ask for that permission. Besides, we ran our connection through the Exchange and he wouldn't have access to that. Maybe he had some other way of communicating. Watching him in the next few days would be interesting.

Thayu got out her reader and we briefly discussed the route we'd take tomorrow. Nicha and I had to speak Isla to make sure that Henri didn't get too suspicious. He was sure to be listening, and I was sure that he was reporting to someone about us.

Meanwhile, the real conversation went through our feeders, because the ship was overhead.

We wondered if we'd just stumbled onto a spying pilot, if spying was a side revenue stream for pilots in general, or if he'd been tipped off by Tamu, or hired by someone tipped off by Tamu.

It was all speculation.

Thayu stared at the open door into the blackness of the night. She was intensely unhappy about the situation.

I don't understand any of these people.

To which Nicha remarked, *There are spies and corrupt people on Asto.*

Of course but at least there I understand why they'll sell themselves to certain people but not to others.

I nodded. It was true, but only once you knew where a person's loyalty ties went. Before that time, you were as much in the dark as here.

Loyalty links are not hard to find out, Thayu commented.

They aren't if you have the highest security clearance. And certainly not always then, either.

"Anyway, I'm going to bed. I'm tired." She rose from the table and Nicha did the same.

"I'll be there soon. I want to check on the guards," I said. *Keep an eye on him,* I told Nicha before he went to his and Henri's room.

I went out the front door to the veranda. The Moon had come up and cast pale light over the water, still as glass.

The two guards sat cross-legged on the ground, leaning their backs against the wall. The air had cooled a bit.

"Mashara," I said, and sat down with them.

They nodded. "Delegate."

"It's actually not too bad out here now," I said.

"It's acceptable." Their moss-green eyes were possibly even greener in the glow of the little light on my reader.

"Are you going to stay out here all night?"

"Mashara will keep this place secure." Which was as much as saying yes, and I wasn't really supposed to ask about their operations in keeping us safe.

"I don't trust the pilot," I said.

"No." Simple. Blunt.

We looked out over the water. The night was absolutely still, with not a breeze of wind, not a sound made by an animal. There were not even insects.

"We'll fly over some of Mr Kray's territory tomorrow," I said. "I'm sure that *mashara* is aware that he is from Indrahui. Is there anything about a warlord from Indrahui that we need to consider?" It was as personal a question as I'd ever asked them. I was uncomfortable with it, which was why I hadn't asked it earlier, because I knew that they would be uncomfortable with it, too. Neither of the men had ever discussed how they came from Indrahui to work for Amarru, who had passed them on to me. I had never even caught them trying to contact their family, although I hoped that they did.

I wasn't surprised that a long silence followed my question.

Eventually, Telaris said, "This man is well-known. He got busted for smuggling Asto-made arms, but he should have gotten busted for countless acts of insane cruelty."

Evi nodded, his face dark. He was no longer looking at me, but sat with his head bent staring at his knees. "Nobody ever cared about all the people he killed, because Indrahui is not a full *gamra* member."

I said, "It's not *gamra's* task to—"

Evi interrupted me. He had never done that before, and the wide-eyed look in his eyes chilled me to the core. "I know, Delegate. I know." Evi and Telaris didn't often refer to themselves in first person either. "It's *gamra's* task to administer the Exchange. And so they do that, but they talk endlessly about which worlds are worthy and which ones have structures in place that obey their laws before they're admitted as members. This world is not a member. But this world satisfies the most important condition: it has an official independent body which can send people to protect civilians. It's a really good one, too. No, it's not perfect. It's bureaucratic. Sometimes it's a bit biased and sometimes there is corruption, and it's slow. And sometimes there are political reasons why they won't or can't do anything. But think of it like this: the *gamra* assembly is as close as we get to this terrible, bureaucratic, silly organisation that's Nations of Earth." I hadn't heard this level of sarcasm from them either. "So, Delegate, if no one at *gamra* says anything about the cruelty of these Indrahui warlords, then who will? We have no Nations of Earth."

That outburst chilled me even more deeply. I looked from Evi to Telaris, who nodded quietly. "Do you know this particular person? I'm sorry if I ask questions that are not appropriate for me to ask."

There was another long and dark silence, in which I imagined the figure of the Grim Reaper floating over the still water. Nothing lived there. Wars and other human stupidity had left this place utterly destroyed.

Telaris cleared his throat. "Delegate, we were taught that it's not appropriate to state a person's personal motivations."

Now it was my turn to burst out. "Oh, just cut the 'Delegate' bit. We're stuck here in this terrible place together. If you have anything on Robert Kray that can help our mission, or that helps me understand the situation, tell me. Use my name. Be or don't be 'appropriate'. I don't care."

There was another long and heavy silence.

I was thinking about getting up and going to bed. I was tired and, to be honest, a bit sick of everyone's hang-ups.

Then Telaris said, "Nothing is appropriate about seeing your sister's baby cut from her body while she is alive, about being forced to watch that, and seeing her life blood seep into the soil. This man, whose name doesn't deserve to be spoken by anyone, ordered that done. He watched it, too. He had the power to stop it. He didn't. He laughed."

Evi cried, "And what does *gamra* bust him for? Smuggling arms! They cared nothing about her and all the other people he mutilated. Nothing!"

I made another important conclusion. "You're brothers?"

Telaris nodded.

"I'm going to kill the bastard with my bare hands," Evi said. "I'll take his body to Indrahui. I'm going to string his guts across the desert. I'm going to cut off his head and feed it to the *garrongi* and when the crushed skull comes out the other end, I'll put it in a box with ribbons, and bring it to our mother." He leaned his head in his hands.

I had no idea what *garrongi* were, and I had a feeling I didn't want to know.

Telaris put a hand on Evi's shoulder. The moonlight that reflected off the water showed that his cheeks were wet. I wiped my cheeks, too. I felt stupid, insignificant, arrogant and ignorant. Of course I never claimed that I knew about hardship, but I professed to understand, to attempt to deal fairly with people.

But every now and then, something happened that made it painfully clear that I knew nothing at all.

17

I SLEPT BADLY. I kept thinking about Evi and Telaris and their family, still at Indrahui. Their world didn't qualify for full *gamra* membership because their regimes systematically excluded several groups of people, and because there was no overarching organisation that had the power to bring warlords to court. Also, *pahemin,* life debt, the system of indenture in which time was exchanged against money. It put poor people at the beck and call of rich ones. It was akin to slavery.

It was hot in the room and I was thinking that Evi and Telaris had the best deal, sleeping on the veranda. Taking adaptation medication always made me feel feverish and jittery, my stomach was still not one hundred percent, the standard of the bed was not great, and the thought of Henri compromising our safety didn't help.

I was wakened in the middle of the night by a soft noise. It took me a while to realise where I was. Apart from the faintest glow of light through an open window, the room was so pitch dark that I could see nothing.

I registered that Thayu was no longer in the bed. I whispered, "Thay'?"

Of course the ship was out of range when we needed it.

She activated her reader and gestured *An intruder* in the bluish light. The light went off again. I slipped out of bed. On my hands and knees, I felt for my bag and my gun in the side pocket. Its weight and metallic feel were oddly comforting.

At home where she had plenty of backup, I'd let her deal with this, but not here where she and Nicha were alone and unfamiliar with the surroundings. And where were Evi and Telaris? Why hadn't they heard anything?

I followed her down the short corridor as silently as I could. I hoped we'd disturbed a monkey or some such thing, even if I knew that nothing grew in this area and there was nothing for animals to feed on.

A faint glow came from the kitchen. Someone had put a light on the table and stood bent over on the other side, checking bags.

Thayu leapt forward and ran across the kitchen. The intruder called out, "Hey!"

She crashed into him. They both fell against the wall and slid to the ground with a thud that made the flimsy structure of the building shudder. The table was shoved sideways, pushing two of the chairs over. The door opened. Evi and Telaris came in both with lights in one hand and guns in the other.

Thayu had wrestled the intruder to the ground. She sat on top of him to keep him down.

Evi directed a light into his face. He squirmed away from it.

It was Henri. Damn, I should have thought of that.

He met my eyes in the space between Thayu's body and her arms and squealed, "Get your fighting machine off me!"

"What are you doing sneaking around in the dark?" I couldn't muster the energy to be friendly. I pushed his bags aside. They were the same ones that had been in the plane. "Did you want to sneak out without us? Leave us stranded here? Why did you think you could get away with that?"

He squealed. "I'll do anything you want but don't tell anyone about me. They will kill me! Please, please."

"Who will kill you?"

"The krayfish! I don't know what you're doing here, mister, but they will kill you, too. Please let me go!"

"And leaving us stranded here wasn't going to kill us?"

"I was just going out. I was going to come back, honest!"

"What have you done that makes you so afraid of the krayfish?"

But he was crying and pleading and saying that he'd do anything we wanted as long as we let him go. I could get any sense out of him.

I noticed something on the floor. He'd been carrying a packet of white cubes, similar to the material I'd been offered by the old krayfish at the shop. The little bag lay under the dining table and some of the white cubes had come out. I picked up one of his bigger bags and pulled open the zipper. The bag was full of similar little plastic bags with white cubes. "You're trying to use this trip to smuggle drugs?" Had he been about to meet up with his contact?

"It's not like that at all! Yes, it's a drug, but it helps to cope with the heat."

What. The. Hell. I picked up one of the cubes. Sniffed it. The material lacked the distinctive smell that my Coldi-produced adaptation medicine possessed.

Nicha frowned at me.

"He says it's adaptation medication," I said in Coldi to him. And then to Henri, "Is this your business? Is this why you have a fancy plane like this, because you smuggle this stuff?"

"Please, mister! I'm not doing anything wrong."

"It's illegal technology. Hasn't been tested on people on a mass scale and there are no approved versions of it." That was the official Nations of Earth position.

"Mister, when you have to work in that heat, you can be dead from heatstroke or you can live and work another day if you take the medicine. That is all the approval I need."

True. I blew out a breath. I was being a hypocrite of the worst order. I took adaptation, and it hadn't harmed me. Sure, there would probably be people who would have bad side effects, and a proper medical trial would be needed before it could be released into the population, but as far as illegal things to smuggle went, this was an area where I was happy not to support the Nations of Earth position.

We'd gone crazy on the poor guy. Evi and Telaris stood at the door, Nicha at the entrance to the corridor, and Thayu pressed his wrists to the floor above his head.

I gestured to her *Let him go.*

She sat back. Henri scrambled to his feet and dropped into one of the two chairs at the kitchen table that still stood upright.

"Where did he get this stuff?" Thayu asked.

"I went into that shop to hire him, and a guy offered me a bag of this stuff. I thought they were illegal drugs and ignored it." The man *had* said that I'd need the stuff. Damn it, he'd been trying to be helpful. "I suspect it's everywhere in this region." Allowing people to survive here.

"As long as that's the only thing he's got," Nicha said from the door. He grabbed Henri's second bag and upended it on the table. The stuff that fell out was just the usual: mainly clothing, a pair of thick-soled shoes—for walking on very hot ground, and a few bits and pieces of technology related to the plane.

Nothing suspicious.

I picked up one of the fallen chairs and set it upright then I sat opposite Henri, looking into his face. He was wide-eyed.

"If you have anything to say to us now, about Mr Kray or your relationship with him or about what you've been hired to do, here is your chance."

"I don't know Mr Kray."

And when I gave him my best disbelieving stare, he added, "I know *of* him, of course, who doesn't?"

I kept staring. He fidgeted, rubbing his wrists where Thayu had held him.

"I sell the stuff to some of his workers. Sometimes." Meaning that he snuck into the building site without Mr Kray's approval?

"Do you come out here often?"

"Sometimes." He looked down. Meaning a lot, I guessed.

"Were you trying to sneak out to meet a business contact?"

He nodded, still not looking at me. "I'm sorry, I won't do it anymore. We can go and do your work—surveys, whatever—tomorrow and then I'll take you back to town as promised."

He still struck me as nervous and flighty.

Nicha said, "It strikes me that these few bags here would hardly be worth coming all this way to meet someone for. These few samples wouldn't last people very long."

Henri let his head sag further. "The rest is in the plane."

I met Thayu's eyes, hoping that she understood. She held her reader and was probably listening to the crude translation that the device would make.

"Who is your supplier?" Nicha asked.

"I don't want them to get into trouble. There is going to be enough trouble already. But I have to eat, mister. I've done nothing wrong."

"Tamu is your supplier, right?"

He nodded. Another piece of the puzzle fell into place.

"What do you want us to do about him?" Telaris asked me in Coldi.

I had to think about that for a while. I still didn't trust him, and still didn't think we'd heard the entire story. "Go back to bed. Keep an eye on him to make sure he doesn't leave the room. I hate to admit it, but we need him. We—"

I became aware that no one paid attention to me. They were all listening. From somewhere in the distant darkness came a heavy *thud-thud-thud-thud.*

18

———

"**A** GYROCOPTER." Henri's eyes were wide. "It's PanAf. They're coming for us."

Thayu and Nicha glanced at each other. *What now?* The ship must have been flying overhead, since we were going through a patch of connectivity.

Gyrocopters means PanAf? Nicha wanted to know.

PanAf or militia, as far as I know.

Why would he think they're PanAf? If they were, why would they come for us?

I shrugged. *Your guess is as good as mine.*

"Quick, quick. We have to go. We can't stay here." Henri's voice rose to a squeal.

"PanAf is not your friend, huh?"

"They're no one's friend. These are corrupt people and they only work for themselves. They're supposed to protect us from the krayfish, but when you complain about them, PanAf soldiers come to take you away and shoot you. Please, they must not find us here."

"You have personal experience with these people?"

He stared at me.

Evi said, "He's right. *Mashara* would be in a very poor position to defend our group from any attack from an airborne vehicle."

And we weren't supposed to be here in the first place. I had to agree that we were probably better off clearing out for a short while. I asked Henri, "Where can you fly us in the dark?"

"Sorry, mister. It's a solar glider. It's night."

"Surely you have some battery reserve. Wasn't that what you were going to do after sneaking out?"

"That was just for me alone. It won't go far with this many people. We're too heavy."

"Then take us across the water to the shore. We're sitting ducks here. We'll find a place to hide there and wait until they've gone."

We grabbed weapons and armour and ran into the night.

In the breathless air, the sound was coming closer. Already, I could see a light further down the shore. The gyrocopter didn't look like it was searching for anything but was coming straight in our direction.

"Mister Kray's mansion is over that hill," Nicha said. "That's probably where they're going."

We all climbed into the plane. Henri activated the battery to power the jet.

The plane took off, gliding low over the water. *Very* low. The glistening surface of the water was not two metres underneath the bottom of the plane.

"Pull it up," I said.

"It's too heavy. It won't go any higher. I'm just hoping that it will reach the shore."

As we kept going, it became clear that it probably wouldn't. The bottom of the plane skimmed the surface a few times. Fortunately, Henri had pulled up the wheels, and the belly of the plane bounced off the water, giving us a little boost each time. The jet would fire and lift us a few metres higher, only to sputter out a moment later.

Henri called, "Battery is flat. I'm going to have to put it down—"

The plane hit the water at full force. It skidded for a distance before bumping into sand. We still had enough speed that various items flew around the cargo hold.

The plane wobbled ominously from side to side, settling on one wing tip and the belly. We were lucky that it didn't flip over.

Henri rose from his seat. "Out, out."

We clambered across the slanting floor. Of course the door was on the high side. Telaris reached the door first. He pushed it open and jumped out with a splash. He helped Nicha out and then me.

We had landed in a very shallow area with sandbanks and mud pools. The ground was so soft that I sank into the mud to my ankles. Great. More yellow stuff on my shoes.

Nicha said. "Step into my footsteps. It's solid underneath."

I did that, but each time the surface crust broke because of my weight, a waft of sulphur would rise up. The stench was so bad that I didn't know how long I could keep this up. Somewhere in the darkness was the plop-plop-plop of bubbling mud. What if someone accidentally stepped in boiling water?

"Use a light," I said. "It's very dangerous here."

When Thayu switched on a tiny light, it became clear just how dangerous. Not only were there bubbling pools, but there was an entire field of structures made of salt and mud that looked like mushrooms. The edges of the "hoods" looked sharp.

We followed Thayu in single file, walking at fast pace across salt ledges that felt crumbly under my feet

After a short while we reached the edge of this little island.

"It's not very deep." Nicha waded in to his ankles, his knees, and then he slipped, falling face-first in the water.

I gasped. Coldi hated water. Like typical Coldi, Nicha couldn't swim.

But instead of going under, he bobbed on top of the water. He bounced up and down, as if sitting in a comfortable chair, but never went in deeper than his waist. "What's this nonsense?"

"It's because it's very salty," Henri said. "When it gets deeper, you can't even wade through it because you keep floating to the surface."

We had to stick to the slippery edge. The moonlight was bright, but not bright enough to see every little unevenness. I slipped twice, making an acquaintance with the salty lukewarm water. Once I landed with my hands in a bed of brittle salt crystals that broke into pieces under my feet as I tried to climb to drier ground.

By the time we reached solid shoreline, the gyrocopter hovered over the research station, floodlights on. Large clouds of dust blew up as it landed on the flat next to the buildings. By the light, I saw a few men with guns come out. Henri gave a squeak. "They're PanAf. What are they looking for?"

The men went to the building. I thought I could hear the sound of breaking glass over the noise of the gyrocopter's engine.

We kept walking away from the water, urged on by Henri.

The men came back out of the building. Stood talking to each other for a while. The guns were clearly visible by the light from the gyrocopter.

They checked the island, but not finding anything, went back inside the gyrocopter. It took off again towards the north.

"Get down," Henri said.

We crouched between a couple of rocks that were not nearly big enough to hide us. Henri threw handfuls of sand over us. Most of us were still wet, so it stuck to our skin and clothes. We sat very still as she floodlight tracked over the shoreline and then moved off to the north. The *thud-thud-thud* sound faded fast and then vanished entirely.

Phew.

The sound died down soon after.

"It has landed," was Evi's conclusion.

"Mr Kray's house is on the other side," Henri said.

"I'm guessing you know a fair bit about that?" I said. I was cranky and tired and filthy. Half our things had been left behind in the house. Was it even safe to go back? There was nowhere to wash so there wouldn't be any point in getting clean clothes. I was going to be the giant yellow mud monster. We could scare away the crooks. Ha, ha.

More seriously, we had no food and no water and we would need both. The water in the sea was way too salty to be of any use. Already my skin was starting to itch from drying salty mud.

Evi and Nicha offered to go back to the research station and collect the essentials. They tramped off through the darkness.

None of us knew what to say.

We were all tired and dirty and cranky. The ground was hard and dusty. I pushed away some of the sharp rocks from underneath where I sat, and got even more dusty in the process. Much as I disliked the salty bath, I now longed to go back to it, because my skin felt tight and itchy. At least the stars were incredible.

Somebody moved to sit next to me. I sensed Thayu's warmth.

"How are you coping?" I asked in a low voice.

"All right." Meaning *I'm wet, cold and I can't see a thing.* Coldi night vision was worse than ours. Then she admitted, "I don't like this."

"Nope."

Another silence. "Are you in contact with my father right now?"

"No."

I didn't know why she asked. Surely she wouldn't ask her father for help. For one, that was admitting weakness, and Thayu wasn't in the business of admitting defeat. Secondly, she would also understand that any kind of action that her father performed would be one that would cause a lot of diplomatic trouble for everyone.

She said, "We should carry our things closer to the water, so that when morning comes, we can get onto the plane straight away."

That gave us something to do, so we picked up our things and threaded our way down the stony hillside.

By the time we settled at a position at the lakeside, the sky was getting lighter.

Nicha and Evi came splashing the other way with the supplies which they had put on a sheet of plastic which they dragged over the ground. They were both wet to the bone and covered in yellow goo and mud all over. We then went back and dragged the plane closer to the shore, which resulted in all of us getting covered in mud and goo.

We tried to clean up a bit, but most of the shore was made out of soft light grey mud and getting out of the water meant getting dirtier than getting in. By now, the lower part of my legs itched so much that I couldn't stop scratching.

Henri wanted to know if we still wanted to fly along the shore and seemed a bit worried when I said we did.

We needed to wait a while before we could leave, he said.

Solar planes were very quiet but the big disadvantage, of course, was that they only worked during the daytime. The battery would take care of getting where sunlight was, but we'd run that flat last night. On top of that, we were on the eastern shore where the light from the rising sun was blocked by the hills at our back. It was frustrating to have to wait in the shade while the mountains on the opposite shore at the horizon bathed in golden sunlight. Wait and sit like dummies for target practice if any gyrocopters came back.

19

───────

I T WAS MIDMORNING before we managed to get off the ground.

The glider flew low over the water before it rose into the air, turning and clearing the hills.

We'd informed Henri of the route we wanted to take: first to the south along the islands and shallow water that surrounded the research station. This was to convince Henri that we really were doing research, and studied the approaches to Mr Kray's house.

A sealed road, a battery of solar panels, some strange contraptions with pipes sticking out of the sand. Thayu took pictures while I prepared the key ones to go to her father. He had been in range before we left but right now he was probably somewhere over the Pacific Ocean.

Even Evi and Telaris helped. We looked like a proper research team.

We followed the shore north, past the station—still no gyrocopters—and continued along the water's edge, taking pictures of the weird salt-encrusted formations. They were mostly white, but sometimes pink or yellow. Henri steered the plane lower and lower.

"So that the krayfish don't see us, mister. There is a house over the next hill."

"Then let us look at this area here," I pointed at a spot past Mr Kray's house. "The water wells up from the ground here."

According to the real Martin Spencer's work, it was one of three spots where there was an underground connection to the Red Sea basin.

Henri veered away from the coast. But while he did so, the plane rose and we got the first view of Mr Kray's house: a couple of white buildings on the hillside surrounded by a long wall, also white.

Thayu was taking a lot of pictures. Her camera was amazingly good and we would be able to see quite a lot of detail on the house.

The pictures she put in the feed showed a white house like a sugar cake, surrounded by palms and a lawn. There were trees along the driveway, and one road led from the gate over the hillside while another went to a shed between the house and the water's edge. There was a solar plant and a tank next to it, as well as a mountain of white stuff which I assumed to be salt from the desalinator that was probably in that shed.

Interesting.

"Look," Nicha said.

The surface of the water underneath us churned. In places it was not very deep. On a rocky outcrop, I saw something that I hadn't seen before: birds. Little white specks sitting on the rocks. Were they nests?

That had to mean there were fish in this water, because what else would they eat?

Life was everywhere. Even in places as hostile as Asto's Crystal Wastelands, there was life. Nature always found a way.

"It's very pretty," Thayu said.

Coming from Asto, I could imagine that she thought it was, but to me this was a scarred and damaged landscape, a frontline victim of human abuse of the planet.

Henri turned around, smiling. "Anything else, mister? We're fully charged."

"I'd like you to go much higher so that I can take a picture of the whole area."

He veered away from the coast, to catch rising hot air, he said. We cleared a couple of hills. Once there was no more water, the landscape returned to its desolate state.

Henri found a pocket of rising air and circled to lift the plane.

The air was hazy here and visibility reduced, so I asked him to come down a little.

We followed the shoreline. We took pictures.

Henri was studying his maps on the navigation screen, tracking a finger across the surface to plot a course. Back to town from here? It looked like it.

Nicha looked at me and pointed outside. *There.* His father's ship must have come above the horizon, because we were going through a patch of connectivity.

I could now see the large building site, too, faint in the hazy air.

Thayu was already taking pictures. The enlargements were still a bit hazy but the software that increased the resolution was very good. It showed the individual trucks standing in front of a shed. It showed us the markings on the trucks.

Behind it was an area where structures were beginning to rise out of the ground.

"It's going to be a power plant," Henri said.

"I guess with all these power outages that will be useful." *You hypocrite.* "It's very big."

"Yeah." A bit later, he added, "I can't go any further that way. The warlord doesn't like it."

"Then turn around. No reason to displease them. I'm here to study the geology, not human structures."

I almost thought he believed it.

We kept going and Thayu took more pictures which she fed to me, and I passed onto the ship. Asha's communicator, Daina, asked us if we could get a clearer view of the far side of the building site.

It will be hard, I let her know. *The pilot is very nervous.*

I see some vehicles that are clearly not local. I would like to get a closer look.

Trucks?

No. Aircraft.

I peered at the picture that I'd sent her and that provoked her interest, but couldn't see anything of the sort.

Henri said, "Shit. I've got another plane in the air."

"It may be a good time to turn back," I said.

He was all too happy to oblige. The plane banked—Thayu got another good view of the building site—and turned around. We had been gliding on the rising hot air, but now he fired the jet engine.

Now that I was on the other side of the plane, I noticed another building, this on by the water's edge. It was a simple, square thing resembling a concrete bunker and the pipes leading to it from the water made me think that this, too, was a desalination plant. However there were no pipes leading away from it, so maybe the water was used as cooling for something inside. Manufacturing?

"Did you get pictures of this building?" I asked in Coldi to no one in particular.

"I did," Evi said.

"What do you think this is?"

"Some sort of industrial plant."

A number of vehicles stood in a walled yard on the building's eastern side. A truck was just coming into the open gate. There were people around it, little black specks in groups. And now a few people ran onto the roof of the building. Two people already stood there. Sunlight glinted on something that stood on a stand between them.

I remembered the gun I'd seen in Dekker's office. *Can be used against aircraft,* Thayu had said about it. This was the area where those guns had been intercepted.

In a split second, my brain put all that information together.

"Get out of here, as quick as you can!" I yelled to Henri.

"I'm already doing my best." He was turning dials and settings on the controls, swearing, of all things, in French.

The jet engine whined but our progress seemed painfully slow.

There was a puff of smoke on the roof.

"They're shooting at us!"

Henri banked the plane sideways while swearing even more in French. It made a sharp dive. I hung onto my seat, and noticed Thayu doing the same thing.

"What are you doing?" I called to Henri.

"Nothing. The solar wing is damaged. I can't get it under control."

A section of the solar sail was flapping loose behind the right hand wing.

Telaris wormed himself from his seat. He was not small and his moving about in the cabin unsettled the plane even more.

He slid into the copilot seat. He said a couple of words to Henri in his halting accent. Henri clicked a few buttons and the plane levelled out. Phew.

And what the hell did Telaris know about flying this machine?

"I'm still barely holding it," Henri said. "We've lost our right solar wing and are flying on jet only. We're going to have to put down somewhere and see if we can fix this, because the battery won't last all the way back."

We glided lower and lower. The building site and the square building both slid from view to be replaced with sand dunes and rocky outcrops.

"I'm going to put down there." Henri pointed. There was a sandy valley that looked quite long.

He turned and lined the plane up.

We went lower and lower.

"What about the wheels?" I asked.

He said, while concentrating on the valley, "No wheels. It will slide over the sand. The solar sails won't fold back in, so they will drag us. It will be a bit rough, but if I use wheels, it will flip. I've done this before."

I hoped so, but damn.

Lower we went, and lower. Henri pointed the nose up. I balled my fists.

Touchdown.

The plane bounced, thudded back onto the sand. The sound of it sliding along the bottom was like a crashing ocean wave. We bounced again, back onto the sand, with a *brrrrrr* over sand rills. The sand dune at end of the valley was coming alarmingly close.

Henri swore. Tried to pull the nose up, but we didn't have enough speed.

The plane slid up the dune, hit a patch of deep sand and stopped abruptly. The force of movement brought the tail up—which fell back down, and the plane tilted sideways so that one wingtip rested on the sand. The solar sail trailed from the wings like an empty sack and it settled around the plane like a deflating balloon. The material was grey and silver on top. It let through some light, but only at particular angles. Draped down from the wings to the ground was not one of those angles, so it grew quite dark in the cabin.

Silence.

Holy shit. There was an exercise I wouldn't be in a hurry to repeat.

"Everyone all right?" Henri asked, looking over his shoulder. His face was shining with sweat.

Everyone did seem to be all right, if shaken.

I undid my seat belt. The back of my shirt stuck to the seat with sweat.

We clambered up the sloping floor to the door. Nicha opened it. When he jumped out, he disappeared up to his chest. He helped Evi out, and then me. I sank to my ankles in the sand. It was hot and stuffy in the space under the sail. I went forward underneath the wing into searing desert air.

"Urgh," Thayu said, coming up behind me. She wiped her face. She wasn't one to show concern, but she had looked quite worried back there.

Evi had walked a little way up the sand dune and I struggled up in his footsteps. The sand was orange-pink and the air cloudless and blue. Those were the only colours in the surreal landscape. The valley had been pristine until the plane cut a deep scar through the delicate patterns sculpted in the sand by the wind.

A breeze whipped up a tiny wisp of sand from the top of the dune. The air was hot. No, it was fucking hot.

The heat of the sand radiated through the soles of my shoes. They were good shoes, too.

If I'd thought it was hot at the research station, it was nothing compared to this.

Thayu was staring at something at the horizon. "I thought you said that this world was nothing like Asto. You could take a picture here, make the sky a bit paler and show it to a bunch of Coldi people, and all of them will tell you that it was taken somewhere near Beratha." Where she had grown up.

We went back down where Henri and Telaris were inspecting the damage to the solar sail: there was a rip in the right-hand sail which made the plane unstable. The projectile had missed us by a hair.

"Can you fix it?" I asked Henri. He and Telaris had taken our things out of the luggage compartment and had unpacked the repair kit.

"We'll have to, right?" He wiped his face. "Yeah, I think we can fix it." He held up a length of new sail sheeting with creases showing where it had been folded in the emergency kit. "We got this patch. It's not quite big enough, so we may have to cut it."

"Stick the whole thing on. Glue works better. Use tape for the smaller rips," Telaris said in his typical clipped accent.

"How come you're so familiar with this type of plane?" I asked him in Coldi.

"Everyone uses these on Indrahui."

"Is this plane imported?"

"No, but the technology is."

Well, that was . . . disturbing. Here was I thinking that only illegal Coldi technology had infiltrated Earth's remote areas.

Evi started unscrewing the solar sail's attachment points from the wings of the plane. Thayu and Nicha went to help him, while Telaris pulled the entire sail so that it lay neatly spread out on the sand. I went to help, but they sent me back to the shade.

"I don't want to let you do all the work," I protested.

"You'll get your chance," Nicha said. "Let us do this, because it's too hot for you and we don't want to have to do the work *and* try to get your body temperature down to stop you from dying."

I sat down in the shade of the plane, but it wasn't very cool. After a while, they sent Henri to sit with me. He slumped down, wiping his face.

"Dunno how hot it is, but they just keep going," he said.

"They grew up in a place where it's very hot." That was true only for Thayu. Nicha had grown up in London, and Evi and Telaris had grown up on Indrahui; and although there were lots of deserts there, the climate was overwhelmingly cool.

"They're from the same place as Mr Kray, right?" he said, his tone hesitating.

"Not really."

"The black ones are. They're not African. They're from . . ." He turned his eyes to the sky.

"Do you know this warlord Mr. Kray?"

"Well enough that I know I want nothing to do with him. And that's not fair, I was asking you questions."

"You can ask questions, but most of my answers would be long and boring. Some people find geology interesting, but most do not."

He gave me a *yeah, right* look that told me not to push my luck. I changed the subject before he started questioning my identity. "I like your plane. I'd never seen one of these before."

"These are made in Sudan. They're a real African design." And he was proud of it, too.

Was he putting on an innocent face as much as me?

We went back to watching Telaris direct Thayu and Nicha. They lined up both sides of the ripped sail and put them where they would belong if they sail had been intact. A strip of fabric was missing, but that didn't matter, Telaris said. As long as the patch covered enough of the surrounding fabric.

Thayu went to spray foamy glue over the ripped wing, and then they allowed me to help lowering the patch in place. When rubbing it so that the two layers lay over each other as smoothly as possible, I had to stop because the fabric burned my hands. Henri was carefully crawling over the glued material to snap in tiny rivets that would make sure that the two solar layers were connected, while Telaris used tape made from the same material to fix a few smaller rips.

"That's done," he said when he finished. "Ready to go."

"The glue needs to dry for an hour or so," Henri said. "Otherwise it will come apart when we try to fold the sail. Let's see how we can best take off from here. If we can push off from a hill, the hot air will give us extra lift."

Jerking his head at the dune where we had been stranded, Telaris said, "Maybe have a look around what the other side of the hill looks like. Maybe we can drag the plane up there and slide down if that side is steeper."

We left Evi and Nicha with the plane just in case there was trouble and trudged up the hillside to the top. By now it was midafternoon, the hottest time of the day. I was sweating so much that whenever sand whipped up from someone ploughing through in front of me, it stuck to my arms and face.

At the top of the hill, a welcome breeze made me shiver. There was another valley on that side, and it was not as wide as ours, but the dune that we stood on was much higher than those on the other side.

"This is perfect," Henri said. "We push off. We use the engine. We fly in that direction—"

He stopped talking.

A vehicle crested the hill and came into the valley, followed by another one.

Henri yelled, "Run!"

20

HENRI RAN, TRAILING a spray of sand down the dune, but Thayu dropped to the ground, pulling me down with her, and aimed her gun. . . .

But another truck came over the hill, and another one. There was a whole convoy of tank-like vehicles, carrying rocket launchers on the roof.

They were huge things, solid square looking things painted in the same colour as the sand.

They had huge wheels with deep-threaded tyres that churned up clouds of sand and dust.

Thayu put her gun away. She elbowed me in the side. "Come on. We have to go back."

But a couple of trucks had come into that valley as well.

They stopped next to the plane, where Nicha and Evi had been folding the repaired solar sail ready for take-off. The truck doors opened and a number of soldiers carrying big guns jumped out. They shouted in a language that I couldn't make out.

One ran after Henri, who turned around again and set off in a panicked run back to us. The soldier following him must have springs in his shoes because the deep sand didn't slow him down at all. He caught Henri by the back of his shirt. Henri squealed.

Of course they had seen us. Thayu stood next to me, all her muscles tense. I didn't need the feeder—which didn't work right now—to realise the precarious situation we were in, and that we didn't have the reserves or the position to fight back.

A fool is the person who starts a fight without being certain of victory. A Coldi proverb, and I couldn't remember who first said it. Why did I even think of this shit?

They came closer, pointing guns at us. They were all local men, mostly very dark-skinned. They spoke with Henri, not in a friendly way. He whimpered.

Another man gestured with his gun and yelled something at us.

I presumed it to mean "get in the truck".

They opened the back door of the closest truck.

A couple of others came forward to search us. None of the ones I could see were Coldi. They were all locals, Africans or descendants of Arabs.

They checked us for weapons. When Thayu yelled at them not to dare feel her up, they backed off a bit. Thayu was not normally the type to request special consideration—Coldi women were at least as strong and often stronger than men—but it was my guess that she probably had a weapon stashed away somewhere that she wanted to escape attention. Was it in her belt buckle? In her socks? Thayu could hide weapons anywhere. They got my gun, and divested Evi and Telaris of their weapons. All the various guns and knives made an impressive pile in the sand.

The soldiers pushed us up a narrow ladder into the back of the truck. I expected it to be hot inside the cargo hold, but the air was quite cool.

Henri was yelling at the men in a local language, but they didn't react at all. They simply left the cargo hold and shut the door.

Henri banged his fists on the metal panel that made a loud, hollow sound.

Telaris told him to calm down. Henri looked up at him—since Telaris was about a head taller than he was and probably twice his age.

"They can't take me!" Henri squealed.

"It looks like we have little choice in the matter."

"But my plane!"

I said, "You are not getting out of here by making a lot of noise and breaking your hands."

Henri looked at his hands. He shrugged. Leaned against the wall and let himself slide to the ground with a theatrical sigh.

"I have a wife and three little boys. Who is going to look after them?"

He did? He looked barely old enough to have finished high school.

He spread his hands and looked at the ceiling. "Come on, what is this? Don't they know who I am? Everyone knows Henri the pilot."

Apparently not.

The only light in this cargo compartment came in through a tiny window in the front of the cabin. Thayu stood on her toes to look out through it.

"Swanky," she said.

She stepped aside to let me have a look. The cabin had a number of rows of seats with small tables between them. The seats were covered in leather and the men—I counted eleven including the driver—sat there laughing and talking, oblivious to us behind the little window.

The vehicle started moving. I sank down on the hard metal floor with my back to the wall.

Henri sat swaying from side to side. His eyes were wide. "They will destroy my plane. I won't be able to work anymore. It's my complete life savings. I wanted to buy my wife a shop."

The truck kept going for quite some time. It powered up sandy hills with the engine churning and slid down on the other side.

"Wonder where they're taking us," I said in Coldi to Thayu.

Nicha stood watching through the little window. "I can't see anything out there except desert."

It took about twenty minutes before the truck stopped.

"We're at the white house," Nicha reported.

Henri whimpered. "That's what I was afraid of. They're taking us to Mr Kray."

The driver spoke to someone outside and then we kept going.

"We're going up the driveway," Nicha said.

"No, please," Henri moaned.

"We've done nothing wrong. We're researchers and we've got the documents to prove it," I said. "There is no need to be afraid."

It was the biggest nonsense ever and no one replied to that statement. Only Evi nodded, his face serious. He held his right hand clasped over the empty bracket on his belt where he normally held his gun. Clearly he wanted to see Mr Kray, because he wanted to kill the man who had cruelly killed his sister. Whatever was going to happen in that house, one thing I knew: only one of the two men—Evi or Mr Kray—would make it out alive.

The truck stopped. The men got out and a moment later the back door opened. One man shouted something that probably meant "get out". He was an African man with a bald head shining with sweat, little piggy eyes and a round face. He wore a sand-coloured military-style outfit with lots of pockets on his trousers and a flak jacket. He had no front teeth.

Thayu went down the ladder at the back of the truck first. She faced the guard, giving him a hard stare. He was taller than she was, but I thought I saw him retreat ever so slightly.

I clambered down the ladder next, emerging in the hot brightness of midmorning. Sunlight belted onto the white walls of a blocky, two-storey house. Ouch, my eyes.

A few more military-style guards waited in the shade under the awning that sheltered the entrance of the house. They were all locals, looking dapper in their desert-coloured camouflage gear.

Evi came out of the truck behind me. He yanked his arm free of the grip of the man who held his uniform. He yelled. "No need to nanny me. I can walk myself."

The guard reached for his belt—

"*Mashara.* That's not necessary."

"My apologies, Delegate." Telaris wormed himself between me and his brother and pushed Evi back from the nervous guard. While Nicha came out of the truck, Telaris spoke to Evi in Indrahui on a low voice. Evi jerked his head, his expression angry. Telaris spoke more calming words.

The guards indicated that I should go up to the door. On both sides, Roman-style marble pillars supported the awning. A red marble ramp led to the entrance, a glass door in a wall made from glass floor to ceiling. The hall was sterile, near-empty. White marble on the floor looked bright and there was a pond in the hall where a couple of lazy goldfish swam about. The far wall was made of glass as well so that we could see through into a lush green garden with a swimming pool and tall date palms in the courtyard.

A little African boy in a white uniform with gold piping opened the door for us. He looked like an absurd living doll, bowing and smiling. In the middle of the fucking desert. The whole charade was ridiculous.

"Is anyone going to tell us why we're here?" I asked. "We were simply doing our work."

The boy bowed again. "Go see Mr Kray, sir. Come inside. Mr Kray knows everything."

The difference in temperature between outside and inside was incredible. The house was spotlessly clean, too, and the air was fresh and cool.

A couple of couches surrounded the pond in the hall, with cushions of white leather. White marble lined the floor, the walls that were not made of glass were also white, the ceiling was white. There were a couple of giant pots with palms. The leaves were green, but the glaze on the outside of the pots was white, of course. Three statues of stylised cats, also white, were each almost as tall as a person. On one of the couches lay a real white cat, its tail curled around its body. As we came in, it raised its head, rose to its feet and jumped soundlessly to the ground.

A second young boy in white uniform came out of a hall to the left.

He bowed. "Come, sirs. You must get changed, be clean and rested, sirs, before Mr Kray will see you." He looked pointedly at the floor, where we had left a trail of dried mud that had come off the soles of our shoes. My clothes were indeterminate grey with dried mud from our escapade on the shoreline. My hands were caked with grime, which had found its way under my nails. There were stripes over my arms from where drops of sweat had run down. Nicha had also taken a tumble in the water and looked similarly dishevelled.

We followed the boy into the passage, tracking more bits of dried mud across the floor. To the right stood a small table with on it a bowl of decorative squash. Next to it stood an empty vase. The whole arrangement was not dissimilar to the tables that influential Coldi people displayed in their halls to inform visitors of their mood. If it stood here with that intent, then what did it mean?

Thayu gave me an odd look. I guessed she had the same thought. A flicker of concern went over her face.

The young servant led us into a luxury bedroom where there was a huge white bed and mirrored wardrobes along the back wall. The floor-to-ceiling window looked out over a little courtyard with a burbling fountain and bright green grass.

"You stay here. You see Mr Kray."

He bowed again and turned to the door.

"Wait. Does this mean Mr Kray will come and see us in this room?" I glanced at Evi. Such a meeting would probably not go well.

"Mr Kray is very busy." The boy's Isla was probably not good enough to understand the insinuations in his halting statements. "You stay here. You see Mr Kray."

He showed us a cavernous bathroom off the room looking out onto the same courtyard. The colour scheme was getting a little monotonous. The floor was pristine white, the bath was white, the towels were white.

"You clean and wash. Get clean clothes. You see Mr Kray." He gestured at the wardrobes at the back wall.

He bowed and backed away to the door.

"When will Mr Kray see us?" I asked him.

"You see Mr Kray."

He didn't seem capable of saying anything else, so I let him scurry out of the room.

The first thing Thayu did when the door shut was walk around the room and inspect it for bugs. Finding no obvious ones, she inspected the cupboards and the bed. She didn't find anything there either.

Thayu tried the sliding door to the courtyard. To my surprise, it opened, letting a waft of hot air into the room.

The white cat had followed us into the room when the servant had let us in. It now slipped out the door into the courtyard—past Thayu who hadn't noticed it and gave a gasp of surprise. An alarm started wailing.

A big guy in a white uniform with gold piping burst into the room. He was a dark-skinned African and looked frankly ridiculous in his uniform. If I hadn't known any better, I would have thought that Mr Kray was a colonial-style white man in the same way that the Nations of Earth diplomats were very much into Victorian customs and clothing right now. The servant was making a big fuss, waving his hands while speaking rapidly. He had his front teeth.

"I don't think he likes us going outside," I said to Thayu in Coldi.

"You're kidding, right?" She snorted and pushed the door shut.

But the man went past her and opened it again. He went into the courtyard, out of view of the window, and came back a bit later carrying the cat, all paws sticking up. It gave us an accusing look. He put it on the ground where it scurried away, tail held high. It turned around at the door, twitching the tip of its tail.

The beefy servant bowed and left after saying something while waving his hand at the cat.

Mr Kray obviously didn't like the kitty to burn its tootsies on the hot ground outside. If there were any mice in this place, they were likely to be inside.

When the beefy guy was gone, the cat sauntered up to Nicha, going *mreow* and butting into his leg.

I'd long since decided that the awkwardness of Coldi around larger animals was genetic, because, despite having lived on Earth for most of his life, Nicha really wasn't fond of people's pets. He tried to push the kitty out of the way with his boot—spilling more sand over the floor—but it started headbutting his other leg.

I decided to rescue him from the kitty before things got unpleasant. I picked it up and dumped it in the middle of the room, but as soon as its paws hit the ground, it scooted back. Now it ran up to Thayu, jumped on the couch where she sat looking at her bug detection screens and wriggled under the screen onto her lap.

Fortunately, my father also had a cat named Myra, and she had become familiar with the concept of cats and the irony that they loved Coldi people because of their high body temperature.

So we were spared the sudden jump to her feet and the yowling of the cat as it was unceremoniously tossed to the ground. But impressed by this white fur ball on her lap, Thayu was not. It lay down, as if the whole world belonged to it, and curled its tail around its body. Thayu spreads her hands in a *what the hell?* type of gesture.

I said, "Let's go in the bathroom. Cats hate water."

There were nods all around. Evi and Telaris had hardly said anything since arriving at the house. They sat next to each other, brooding black giants with moss-coloured hair and bronze curls.

As they got up, I realised something. "Wait, where is Henri?"

He was not in the room with us.

As far as I remembered, he hadn't even come down the corridor with us. Had he even entered the house, or left the truck?

A chill crept over my back.

Thayu and Nicha gave each other a meaningful look. They knew something? I gestured in the direction of the bathroom. Somehow, it seemed a safer place to have a discussion than the living room, given that Mr Kray was probably trying to snoop on us.

The bath was set in the middle of the room, a circular basin that, with a bit of squishing, held all five of us. Fortunately also, with five people in the bath, it didn't need so much water.

We sat on the ledge around the perimeter while the water splashed into the basin and rose around our feet, legs, backsides and waists.

Thayu and Telaris held a conversation in code. It was about bugs, but that was about the extent of the meaning I could glean from it.

The kitty remained at the door and stalked away when I flicked water out of the bath. It jumped on the couch with a glowering look at us. I went to shut the door after it.

"Henri," I began.

"He was kept in the truck when we got out," Nicha said.

"I didn't even see it," I said. "I was too concerned about my own backsides. Still am. I don't like what's going on here."

He shook his head. "No. This . . ." He gestured at the bathroom's white interior. "Putting enemies up in your house in luxury is something Ezhya would do. Anyone from the Inner Circle, really."

"He's Indrahui. Do those warlords play games with visitors as well?" I looked at Evi.

He shook his head. "They're more likely to throw them in the dungeons."

Well, maybe that was the next step. "Thay'?"

She licked her lips. "That arrangement on the table in the hall . . ."

"Yes," Nicha said, as if glad that someone finally mentioned it. "I noticed that."

"What does it mean?" I asked.

Thayu said, "It's ugly. It means that everything is broken and all associations disbanded. It means that people will be killed."

Nicha added, "But also it wasn't quite complete. If Mr Kray really intended it to be a Coldi arrangement and cause offence with it, he would have included an offensive object, like a broken gun or something."

Evi said, "At Indrahui, we don't have that custom with the arrangements in the hall. It could be a coincidence. How would he know that he's getting Coldi visitors who can interpret it?"

"That's the question, huh?" Thayu said, in a tone that indicated that it wasn't much of a question for her. "Henri or Tamu?"

"I don't think Henri knows anything much," I said.

"Why isn't he here with us, then?"

"Because they don't want him to find out much either. He's been flying supplies to them. I think they'd like to keep him."

But I realised something else. The broken gun that Nicha said was missing from the arrangement in the hall. I'd seen it, in Dekker's office. Was this a ridiculous coincidence, or some practical joke played on us? And if so, who was playing it? Danziger? Dekker? Or Mr Kray? Did this scheme go all the way to the top?

21

____

T HE QUESTION WAS what to do now. How to get out of here, and whether to worry about Henri. The others said to just worry about ourselves, but it didn't feel right to me. Living and working in this area, Henri would know more about Mr Kray and weapon smuggling than we did, but I didn't believe he worked for anyone. If anything, he'd seemed more terrified of the soldiers than we were.

We discussed what Mr Kray intended to do with us. It could well be that he believed we were a scientific team, but I wasn't holding my hopes up. Neither were the others.

And then the order to dress in clothes from the wardrobe full of white kaftans?

"I'm in this house because I have no choice, but I'm not wearing any of this vile man's stuff," Evi said, a deep hatred in his voice.

Telaris nodded, the expression on his face intense.

Nicha said, "Take it easy."

But I agreed with them. We should rely on this man's property as little as possible.

So after we got out of the water, we washed our clothes in the bath.

I was annoyed that all my things were scattered over the area: some stuff left behind at the research station, some in the plane. I didn't think I'd left anything incriminating in any of those places, but a change of underwear would be nice.

Evi risked the alarm and took all our wet things into the courtyard. He seemed disappointed that it didn't go off and didn't bring in the servant in the prim suit, because Evi was stark naked and very black in all sorts of interesting places, including the palms of his hands and soles of his feet. Indrahui had blue tongues.

There was no obvious place to hang the wet clothes, so he draped wet shirts and pants over the bushes.

"Hot out there, but our stuff should be dry soon," he said, when he came back in and joined us while sitting at the edge of the bath. Nicha had pulled out the plug and the muddy water gurgled down the hole.

We agreed that we would hold onto the scientist and team story as long as we could.

"It's not going to stand up much longer, mind you," Telaris said. "As soon as he sees us, he'll know something is up." *Us* meaning himself and Evi. Indrahui. He would know that he had been recognised. He probably already knew. If we could only find the damn bugs that spied on us.

Evi nodded, his face grim. "Something *will* be up." The two of them always had a brooding appearance, but right now they looked terrifying.

They were here only for one thing, and it wasn't sitting in the bath.

"How about we try to avoid bringing you two into a meeting with him?" I asked.

They remained quiet. Evi said, *"Mashara* goes where the delegate goes."

"But I'm a scientist, not a delegate."

"Amarru's orders."

"All right then. If we're called into a meeting you can stay outside and observe the area as much as you can."

"We'll go inside with our scientist," Thayu said. "In case someone decides to do something stupid." I had no doubt that she'd still managed to smuggle a weapon inside, even if I had no idea how she did it.

Evi wasn't happy with that, but that was how it usually worked and how we planned it.

Telaris went outside to check on our clothes, still stark naked.

"I don't understand why the other door is armed and this one isn't," Thayu said.

"There is a sloping roof directly above our head here," Telaris said, coming back into the door with an arm full of shirts. "If there's more than one of us, we could boost each other up and have a look at the rest of this place."

"We'd have to wait until dark, though," Evi said.

"And hope they don't have floodlights all over," Nicha added.

"Or vicious guard dogs," I said.

Thayu shuddered.

They all agreed. Dogs would be really bad news.

Telaris distributed the clothes. "The rest wasn't quite dry yet."

"What about we can try to tap into some sort of security network?" Thayu said. "Seems less risky than going outside and being discovered by Mr Kray's clown guards, or the serious ones. Or having to face *dogs*."

The team liked that idea, and what was better, it could be implemented immediately, if Thayu could locate the bugs that were likely to be in the main room, and maybe in the bathroom, too.

The discussion about bugs finally drew Evi out of his brooding mood. He and Telaris—Thayu and Nicha, too—hated being passive, and liked moving forward on their own terms, even if the situation was risky.

I had a good team.

Telaris went back into the courtyard and retrieved the rest of our clothes, which were almost dry after barely half an hour out there. Again, the alarm did not go off.

"It's really strange," Thayu said. "Why arm that door and not this one?"

No one could answer that question.

I got dressed. My shirt and pants had gone stiff in the sunlight, and I didn't doubt that, were we in Barresh, Eirani would have a fit with their lack of cleanliness, but they smelled of sunshine and *felt* fresh.

Thayu was already going around the room for a second inspection for bugs when both my feeders burst into life.

Notice you stopped moving. This was Asha himself.

We're inside the house. We had an issue with the plane.

Are you restrained against your will?

Not yet.

We will be going into geostationary orbit so that we can observe the area constantly. We have discovered other construction sites nearby. Not all of them obvious. Will send you images.

I suspected that Thayu was already looking at those images, because she had abandoned the search for bugs and leaned against the wall next to the mirror-fronted wardrobes. The white cat sat at her feet.

I told Asha, *We will find out as much as we can about what these people are up to.* Not mentioning that we'd have a little trouble getting out of here.

This man Romi Tanaqan is not be underestimated. He's smart, can be nice and entertaining if he wants to. Even at Indrahui, he managed to woo clan leaders and officials. They would come to his house, only to be killed or subjected to unspeakable cruelty. This is another reason your cover would work well. He is interested in power and knowledge. A scientist would intrigue him.

That would be good if I were actually a scientist. I was hoping that he wasn't going to grill me on geology.

Let me know if you need any assistance.

I will.

But I knew one thing for certain: calling him for assistance was the very last thing I'd do, because if I did, he wouldn't risk his troops by putting them on the ground fighting a land war. He'd do something from orbit. And if that happened, Nations of Earth would revoke my citizenship faster than you could say *alien invasion.*

When he signed off, I went to look over Thayu's shoulders. She was indeed studying satellite images of building activity in the desert.

The shape and design of a rectangular site in amongst sand dunes followed the outlines of the old Coldi plan. On the far side of the main site lay only a patch of churned earth. There was nothing to see there, at first glance, except that the colour of the soil was slightly darker in a clearly artificial, perfectly rectangular area. Closer inspection revealed a driveway that disappeared under the ground and appeared to be the entrance to an underground building. Now the image I'd seen earlier made more sense. What we were looking at was not the foundation of some project yet to be built, but an existing building which was mostly underground.

Then I noticed the locality coordinates at the bottom of the image. "Hang on, this is not even close to where we are."

Thayu shook her head. "No. He says they discovered three similar sites in the northern half of this continent." The other localities were in Algeria and Egypt.

Nicha, Evi and Telaris joined us in studying the image, but neither had any idea what might have been built under the ground.

We chalked it up as "another place someone should have a look", but right now, we weren't even sure how to get out of this one.

"How are you going with the bugs?" I asked Thayu.

"I can't find any," Thayu said. She looked unhappy.

Nicha said, "This house is new. The bugs are probably built into the walls."

Thayu argued that even if that was the case, her scans should be showing some activity. Nicha said he didn't believe that bug could be shielded, so they walked around the room studying all the places where bugs should be hidden if there were any, mainly in the ceilings and corners, above the doors. And finding nothing.

"How about you check places where you *wouldn't* put them?" I said.

Thayu gave me a *don't be stupid* look. "But . . . you wouldn't put them there."

"*You* wouldn't. Maybe they've had different training and would put them somewhere else."

"But if you put them somewhere else, you wouldn't get as good a view of the room. That's why everyone puts them in the ceiling."

"They could be for listening only."

She spread her hands, looked like she was going to argue, but then let them sink. "Who is part of the security here?"

But I did notice that she checked under the table. It would have been nice if she'd found anything there, but my luck didn't go that far.

The beefy servant came back, wheeling a trolley. On the top stood a stack of porcelain plates, a set of cups and a jug, all of them white.

The bottom shelf held a large tray with a silver lid. The servant took this tray and put it on the table. He had to push some of our gear aside to do so.

"Your dinner, sirs," he said, and bowed.

"When is Mr Kray going to see us?" I asked.

"Yes, yes. Be patient. Mr Kray is busy. He'll see you as soon as he can. You can stay here tonight. I assume it's comfortable?"

"It is, thank you," I said. Mr Kray is busy, my hat. I had a suspicion that keeping us here had been the aim of capturing us in the first place.

The servant bowed and left.

On the covered tray, we found a selection of spring rolls, salads, smoked fish and little pancakes. There was nothing that Nicha and Thayu or Evi and Telaris couldn't eat, but Thayu wouldn't let us touch it until she had inspected the trolley and trays for bugs.

She found none.

"It's got me baffled," she said, while Nicha was using his testing wand for analysing the food for poisons. "I can't believe that there wouldn't be anything. If he was a local warlord, yes, but he's from *Indrahui*. He'd be smarter than that."

And smarter than to have an alarm on one door but not the other.

Nicha said, "It's safe as far as I can see."

Evi still looked dubious. He would probably have been happier to refuse the food, but the need to stay healthy to perform his job took priority.

As we made our way to the couch, the white cat followed us. I didn't want it to upset and of the others, so I held up a piece of fish, which it duly demolished.

This meant, of course, that I was going to be its next most favourite thing. It jumped onto the couch next to me, but after another piece of fish, it was happy to sit on my lap and let me eat the green bits.

Considering that we were in the middle of the desert, the food was extraordinary. Mr Kray sure liked luxury. When we finished, we expected the servant to turn up to take the dirty plates away, but no one came.

It was fast going dark outside. The white cat had had folded its legs underneath its body, had its eyes closed and sat purring heavily on my lap. It was a bit hot, but I judged it better than letting it disturb Thayu or Nicha.

Thayu was prowling across the room, impatient, because she wanted to keep looking for bugs, and didn't want to be caught in the middle of something that looked suspicious when the servant came in to pick up the remains of dinner. And she was annoyed because he didn't show up.

Eventually, Nicha said, "Stop pacing. I know how to get him to come. We'll open the door to the courtyard and the alarm will start ringing."

That idea met with approval, so he rose and slid the door open. . . . Nothing.

Well, what the hell?

"The guy who was here before must have turned the alarm off," Nicha said.

"Why would he do that while we're in the room?" Telaris asked. "That makes no sense."

But I realised: there was another difference between now and this afternoon. Maybe the *doors* had no alarm, but . . . "Thay', come here with your scanner."

She frowned.

I pointed at the purring cat.

Her frown deepened, but she held her scanner close to the white fur. I could see the screen, and I could see the jump in wriggly lines.

"There is your bug."

22

———

W E ALL GATHERED around the cat, which kept its eyes closed and kept purring.

"That's interesting," Thayu said. Her face showed that she was just about as unsure what to think of this as she was about the concept of cats in general.

I stroked the cat, digging my fingers into its white fur. All I could feel was soft skin, muscles and bones, all vibrating with the cat's purring. I couldn't feel anything artificial. It made me nervous. I normally didn't mind cats, but right now I wanted to toss it out the door.

Thayu gestured to the wardrobe.

I got up from the couch still carrying the cat. It had opened one eye and looked at me balefully.

"Look," I said, and pulled some of the clothes off their hangers to make a little nest on the floor. My father's cat Myra loved nests of dirty laundry. The cat was happy to lie on the pile. I shut the door. That was one problem solved. We went back into the bathroom, where we sat around the empty bath.

"That's one of the more interesting places I've ever seen a bug," I said.

"It's cruel," Evi said. "I should have known that he would do something like this. He does it with people, too."

"People?" I felt sick.

"Yes, on Indrahui, he would occasionally free his prisoners of war. They'd have sensors and explosives implanted, and when they arrived home . . ." Evi made an explosive motion with his hands.

Thayu's face showed the horror I felt. "That's stupid. What's the point of that?"

"I would use a lot of words that are stronger than stupid," Nicha said.

Evi said, "The point of Tanaqan is that he uses everything and everyone around him to gain an advantage. And he loves seeing people being cut to pieces in front of him."

Telaris said, "That cat has got a radio chip that's receiving and sending. We can figure out the frequency and then we can try to get into the network that it sends to."

"You make that sound simple."

"It can be," Thayu said. "Usually, though, it isn't. Some of these networks use *really* complicated passwords."

Evi took his reader from his pocket and unfolded the screen projector. "Let's get started. We've got some serious work to do."

Thayu said, "Can I suggest that we keep working in the bathroom while anyone who is not needed here goes into the other room and keeps an eye out if anyone comes in?"

"Some of us should sleep, too," Nicha said. I guessed he wanted to be part of that group.

I was quite useless at technology, so I was also assigned to the guard and sleep team that would remain in the living room. Thayu and Evi would go into the bathroom.

Thayu accompanied me into the little passage that went into the living room, where she held me back for a kiss.

"Good night." Her voice was soft.

I was about to breathe in to protest, but she said, "No, you are really worth more to us when you're rested."

"That really vouches for my computer skills."

"We may need your cat-handling skills later." She brushed her armour. The surface was dull dark grey. "That animal has been putting hair all over me."

"That's the first time I've heard you worried about your appearance."

She grinned and we each went our own way.

Telaris insisted on keeping watch by the door, and told me and Nicha to go to sleep. We got into the big bed with the white cover. I was asleep in minutes.

———

It was still dark when Thayu shook my shoulder.

I lifted my head, squinting into the light she shone in my face. "What's going on?" I squinted into the glow, having trouble figuring out where I was.

"Come. We've found out some interesting things."

Nicha was already sitting on the edge of the bed, looking unimpressed with the fact that it was still dark outside.

I stumbled from the bed feeling stiff—what had I been doing yesterday?—and followed her into the bathroom. Evi sat with his reader on a bench intended for putting one's clothes, leaning with his back against the wall. The light from the screen made his face blue. He motioned me to join him.

I did.

His screen displayed an image in bluish-grey hues, showing a corridor where a man in a white uniform stood guard in front of a door.

"That's outside our door," he said. "We managed to get into the security camera network."

He flicked to another image showing a gun mounted on a stand. "And in case we'd intended to climb onto the roof from the courtyard, just as well we didn't, because these are up there and they're attached to motion sensors."

Another image, this one of a luxurious office with a big wooden desk with a high-backed chair.

"This is bigger than the *president's* office." More luxurious, too. A couple of antique oriental vases stood on a table in the corner. An old bookcase held a collection of old tomes with gold-embossed lettering on the spines. A low table with carved legs sat in front of an old-style leather couch. Old paintings of sailing ships hung on the walls.

"You might find this interesting." He picked out a section of the image of a cabinet behind the desk and enlarged it.

On the top rested a number of photo display frames. Evi panned through the selection of photos. Most of them featured Mr Kray in places like Paris, Rome, New York, and even inside the main assembly hall of Nations of Earth. It made me kind of sick to see his toothy smile—no canine teeth—against the backdrop of the floor of the hall. All the seats where Danziger's helpers and committees would be sitting were empty, except for a guard who stood next to the president's chair. I guessed this was taken during the open hour for tourists.

Hey what was that?

Another photo showed people sitting at tables at some official dinner party function. It had to have been a while ago, because Danziger was in the picture, looking a lot younger than he was today. He was smiling at the camera, holding his arms over the shoulders of two people. On one side was a dark African man I recognised as a younger version of Lucius Brown. On the other, Robert Kray.

Shit.

I stared at Thayu. "Danziger is friendly with these guys?"

Then why did he tell me . . . No, wait. I had not seen Danziger when I was called back. And even though the message I'd gotten was under Danziger's letterhead, Simon Dekker would have access to that. In fact, Dekker had specifically told me not to contact Danziger. Or the press. And he had made threats about it, too.

So what?

Dekker was trying to manoeuvre behind Danziger's back?

Maybe Dekker was trying to clean up messy business from Danziger's past, prior to the election? *Do not go to the press* certainly fitted with that line of thought. But why not contact the acting president? Because he was not supposed to know that this was happening? He was not supposed to "remember" the time when this picture was taken? He was using his aide and an unfortunate Nations of Earth employee, whom he hated anyway, also known as Cory Wilson, to clean up the mess?

My heart was hammering.

Evi flicked to the next image. It showed an underground passage with a walkway on one side suspended over a couple of large pipes that disappeared out of view into the darkness of the tunnel.

"Water?" I asked.

"*Mashara* is fairly certain about that. This tunnel is not far from this room. It leads all the way under the hill to the main site in the next valley."

The next image showed a large hall. People worked at benches assembling things. Many people. Local people.

He showed me a shot taken from a different angle. A woman in traditional garb was putting long things in a wooden crate. Wait—

"Are those guns they're putting together?"

"Indrahui-style plasma guns, Delegate."

The type I'd seen in Dekker's office. A few men were assembling crates next to the women's workbench. Closed crates stood against the back wall in stacks of three. There were at least thirty. If every crate contained twelve guns . . . "That's a lot of guns." Also, if they produced this many guns, it was a wonder that they hadn't been noticed before. How long had this been going?

Everyone had been wrong about these guns. They weren't importing them. They were *exporting* them.

My head was reeling.

"Where do they sell all of them?"

"*Mashara* has been sent this image."

It was a much-enlarged satellite image, no doubt one sent to Thayu by her father. It showed some sort of nomadic settlement with tents in the desert. At least ten or twelve tents stood in a circle, with a fireplace in the middle.

To the side of the camp was something that looked like a drinking trough surrounded by longitudinal specks. They were camels.

"They trek through the desert? How hot does it get there?"

"They take adaptation."

"What about the camels? I know they're animals of the desert, but I don't believe they'd happily travel through that area."

"They take adaptation."

"The *camels?*" But as I said that, I knew that it was true, and so brilliant that no one would have suspected it for a long time. They'd produced weapons, loaded them onto camel trains and carted them across a desert everyone said was too hot to traverse, but which they could cross using adaptation medicine brought to them by Henri. Damn. That was where our pilot came in. And he was probably in a lot more danger than we'd first thought. Sure Mr Kray didn't appreciate him bring nosey foreigners to this area as a side job.

Actually, knowing what I knew about Romi Tanaqan, I was wondering if Henri was still alive. That thought chilled me.

Evi went back to showing the security camera images, now showing a passage with counters on both sides where people lined up to collect trays and parcels. In the rooms behind the counters, I could see racks of clothing, or people cooking, or tables full of knickknacks made from rubbish like we'd seen in the city: cups or lights made from cans, sandals made out of tyres and door mats knitted from plastic bags.

"It's a whole underground city," I said.

"This is not the only one. There are ones in Egypt and Sudan."

Thayu said, "No wonder that all these people disappeared. They work here."

Evi said, "They don't just work. They have been sold in *pahemin*. Only their families don't know this."

And those families wouldn't understand that if the worker defaulted on their commitments, everything the family owned was at risk.

"I wonder what Dekker thinks we can do about this. It's a massive operation, much more extensive than Kazakhstan ever was." That had only encompassed a few Zhori bases inside old buildings and in the field. It had only concerned itself with the sale of weapons, and had never been touted as a solution against the incredible poverty in the area.

You don't need to do anything about it. That was Asha in my head again. If the ship was moving into geostationary orbit, he would be able to communicate with us any time of the day. Fortunately, he would also be a lot further away. *Take pictures. Pass the information to us. We will make maps and run any images of people through face recognition. We will find the criminal elements.*

And what will you do? Oo-er, that was a cocky question with a cocky pronoun.

We will pass it on to the appropriate authorities. The answer was equally cocky. I didn't believe him and he knew it.

Pardon the inappropriate analogy, but I wished I could get this damn monkey off my back.

Evi flicked to the next image, which showed a hall with many seats that were all empty. There was a small stage at the front of the hall where a dais stood with a curious symbol on the side facing the audience.

I frowned at Evi. "What's that for?"

"There appears to be some kind of convention in progress now."

He changed to the next image: a large dining hall where people wearing dinner suits and fine dresses were seated along tables laden with food. There were hundreds of them, Africans and non-Africans alike. People wearing white aprons walked between the tables serving the diners.

Mr Kray stood in the middle of the hall. Like all Indrahui, he cut an imposing, tall figure. His dark skin stood out against his white suit. His hair was shorter than in any of the previous images I'd seen of him and he'd died it a convincing pepper-and-salt grey. He was facing the camera and most in the audience had their backs turned to the camera.

"What is this about?"

"*Mashara* is still trying to establish this. Also who these people are. At this stage, *Mashara* does not know."

But even if we couldn't see who they were, their clothes marked them as rich and influential people, and here they were, wined and dined by the most notorious war criminal in all of *gamra*.

23

———

"I THINK WE SHOULD use this conference of his as an opportunity to get out of here," Thayu said. "I'm sure he has to be careful that these beautiful people don't get any wind of trouble, because they don't like to get blood or dust on their pretty clothes."

"The guards will be more nervous with all those important people here," Nicha said. "They can't afford any trouble either. That's why we've been locked up and forgotten. He probably intends to deal with us once everyone is gone."

I now also realised why Tamu had complained that it had been busy the previous week in her hotel. This many different people travelling to this region at Mr Kray's invitation for this conference would need a host of servants and others to look after them. The guests would have stayed in swanky hotels in the city. The workers were more likely to stay in Tamu's hotel.

I agreed with Thayu: Mr Kray was preoccupied. This was the best time to try something. We studied the detailed 3D scan of the building and underground passages that Asha had produced, from his scans and the information collected by us.

The tunnel that led to the main part of the project was 2.4 kilometres long. It had a walkway along its entire length and, apart from the house, and the pump station further down towards the shore, there were no other entrances. The only exit was in the factory hall of the underground settlement.

The trouble was how to get to the tunnel, which had an entrance at the end of the corridor where we were.

"We no longer have weapons," I said.

Nicha said, "First lesson in defence: in the hands of a skilled fighter, a flower can be a weapon."

That was the proverb that his father was trying to get credited to his name. It needed to have seen a certain number of documented cases of use before it could be official. I didn't think this counted as documented use.

It does, said a dry voice in my head.

Thayu, Nicha, Evi and Telaris were discussing whether the best option was going out the courtyard door, or the room's door into the hall. I had the feeling they were deliberately ignoring me, telling me ever so subtly to shut up. I told them to go into the bathroom and that I'd take Telaris' position by the door.

Once the four of them were gone, I became aware of an odd sound, like something being dragged across a rough concrete floor.

The sound came from the back of the room. As I got closer to the back wall, something in the wardrobe went *mreow*.

Ah, the cat had woken up. I opened the door a crack and got rewarded with a scratch over my toes. Ouch.

OK, kitty was unimpressed. I shut the door again, and the cat resumed scratching the back of the door.

It was an awkward situation. I hated doing this to an animal, but also couldn't risk it walking around transmitting stuff we couldn't allow people to hear. I had no idea how to deactivate the bug. Normally Thayu would rip cords out of the wall and cut them. I guess Mr Kray killed animals when he didn't need them anymore.

I sat on the couch.

The cat scratched the back of the door.

I found it hard to listen to. I hoped that when we left, someone would free the cat. I hated it when people were cruel to animals like this. Or like giving adaptation to camels. Whose idea was that?

It was just getting light when Nicha and Telaris came in.

I began, "What is—" but Nicha motioned to be quiet. Next he gestured *Get your things.*

I scrambled to collect my reader, my shoes and socks, and put them on. Urgh, those shoes smelled bad.

When I was ready, I nodded to Nicha. He made a signal. Evi came out of the bathroom, followed by Thayu. She carried a strip of plastic that looked to have been removed from a cupboard or some piece of furniture. She took it to the door, and knelt. Very carefully, she inserted the strip between the door and the doorframe where the lock was. After a couple of minutes of wriggling, there was a click. Thayu nodded and rose, while keeping the plastic strip in the door. Then Evi yanked open the door and Nicha ran through.

A shout in the corridor was followed by a heavy thunk.

A few moments later Nicha came back, studying a gun in his hands. It was a model like Simon Dekker had shown me, except this one was complete with a plasma chamber. He gave it to his sister, who studied it. "Interesting model."

"Didn't you just show me that there's a bug outside the door?" I protested. "They'll have seen you."

"*Mashara* disabled it," Telaris said, his tone smug.

Clearly, Mr Kray had not expected trouble, because there had only been one guard outside the door, and as Nicha told me, he'd been dozing. He now lay unconscious on the floor.

Thayu went over his clothes and divested him of other things that might be useful; some sort of entry pass, a reader and a knife, which she gave to Telaris.

"Come." She led the way further into the house.

We walked as quietly as we could. It was in the very early hours of the morning, and outside everything was still pretty dark. Inside the house there was no activity and even our very careful footsteps sounded loud.

We found the tunnel entrance at the end of the corridor easily enough.

A few flights of stairs led down into the ground. Unlike the house, the stairwell wasn't air-conditioned. The air was breathless and hot.

We came to a door at the bottom of the stairs, where Telaris and Thayu disabled another camera before leading us through. It led to the mesh walkway in the tunnel. The giant pipes ran in both directions underneath us. It was so quiet that I could hear the water sloshing inside on its way to the house, settlement and the factory.

We started walking. The passage was lit only by the occasional green emergency light on the ceiling. Our footsteps sounded loud on the metal of the walkway.

Thayu was walking first with her scanner. Every now and then she would stop and turn around, holding the scanner in front of her with her arms outstretched.

Telaris said, *"Mashara* has established that there are bugs in this passage. We will have to disable them."

Thayu gestured. "Up there."

Nicha went a few paces back, approached at a run, and jumped up the side wall. He reached for something on the ceiling, and then tumbled to the ground with a thud that made the walkway shudder.

"Nich'!"

He rolled to his feet, got up and came back to us, grinning and holding a tiny square box dangling on a piece of electrical cord.

As we progressed through the tunnel, this process repeated itself a few times. It was slow. I knew the tunnel was 2.4 kilometres long, but it seemed much longer. It was hot and humid because the pipes leaked a bit in some places. Nicha made enough noise for a herd of elephants, and he was starting to look dirty, with smudges of moss and algae on his hands and clothes. We couldn't just shoot the bugs down, Thayu said, because we had only one gun, which was only one-third charged and we might need it later.

I still felt we made enough of a ruckus that a reception committee would be waiting for us when we finally came out of the tunnel.

Finally, the end was in sight—or at least some place where the tunnel opened out and there was more light. An oil-scented breeze wafted from that direction. And a good deal of noise: clanging and hammering and clicking and zooming. I guessed this was the factory hall that we'd seen.

Closer up, I could see into a big hall where the pipes crossed close to the ceiling. At the entrance into the hall, there was a metal grate with a guard on the other side. If the guard in front of our room had been half asleep, this one was very much awake. And he carried a very big gun.

Thayu motioned *stop*.

We did, crouching against the side of the tunnel in the darkness. The tunnel's wall was rough and dusty here. My hands felt filthy. If that guy with his big gun decided to turn on the light in here, there would be absolutely nowhere to hide. A lot of hand signals were passed between Thayu, Nicha, Evi and Telaris.

Then we started moving again, slowly this time. Telaris motioned for me to stay at the back.

Closer we came, and closer, creeping in single file along the tunnel's wall.

And closer, and closer.

Not ten metres away from the grate, we stopped again. Telaris took one step away from the wall and drew himself up to his full height. He lifted his arm and threw something that flashed in the light and flew through the passage, between the bars of the grate.

The guard stiffened, and fell sideways.

We ran to the grate. It was locked, but Thayu fired at the lock. The metal glowed, and globs fell down. She pulled the grate open enough for one person to go through. The guard lay in a pool of blood with the haft of a knife sticking out of his temple. Evi dragged the body into the tunnel where it was not clearly visible save for the fat bloody trail on the floor.

I felt sick.

We had come out of the tunnel on a platform above a factory floor. The big water pipes crossed the hall, supported by brackets on the ceiling. On the ground floor, twenty-five or so local people stood at tables putting weapons together. Attaching handgrips, clipping in plasma chambers, screwing on sights, packing complete guns in crates by the dozen. At the far end of the factory hall people were working on the gun parts: machining barrels, welding, cutting, pouring red glowing resin into moulds. A bank of shelves contained smaller boxes with parts that were clearly imported from off-world: parts of mechanisms, rivets and strips made of Hedron steel with its characteristic purple sheen.

Guns. A whole factory of them.

The noise and smells of plastic and oil wafted up to where we stood.

I said in a low voice, "I guess this is the part where we go gun shopping."

"Yup," Thayu said. She had our only gun, so she led the way down a couple of flights of metal stairs. We were about halfway when people at the gun assembly line started noticing us. They looked with wide eyes but didn't move from their positions.

Someone yelled, "This way, mister, this way!"

I thought I recognised the voice, and indeed it was Henri. His cheekbone was bruised, and he wore ankle braces with chains attached to the workbench. His clothes were ripped. He looked dreadful, but I was glad to see him.

Thayu ran to him. The other workers scrambled away from her. She fired at the chains until they, too, fell apart into molten globs.

The factory workers who had scurried away were returning now that they'd figured they weren't going to be shot.

"Free as many people as you can," I told Henri. "Take them outside."

"Please, mista," an old man said. "No good can come from trying to help us. If we leave, they will find our families."

Many people nodded. There were at least twenty, all local people, most of them men, and numbers were still growing. There had to be at least a few hundred workers in this hall.

They were skinny, filthy. Some had weeping sores from burns or other injuries. Some had no shoes. None of them had overalls or anywhere near appropriate gear for working on a factory floor. But all the ones I could see had their front teeth. *Not* krayfish.

"How did you end up here?" I asked.

"He promise us money," a woman said in heavy accent. "He says: money if you work. We said: we know how to work, give us money. He says he look after us. Then we get here, no money. We get food, but not enough. We complain. Few days later they bring your brother or sister. Sometimes they bring your old mother. They make them work. You try to escape, they kill you."

Evi and Telaris gave each other a dark look. Evi lifted his chin, an Indrahui way of indicating *yes*.

These people were under *pahemin*. They were indebted workers, Indrahui-style. They'd bought into it without knowing what they agreed to.

I looked at Henri and had another chilling thought. "Who actually owns that plane of yours?"

The expression in his eyes told me enough.

Someone shouted on the other side of the hall.

"Let's go," Thayu said to me in Coldi.

"But . . ." I spread my hands. These people needed help.

"Any of these weapons that we can use?" she asked.

I translated the question.

"You need to attach the plasma chamber," Henri said. "We don't assemble them here. The krayfish do that. Those are packed and stored separately."

Made sense. "No gun shopping." I told Thayu what he had said.

She didn't look impressed.

The shouting on the other side of the hall increased. Likely some bug or such trivial thing as the presence of a dead body had alerted guards that we were in the building and they were coming to ferret us out.

"Quick!" Thayu called.

She took off across the hall.

"Keep safe! Try to get out!" I called to Henri while running after her.

24

W E RAN ACROSS the factory floor, between the benches where some people were still working. Once, Thayu almost crashed into a grey-haired man who crossed the aisle while carrying a crate. He gave a cry and stumbled back, almost toppling over. His work mates all scurried out of the way. They made no move to speak to us or ask questions. Many stared at Evi and Telaris with wide eyes and *cowered*. If ever Indrahui intended to build goodwill here, they had a long way to go.

A passage led away from the hall, and two guards stood at its entrance. At our approach, both reached for weapons. Thayu made short work of one with the gun while Evi threw a metal bar he had picked up somewhere at the other guard. It hit the man on the side of the head.

The guards both slumped to the ground. Both locals, too. I could hardly believe Mr Kray was the only offworld person in this place, but it was starting to look like it.

Thayu kicked the men's guns aside. One had carried a big gun of the type I'd seen in Dekker's office; the other had two smaller guns.

"Take those." She dropped to her knees next to the bodies to search them for other useful items. The one she'd shot wouldn't be getting up anymore, but the other man might live. For someone who didn't like people getting killed, I sure spent a lot of time in situations where that happened.

The men's belt pouches contained an assortment of gadgets that she stuffed into her pocket.

She handed the big gun to Evi, and the others to Telaris and Nicha. "You'll have to do the shooting. Mine is almost flat. It's for show only."

They all inspected the weapons with the same cold, calculated military look. It chilled me.

Telaris flicked the switch to turn the weapon off and on again. He pushed another button bringing a small display to life. "Made locally?" He seemed impressed.

Behind us, a whole audience of the factory floor's workers had assembled in the hall. They stood there looking at us, like a silent crowd of ghosts. Their eyes were hollow, their hands marked with cuts and burns. Some people wore dirty bandages.

Most were thin to the point of being emaciated.

I shivered. The Indrahui *pahemin* debt system was notorious. There were whole generations who would never be free from indenture to the warlords. As long as the people were dependent on these warlords, they could not protest against them. They would not pass on any information to anyone else. The warlord owned these people. He owned their children, their voices, the products of their work. He owned their future.

We continued further into the passage with Thayu in the lead. I had no idea where she was going, but she seemed quite confident, occasionally glancing at the map her father had sent us. She led us into a side passage and ducked into a stairwell, going up. One floor above, we came out into a soft carpeted corridor. There were doors on both sides, with little numbered signs. It looked like an expensive hotel. The air was cool and clean, there were plants in large pots along the walls next to each door, the light was muted. The place was deserted and eerily quiet.

What now? I met Thayu's eyes, but she held her finger to her lips. With a jerk of her head, she motioned Telaris to come over. They each took up position on either side of a nearby door on the right-hand side.

The door opened and a cleaner wheeled a laundry trolley out

of a doorway. She stopped. Looked at Evi. Her eyes widened. Telaris grabbed her from behind, putting a hand over her mouth. He dragged her backwards into the room.

She went, "Mmmmm!"

"Be quiet," Telaris said in Isla.

He forced her to sit down on a chair. She strained against the pressure of his hand on her face. "Hmmmm!"

"Quiet," I repeated Telaris. I crouched so that my face was level with hers. "Do you want to leave this place?"

She nodded behind Telaris' hand. She was a local of the dark African type, probably no more than eighteen years old, pretty and soft-skinned. I gestured for Telaris to take his hand away.

She began, "My brother . . ."

"He works in the gun factory?"

"Yes. I'm afraid for him. People have told me that he is sick. I haven't seen him for years."

"What is your name?"

"Sara."

"Sara, would you like to help us so that you and your brother can be free?"

Her eyes widened. "Do you know that they can kill me just for talking to you?"

"Not if you help us, you won't be killed. We'll be letting all of you out of here. We're here to shut this place down."

"Delegate, have a look here," Evi said from the other side of the room.

Evi had moved a curtain aside. What I had taken to be the room's back wall was in fact a window. It looked out over a large hall. There was a blue swimming pool to one side. Big pots with palms stood around the edge. On the other side people sat at tables. These were all the dinner guests I had seen before but they were now having a breakfast meeting and wore more business-like outfits.

Waiters and waitresses in white aprons moved between the tables carrying bread and coffee.

I could almost smell it up here. My stomach rumbled.

They were listening to a man behind the dais that we had seen earlier. Because they sat at tables instead of in rows in an auditorium, I could see some of their faces. I hadn't expected to recognise anyone, and I didn't; but I could tell they represented a wide range of groups from all economic backgrounds. There were clean and cultured people in suits and wizened, wrinkled elders from desert tribes. There were West Africans and North Africans and Arabic Africans and people from local tribes.

No Coldi.

No other Indrahui or anyone else from off-world.

Mr Kray was again dressed in white, which contrasted sharply with his very dark skin. In the flesh, his impressive size stood out even more.

Evi raised the gun and pointed it at Robert Kray's head. The expression on his face was intense with hatred.

Sara gave a little squeal and cowered behind the couch.

For a moment, I was afraid that he was going to shoot, giving away our position, bringing guards up here, making sure that we'd never complete our mission, making action by that ship in orbit a certainty.

Telaris said something in Indrahui in a low voice. Evi let the gun sink again, blowing out a deep breath. He gave me a startled look.

"*Mashara* apologises." He wiped his face. "*Mashara* must not let anger get in the way of the mission. The shot would have been no good going through the glass anyway." He put the gun in his belt. "But I'll kill the bastard the first time I get a clean shot."

I didn't know what to say. I had no sisters or brothers, let alone ones who had been cruelly killed by a warlord whose face I'd got the chance to see through the sight of a gun. If I was in Evi's position, I didn't know if I'd be disciplined enough not to push the discharge button.

The subject of their hatred continued to speak, oblivious of his temporary reprieve.

"What is this setup anyway?" I asked in Isla, turning my attention back to Sara.

"Mr Kray likes giving parties that go on for days," Sara said. "We have to cook the food and serve the food. He gets his own people to bring the food, because the men from the factory floor would eat it."

"Who are 'his own' people?"

"They're the ones who are most loyal to him. The krayfish. You get points for doing certain things, and he judges if you're trustworthy. If you have enough points, you go into the guard. You can get a gun. If you're a girl, you can live in his house and clean and cook there. They take your teeth." She grinned, showing her intact front teeth.

She was still only mentioning local people. "Are there many people like her or him?" I gestured to Thayu and Nicha.

She frowned. "I thought they were both girls."

Nicha snorted. Thayu's face had a puzzled expression, and through our feeder I was getting signals that she was annoyed and thought she should really learn Isla.

You should, I told her.

That made her even more annoyed.

"They both have long hair," Sara said.

True, and the differences between male and female Coldi was very subtle. I no longer had trouble with it, but I remembered when I did.

Sara shook her head. "There are no people like them."

The implication of this little statement was huge: no Coldi meant no Zhori clan and no connections to the Exchange. So Romi Tanaqan had bought advice from the Zhori and had then started his own illegal settlement?

"Any people like them?" I now indicated Evi and Telaris.

"They're like Mr Kray," she said, her voice uncertain. Clearly, anyone looking like Mr Kray frightened her very much.

"Anyone apart from Mr Kray?"

"No. He's the only one."

"Does he have family?"

She shook her head. "There are a couple of girls who don't mind sleeping with him, but none have children."

"Don't mind?" Evi asked.

"Well, I hope it's all right me talking about these things, mister, but he's pretty big, in the downstairs department. He hurts the small girls." Her skin went even darker than normal.

Yes, I knew what she meant, having seen Evi and Telaris naked, and yes, the subject was embarrassing. I steered the conversation in another direction. "Has anyone told you where Mr Kray comes from?"

She shook her head. "There are rumours, but no one knows for sure. Mr Kray is black, but he looks strange." She cast Evi a nervous look. He was at least a head taller than her, and was clearly unimpressed with her remark about Robert Kray's size in the men's department. "I thought he was just odd, but I see that he's a different type of person. They say that these people are from other worlds. Like the Moon. It looks quite small in the sky, but when you get closer, it's as big as the whole world. You can live on it."

"Yeah, that's close enough to the truth." It never ceased to amaze me how certain areas of news completely bypassed otherwise intelligent people. Like when Thayu and I visited New Zealand, people would often ask us if I knew that president Sirkonen had been shot *by aliens!* never mind that I'd been in the room with him.

Different worlds, I guessed.

"So, who are all these guests?"

"He calls them the African Forward Thinking Group. They meet once every couple of months."

"Who are they? Government? Political leaders?"

She frowned. "Sorry. I don't know any of them. They're important people, that's all I know."

"Do you hear any of what he tells them?"

"A lot of the same things that he tells us: that he wants this area to become independent and have industry. That we will always have jobs, and there will be enough money to buy imported things. The sad thing is that the boys very much want imported things and they believe every word he says. But only Mr Kray's close friends ever get anything. Not even all the krayfish, although they get enough so that they don't leave. The ordinary workers just stay here and stay poor."

In the hall, Robert Kray was showing a clip of a farm in the middle of the desert, taken from a plane. The contrast between the green fields and the surrounding desert was almost painful. The crop was some kind of broad-leaf plant, I had no idea which.

Thayu said, "That's *moya.*"

Moya was the standard staple crop that fed large parts of Asto.

It was a large-leafed plant, about waist high, that produced fruit reminiscent of a pineapple, except that it was very dry and woody and needed to be ground into flour. I'd seen plenty of pictures of street vendors in Athyl's outer circles crouching over a hotplate to bake the flour mixed with water into pancakes.

To grow these plants in the desert was smart and highly illegal. Asto's plant species were adapted to extreme heat. They also carried diseases against which Earth had no defence. Many species were invasive, or poisonous.

Nicha said in Coldi, "It's like he's taken the idea of a Coldi colony in the desert and made it bigger."

"And there are no Coldi people involved," Thayu said. "I don't understand."

"I don't understand why Danziger has allowed this to exist."

"He doesn't," I said. "Isn't that why we're here?"

"But why let Mr Kray get away with it this far? You can't tell me that no one knew."

No; Nations of Earth, or at least PanAf, would have known.

"Well," I said. "My hunch is this: for many years, Nations of Earth has given vast amounts of money to PanAf as part of the Copenhagen agreement" —the 2061 treaty that determined compensation paid by richer countries to the third-world nations who had seen their viability reduced because of temperature increase or rising sea levels— "but Nations of Earth has been frustrated because this area has never been anything other than a vast money pit, while other nations have used the funds to get ahead and have something to show for it." Like Pakistan and Bangladesh, once basket cases, which were now quite well off. "I'm guessing that the vast amounts of aid given to this area by Nations of Earth are getting in the way of Danziger's other promises to other areas, so when some guy comes along with plans like these, he'd be excited, especially when that guy is a friend of his friend Lucius Brown."

"He'd only be excited until he discovered that this scheme is set up by one of *gamra's* most wanted criminals, and is therefore unlikely to be benevolent."

I nodded. "Something like that. And with those photos in Mr Kray's office, I'd have to say that Danziger knows about it." *And somehow, Danziger had not realised at first that Robert Kray was not an African.* That was something I could believe about Danziger, too, because of his limited knowledge of *gamra* and his refusal to accept advice from people who were in a position to give it.

"This is nothing more than the worst kind of slavery," Thayu said, glancing at Sara. "Even in the Outer Circle, we don't allow this."

"It's the production of illegal weapons under everyone's nose, and with their approval, too," Nicha said.

"The man is a criminal of the worst kind," Evi said. His voice wavered with anger.

They all appeared shocked by the brashness of the scheme.

I said, "Danziger didn't see me that night when we were called back to Rotterdam because he wanted Dekker to clean up his dirty laundry. Because of the election. He also didn't want to renege on any deals he had with either Lucius Brown, a friend, or with Mr Kray, because the krayfish would kill him. So he asked me instead, citing the presence of *gamra* people, which he already knew about. At least this way, if there were any assassinations, the person killed would be me."

"You're already dead," Nicha said.

"Yeah, I think I'll rise from the grave soon." I was going to make a zombie joke, but none of them would get it.

Thayu snorted. "It really astonishes me what sort of behaviour you tolerate from your superiors—What?"

I was shaking my head. "Danziger is not my supervisor. Dekker told me not to bother the president with any of this 'because campaigning is tiring', but I think I might just ignore that order. I might also send a copy of all this to Flash Newspoint."

Down in the hall, Robert Kray was still speaking.

The wall behind him held a large screen. On it was a map of the northern half of Africa, indicating a couple of locations in red dots. Ethiopia, southern Egypt, Libya—was that the original site? —and Nigeria. Dotted lines connected these locations to each other and to another dot at the top of the map. A ship in the Mediterranean? Or—I felt cold—a satellite in orbit?

Thayu was busily taking pictures.

This guy was planning to take the whole northern half of the continent with the knowledge of all these people.

I felt increasingly sickened by this man's tricks. Using the old Coldi plans would assure that when *gamra* found out about the intent of the plan, Asto would be blamed.

25

———

"SO, WHAT ARE WE going to do?" Nicha asked. "There are way too many people here and there are only five of us. There is no way we can barge in there with guns and hope to get out alive or even just get the guests out alive."

Asha's voice in my head said, *I have the locations. We're calibrating actions.*

My heart skipped a beat. *No.* And after a panic-filled breath, *That's not necessary. There are many innocent civilians in this area. I'm confident that we can resolve the issue without the use of military force.* Damn, I'd thought that he wouldn't be able to do anything from that distance.

I said to Thayu and Nicha, "One of our most powerful weapons will be information. All these people here look important. They need to know what's really going on." I turned to Sara and continued in Isla, "We need your help." Hell, we *all* needed each other's help to avoid any "action" from orbit.

She nodded, eyes wide.

"Is there a place where Mr Kray or his secretary stores the details of all these people who are here?"

"There is, in the office downstairs, but I don't work there."

"That's all right. Can you get us some uniforms like the one you're wearing?"

"Men's or women's?"

"Women's. Two sets."

Nicha protested, "Hey! What do you think I am? A drag queen?"

I said in Coldi, "These are the type of people who will find a woman less threatening." Back to Isla. "Can we use the bathroom here?"

"Not this room, but there is an empty room on the other side of the corridor."

"Take us there, then."

Sara did. The room was much smaller, but contained a double bed, a single bed, two chairs and a wallscreen that, when Evi turned it on, displayed details of what was going on in the hall downstairs.

I asked Sara to bring us something to eat while she was down there.

Sara went to get uniforms, and we studied the layout of the building. The foyer in the bottom floor of the accommodation wing was next to the pool, and a little room behind the reception desk held the computers with administration details.

Sara came back with coffee, bread, rolls and jam, carrying a bundle of clothes over her arm. We demolished the food and then Thayu and Nicha went into the bathroom carrying the uniforms.

We discussed the plan: get the guest list and send a message about the weapons factory and the illegal alien crops to the guests. Make sure that all those who wanted to leave could do so.

I prepared a message and photos. "I think I should sign with my real name."

"The risk will be increased, but *mashara* agrees," Telaris said

Evi burst out laughing. It was such a rare sound that I looked behind me. Thayu and Nicha had come out of the bathroom, both dressed as waitresses. I don't know which of them glowered the most: Thayu because she had to wear a light blue dress that showed her nicely-shaped legs, or Nicha because he had to wear a light blue dress that showed his nicely-shaped legs. He had also stuffed hand towels down his shirt to give the appearance of breasts.

I stifled laughter.

"Remember that I'm doing this for the good of the world,"

Nicha said. He took the cup he'd left before going into the bathroom and gulped the remaining coffee.

Thayu sat on the bed, a dark expression on her face. The uniform did, in fact, look quite sexy on her, since Coldi women were always quite sturdy and the shirt was tight around her breasts and shoulders.

The two of them looked so much alike.

We went through the plan. They were to go down to the office, and Thayu would break into the computer while Nicha guarded the door. A simple thing, Thayu said. They knew where the office was, and breaking into computers was easy.

They left.

I sat in one of the armchairs, making a list of all the people outside the settlement to whom I needed to send as much information as possible: key Nations of Earth officials, Melissa Hayworth and the head of the Special Services branch of the Nations of Earth guards. I deliberated sending the information to Danziger, but Dekker would probably intercept it.

I chose the most incriminating of Thayu's pictures: the trophy picture on Mr Kray's desk of Danziger with Robert Kray and Lucius Brown, the image she had just taken of Robert Kray standing in front of the map with all their planned settlements. The crops in the desert. A wide-angle picture which clearly showed all the important guests sitting at dinner.

Then I wrote a message, explaining what we had found out. It included relevant text of the laws that prohibited unauthorised imports and especially the culture of non-Earth plants. I included pictures of those plants and effects of the diseases they could carry. I included pictures of the original settlement plan by Mizha in 1975 and the number of deaths attributed to the Kazakhstan disaster. I even included vague hints that *gamra* wasn't happy with the situation either, and that there might be some kind of military action if nothing was done about it.

At the end I said, *I advise that everyone get out of here as quickly as you can by any possible means that is safe.* I signed with my real name and attached a scan of my tag that could only have been taken by someone with access to that tag, and the tag itself only worked if a person was alive.

I was still perfecting it when the door opened and Thayu and Nicha came back. Thayu gave a thumbs-up, passed me the list, and both of them first disappeared into the bathroom to get changed back into their regular gear.

A quick glance at the attendance list revealed that the guests came from countries all over the northern half of Africa. There were many from Sudan, a country that had done surprisingly well out of the violent changes in the last seventy years or so. It had been one of the first countries to go one hundred percent solar, even when cells and batteries were a lot less efficient than they were now. They sold power across the borders. With the money made from that, they had pioneered low-cost versions of everything: power stations, cars, planes. Lately, they had been into cloud seeding to produce artificial rain. They were also experimenting with large-scale controlled-climate habitats.

There were people from Egypt, the hotbed of several radical religious groups; Algeria, where some of the Zhori were said to have gone; Senegal, where huge camps held hundreds of thousands of environmental refugees, most of whom had been there for generations with no hope of ever returning to their parched home countries; Nigeria, Morocco, Libya, and so on, all countries that were deeply affected. Many that were broke, near-defunct and lawless.

Some of the names were marked with different colours. Sara had gone back to her work, so I couldn't ask what the colours meant.

Thayu said that her father had run her pictures through a face recognition process and had names on several people.

I was happy to see that at least some names were the same as on the attendance list, although there were also disturbing discrepancies. The people whose names appeared in both lists were mostly from middle layers of government. Not members of parliament themselves, but assistants of members of parliament. Some of them had to be tribe elders as well, but I gathered that face recognition wasn't useful for people who didn't frequent places where they were likely to be picked up by some sort of database or security camera.

"Why are there people on this list who are not on the face recognition result?" Nicha was looking over my shoulder.

"Because face recognition is not perfect," Thayu said.

Telaris said, "Because they use alternate names?"

As he said that, a chill crept over my back. There would only be one reason for people to do that: if they didn't want to be recognised. "Maybe they're military people?"

And, also, those people were the ones whose names were marked with colour-coded labels. Did they indicate how much these people had paid to be here and be part of "A new wave of development in Africa" that Mr Kray was pushing?

I glanced at the wallscreen. In the hall, the guests were now eating breakfast.

People were engaging in lively conversation and the scene looked just like those "working" breakfasts I'd sometimes attended at Nations of Earth.

With one press of a button, I was going to disturb their illusion of progress and self-determination.

"Everyone ready?"

Thayu, Nicha, Evi and Telaris all nodded.

I pressed *send*.

Downstairs, in the hall, a lot of people groped for their readers at the same time. Read my message. It grew very quiet. People were looking at each other from the corners of their eyes, clearly not sure what to do.

Then a man rose. He was a bearded fellow, wearing a flowing blue robe characteristic of some of the Arab desert tribes. He shouted angry words, but his accent was too strong and the quality of the recording wasn't good enough to make out what he said.

Several other people rose. An argument broke out between a couple of guests. One man pushed another in the chest, causing him to fall on top of the table behind him. The woman who sat there yelled at the aggressor.

A couple of armed krayfish guards ran between the tables, but they completely ignored the skirmishes and went to Mr Kray, who sat at a table in the middle of the hall. He rose. The guards surrounded him with their backs to him, and started moving out of the hall.

The poor person in charge of recording the event had no idea where to point the camera. It swung around wildly, showing a number of people leaving the hall past the side of the pool, or swinging back to the argument in the middle of the hall, or Mr Kray now making his way between the tables surrounded by guards. People around him yelled at him. One of the guests had climbed onto a table in order to speak to him.

Sounds were all garbled. Orders being shouted, people asking questions, yelling at others. Over the top of the noise came a very loud bang.

The camera swung back to Mr Kray. The man on the table froze and jerked, and fell backwards between the tables. A red spot bloomed on his chest.

People nearby screamed, running from the scene.

The camera feed went black.

"Well, shit," Nicha said. "I guess our camera man has been ordered to stop recording."

Although the screen had gone quiet, we could still hear sounds of yelling through the floor and several walls.

"Maybe it's time to go," Thayu said.

"We've done nothing yet!" Evi protested. He'd been watching the screen intently, his hands clasped tightly while leaning his elbows on his knees.

"We've got enough incriminating information for authorities to draw the necessary conclusions."

"Authorities! Pardon the abandoning of protocol, Delegate, but do you know what men like this do with authorities?"

"My guess: they buy them and corrupt them. That's why we're here. We have proof of corruption that goes all the way to the top. We take it to Amarru and Nations of Earth. They will have reason to act."

"By that time, this evil man will have disappeared. He will go somewhere else and start again. But all these people, the innocent, the opportunistic and the hopeful, will have lost their livelihood and often family members. Not to mention their front teeth. They had hope that life would be better. That someone could do something useful with this hot desert that—let's see—was here not because of something *they* did, right? Because this land was written off because the world grew warmer, and that had nothing to do with the poor countries in this region."

His reaction took me aback, but he was one hundred percent right, and it was precisely the reason why a lot of the wars had happened.

I got up and faced him. He was a head taller than me and very imposing. Behind him, his brother was making cautious noises in Indrahui.

"What would you do in this situation? I can warn Nations of Earth. I can warn Amarru. They can send people. I can't possibly allow Asha Domiri to interfere."

"Why not?"

"Because he'll be committing an act of war."

"Don't Nations of Earth want this solved?"

"Yes but . . ." I lifted my hands.

"Haven't we just warned everyone to get out of here? All the guests are leaving. All the factory workers should be leaving as well. The only ones left would be this vile man and his vile assistants. He's not even a citizen of any country or *gamra* entity and his henchmen are soldiers who know that the risk of signing up to fight for a warlord is that you may die."

But . . . I let my hands sink again. Yes. I could tell Asha to destroy these buildings and the fields. But. "No. Much as it would make sense—"

"It would solve the problem—"

"—Much as it would make sense, I can't allow that. We're going back to Athens and Rotterdam. We're going to present our information. Lucius Brown will find himself out of a job. Heck, even Danziger might be forced out of the race—"

"The president is an idiot, but he's not guilty. He can resign for all he wants, and Lucius Brown can be punished as much as Nations of Earth wants, but there will be no point unless we stop this vile man."

Ouch. Right again.

Evi's moss green eyes met mine, intense. Why had I ever thought that he was timid? Right now, he frightened the hell out of me. I didn't even want to think about what would happen if

Nations of Earth assembly got wind of a strike from orbit by the Asto army.

"Can we have this discussion later?" Thayu said. "If we wait any longer they'll have traced the message back to this room."

"We are going back to Athens," I told Evi, still meeting his eyes. "That's final."

He nodded curtly and went to gather his things. He was unhappy. Oh, he was very unhappy. Nicha gave me a look I couldn't interpret.

I said, *Well then, what would you do?* I was getting really annoyed.

He said nothing. The feeder told me that he was thinking of Kazakhstan, of the mess and protracted fights, of all the innocent civilian lives lost. And no one there was even forced into *pahemin* indenture structures. A generation or two of this, and no one would even be loyal to PanAf anymore.

I get it, Nich'. Stop it.

I *couldn't* possibly authorise Asha to strike.

Could. Not.

End. Of. Discussion.

26

W E WENT INTO the corridor. Already a good number of people were running out of the stairwell to their rooms. We struggled down the stairs against the stream and came to the foyer. A couple in African garb protested loudly at the front desk. They wanted the first flight out of here, they said. The girl at the desk seemed flustered and nervous. I heard her mention Mr Kray's name several times. A large group of people were watching, many of them holding their suitcases. *They* all wanted to leave immediately, too. More were joining all the time.

I had expected . . . whatever reaction someone would show when an illegal scheme had been discovered. Anger, nervousness. Perhaps people avoiding each other.

I was not prepared to see this level of apparently genuine outrage. Surely they *had* to be aware that Mr Kray's plans were very dark grey at best. Had not one of these people asked which crop stayed brilliantly green in the hottest desert on Earth, and where it came from?

The foyer of the accommodation wing gave direct access the pool and dining area. A lot of the guests were still coming in. The door was quite narrow so a group of people bunched up outside. Some people had stains over their clothes. Some argued, others were yelling hysterically.

We waited on the inside of the door. I wasn't even sure why

Thayu wanted to go that way. The krayfish would be in that part of the building. I had no intention of getting caught by them.

The vehicles are that way, Thayu said in response to my thoughts. *Unless we have more business here, we should get out as soon as we can.*

Seriously, Thay', just stop acting as if your father is going to attack from orbit.

I was trying very hard not to blame them for failing to understand my objections. I was certain: Amarru had sent me here to stop a direct attack from orbit. Because she understood how much Nations of Earth was attached to sovereignty and how much that would upset them. Even if the target was not under Nations of Earth jurisdiction, the land was.

Thayu squeezed out the door into the hall when there was a little gap between the people who were coming in. We followed close behind her.

In the dining area, a couple of cleaners were already sweeping up the mess of fallen plates and broken glass. There was no sign of any bodies.

A couple of guards stood mulling about at another exit.

I whispered, "Thay'!" I held her back.

She pulled me down behind a planter box. Evi balanced the large gun on the concrete rim and pointed it at the guards between two slender palm trunks. Telaris aimed his smaller gun.

A woman squealed. The guards turned in our direction. Thayu motioned with her hand. Evi and Telaris both fired. A flash of light zapped across the pool and exploded at the entrance to the hall. People behind us screamed. When the dust cleared, the guards were on the ground and a hole had appeared in the wall.

Evi hung the giant gun on a bracket on his belt.

The expression on his face still chilled me. It was not unemotional, it was murderous. He was not here to protect me. He was here to serve justice for the killing of his sister in the bloodiest way possible. If I wasn't going to order that strike from orbit, he would stay here to kill Mr Kray, or be killed instead.

We ran past the pool to the entrance. Thayu stopped briefly to check the fallen guards for weapons, but they had been too badly burned to be of any use.

"We need to be more careful. Someone else is sure to have noticed that massive blast." She glared at Evi, who stared ahead.

Thayu met my eyes. *I'm worried. Is it safe to continue with him?*

I said, "Evi."

He turned to me, dark and brooding.

"It is *mashara's* task to protect the mission, to make sure that we all make it out of here alive."

He was silent for a frightening split second, then he nodded and looked down. *"Mashara* understands."

My heart was hammering.

Thayu led us into the passage off the main hall. "The area where the vehicles are is at the end of this corridor."

A door stood open there and I thought I could already see the large caterpillar wheels of the desert trucks in the darkness.

We ran. I wanted so badly to get out of there, even if only to have a stern talk with Evi, to make sure that his aims were still aligned with that of our team.

A door opened as we passed. A couple of people burst out, and ran after us. From the corner of my eye, I noticed their sand-coloured clothing. They carried guns.

Nicha grabbed my arm, increasing his pace. He was a much faster runner than I was, and all I could do was watch where I put my feet so I didn't trip.

Telaris yelled behind us. He fell back, fighting a couple of krayfish who had grabbed him by the back of his clothes. Evi whirled around, mowing them down with the butt of the gun.

Now there were krayfish in front of us, too, levelling their weapons at us.

A man shouted, "Hands up! Drop all weapons."

We stopped, and Evi and Telaris caught up with us, but the men who had followed them caught up, too.

For a moment, everyone stared at each other. The only sound was that of heavy breathing.

The men were krayfish, dark, tall, muscular Africans. They wore sand-coloured clothing with flak jackets over the top. There were at least ten of them, all of them pointing guns at us. The leader motioned impatiently for us to drop our weapons.

We could do nothing, not even Evi with the large gun. He bent down and put it on the floor. I noticed him glancing at the weapons in the hands of the guards.

Telaris and Nicha did the same. And Thayu, with her useless gun where the charge had run out.

More men came out of doors and side passages. There was a lot of talk and signalling, but I had no idea what any of it meant.

We were frogmarched back in the direction of the pool and hall, then into a side passage. It led to a flight of stairs.

I take it you're in trouble, Asha said in my mind while I followed Evi up the stairs, looking at his broad back.

I met Thayu's eyes. She didn't have a feeder that allowed her to converse with her father—she needed her reader for that—but she looked at me as if she knew what was happening, and wanted me to say *yes,* and wanted me to ask him for help.

I asked instead, *Did you receive all the information we sent?*

I did.

I need that sent on to Amarru.

He chuckled. *You're treating this link as assistance in administration now?*

Amarru needs to have that material as soon as possible. Tell her that it's all right for her to send it to the news services.

I ignored his needling. I really did not want to get further involved. The temptation to tell him to bust these crooks' backsides off the planet was huge.

We arrived at a landing where a pair of guards stood in front of a closed door. One look at us and they opened this door, letting us into a brightly-lit foyer. It was an odd room: octagonal, with such a high ceiling that the walls were taller than a cross-section of the room. The floor was covered in diamond-shaped alternate white and red marble tiles with little gold-coloured metal strips by way of grouting. A couple of couches stood in a circle facing the centre of the room while a flame burned in a basin.

Telaris shuddered visibly. This setup reminded him of Indrahui? I'd never been there, and had assumed I never would; but I was wondering, with so many of *gamra's* security personnel of Indrahui descent, if maybe there was a lesson to be learned on that world.

More guards waited on either side of a set of heavy doors.

They insisted on searching us. Thayu protested, but that only prompted one of the guards to raise his gun at her.

"Let them, Thay'," I said. "They can't do much damage." Every piece of information of value that we found had been sent away already.

"I object to these men *touching* me."

"Try to keep calm."

One of the soldiers shouted something at me, probably to shut up.

They pushed Thayu face first against the wall, hands up. Coldi were a good deal more intimate with friends than most Earth people were used to, but they tended not to touch enemies except after they'd been killed. Thayu let the men go through her pockets, even though she stood stiff with nerves and could easily have wiped them all aside.

They found her readers and a good deal of discussion in their language ensued. They took the equipment off her, placing it on one of the couches.

They also searched Evi and Telaris and took all of their electronics as well.

Evi was eyeballing one of the guards' guns. It was a ground defence weapon similar to the one he'd lost, which the guard carried in a sling over his back.

Nicha was very quiet.

He's recently been on the wrong end of a good number of searches and questionings at gunpoint by Nations of Earth troops. I could see the haunted memories of those on his face.

They didn't find any weapons on any of my team. I wondered where Thayu would have hidden them, because I couldn't believe she truly had no gun at all.

The guards then hustled Evi, Telaris, Thayu and Nicha to the other side of the room. Thayu protested, but the guns were levelled at her again. They were made to sit on the couch furthest away from the pile of electronics that was theirs.

A couple of krayfish guards stationed themselves around the couch.

One of the others now opened the set of double doors and gestured for me to come. "Mr Kray will see you now."

As I went through, my eyes met Thayu's. She made a gesture. I wasn't fully versed in security's sign language, but I thought it meant that they would continue to fight when there was a chance.

Then I went through the doorway and she disappeared from sight. I entered a luxurious living room. The theme was getting a little monotonous. The couches were white, the floor tiles were white, the carpet was white.

Mr Kray sat on the couch, with one leg crossed over the other in a relaxed fashion. I knew he was not a young man, having been at the height of his power when Evi and Telaris were young, but was surprised to see just how old and wrinkled he looked close up.

He wore—of course—a white suit, and when he smiled at me, his teeth were also white. His eyes were dark. I had never seen an Indrahui with any eye colour other than moss green, so I assumed him to be wearing coloured lenses. Although his skin was very dark, I would never have mistaken him for an African, not even the ones from southern Sudan who were graceful, tall and as dark-skinned as Indrahui people.

He indicated for me to sit down on the white leather couch opposite him.

I sat, keeping my back straight.

"Mr Spencer," he said and then he laughed. "British scientist. Geologist, studying the rising of the water. I like that. It's one of the better excuses I've seen for people spying on me. It's not really necessary, you know, because I give out information freely. You want a tour of the site? Simply ask me."

His reply puzzled me. I couldn't believe that he didn't know who I was, but he acted like he didn't. Maybe he was trying to get me to walk into a trap. Maybe I was already in the trap.

Way back in the farmhouse outside Athens, we'd agreed that we'd stick to the visiting scientist story for as long as possible.

So I said, "I didn't come here to spy on you. I've come here to check up on projects we completed five years ago." I wanted to get out of this room. This man could tell me nothing that would incriminate him further. We already had all the juicy details.

But I played the scientist role and asked him about the site and his plans as if I knew nothing. He explained that he had *specially bred* crops that were adapted to the heat and that this would allow people to live in their homelands again. I might even have believed it. I asked him to show me those plants, but none of the pictures he showed me included close-ups of the plants. To my questions of what sort of crops they were, he was evasive, saying that his people would get back to me with all the details.

I wasn't going to argue with him, because that was the task of others. I was meant to collect information, nothing more. If he was going to play this game, I was ready to play it. He showed me maps of all the places where he'd planned to grow crops.

A *lot* of places, most of them in the region's most vulnerable countries.

"Do you have permission to use all that land?"

He grinned. "We own that land. Given to us by people or governments grateful for the opportunities we give them. That land is worthless to them."

Given to him under *pahemin*, except those innocent government people didn't understand the rules of *pahemin*, which were heavily skewed towards the buying and selling of debt. They might merely think that they could finally put useless land to a good purpose. Would anyone have explained to them that once the land was improved, it automatically became the property of the creditor? And he was going to grow crops there that were imported directly from Asto? Once Nations of Earth got onto this, all of northern Africa would belong to him, and he could do whatever he wanted with the people who depended on him for their food.

I had trouble keeping my innocent persona. "Have you started to cultivate the land? I should like to see the desert turned green."

"We started with a few fields around here last year. Most of the seeds are still in storage ready to go out for the summer. Most farmers grow winter crops. Now they can grow summer crops as well."

And I truly couldn't believe that he believed my scientist story. All through his talk about new settlements in the desert, I felt like screaming, *Do you even know that I am the guy you tried to kill?* but he showed no sign that he did. That sickening feeling of doubt returned: we had a hunch that the krayfish had shot the jet in Rotterdam, but we still didn't know that for sure.

He stuck to the promotional storyline. It sounded incredible.

Green deserts, industry, jobs for local people. I was itching to ask him how happy the workers in the gun factory were, when they'd last had a good meal or had seen their families.

A noise of a slap drifted in from the foyer. Someone screamed, the sound cut off suddenly.

Mr Kray stopped talking. His gaze darted to the door.

My heart was thudding. The voice hadn't sounded familiar. I hoped it meant that my team was getting on top of the guards.

Mr Kray turned around and opened the door to a cabinet at his back. "I appreciate that you're busy and I think it is time we got to business."

"I don't have any business here. We have the right to visit this area, and the research station still belongs to the university. I apologise if we accidentally crossed onto your land—"

"Yes, we have business." He turned back, and pointed a gun at my head. "I think I might finish what we failed to complete in Rotterdam. Did you really think that we didn't know who you are?"

Oh, shit.

Thayu.

Yes. We're busy.

Hurry up.

Mr Kray tensed the muscles in his arms. I could see the tendons move where the sheen of the skin changed. I groped for anything I could reach. The times I spent with Thayu training for this kind of situation kicked in.

My chair—

Was made from hardwood. I sort-of half-rolled, half-fell off the seat behind the backrest. He hadn't counted on that and the discharge went over my head—

Picked up the chair. Lifted it to protect myself.

Oof. It was heavy. This was where the slightly higher gravity at Ceren came in handy. I shuffled backwards in the direction of the door.

A second charge engulfed the chair. The whole thing disintegrated, leaving me with hands full of wood fragments and the cloth-covered seat and backrest, which fell on my toes.

I vaguely registered that the door opened—and a gun

discharged. Evi ran into the room, brandishing one of the giant guns.

"Hands up. Put the weapon down!"

I was surprised that Mr Kray put his gun down, slowly. As soon as he did so, I understood why. It was only a small weapon, and because he'd discharged twice in close succession, at the highest power, the *ready* light was still off.

Evi darted across the room and flicked the weapon off the desk. The *ready* light came on while it bounced a few times on the carpet.

"Careful, Evi," I said in a low voice.

Evi didn't react, so I picked the gun up, taking care to keep my hands away from the barrel, which would be hot.

Mr Kray said something in Indrahui. I didn't count myself an expert in the language, but I understood enough that he was trying to sell Evi something. *You'll get a share of my profits if you don't kill me* sort of thing.

Evi laughed, not in a nice way.

Telaris had also come into the room. His gun was smaller than Evi's, probably one of the guards' weapons. In the glimpse of the hallway that I could see through the open door, a body in sand-coloured clothing lay face down on the ground. I could hear Thayu's voice.

Evi spoke, choosing the words deliberately. "I speak to you in this tongue because I will not debase my language further by using it for you. I let you live long enough to tell you that from the day that you came into our village as Romi Tanaqan, and you murdered my sister, I have waited for this day. This is for my people, my friends and family you have killed. For my uncle, for my cousin, for my sister Remani and her unborn child."

His hand tightened around the discharge button—

I called, "No, Evi!—"

The charge released and zapped through the room—

Mr Kray's eyes widened—

And the charge hit him in the head—

And again—

There was a sickening wet squelch, and a spray of moisture. I fell back with the shockwave.

Evi fired again—

Another squelch and spray.

Someone yelled, "Evi! Stop!"

The chair behind the desk, with its occupant, had fallen backwards, but there was blood and unmentionable gore all over the pristine white wall behind the desk.

Charge guns, I'd been told, worked by cooking the target from the inside. Repeated strikes at the same spot led to explosions.

Even the carpet, under my hands, had acquired a dusting of the stuff, as had the front of my shirt, my hands, and, when I wiped my forearm across my face, it came away with pink smudges.

Telaris grabbed his brother's shoulder. "Come on, come on. He won't be going anywhere anymore."

"It is for Remani." Evi's hands trembled. There were flecks of blood on his clothes.

I climbed to my feet.

Blood and bits of unidentified tissue were everywhere. On the walls, on the carpet, on the desk. On the carpet on the other side of the desk lay a hand with only two fingers attached, torn from the rest of the body. I had to look away from the unidentifiable lump of cloth and blood and guts that had once been a body.

While people walked around in the room—I thought I heard Nicha come in—I gulped air, hearing the blood roar in my ears, trying to get my breathing and stomach under control.

Telaris managed to prise the gun out of Evi's hands. "Come, let's get out of here, if you want to tell the family this news."

Evi wiped his face. But his eyes were wet with tears. His hands trembled.

Thayu came into the door, holding another fearsome gun with plasma whirling in the chamber, ready for use.

"Shit." She looked at the carnage, wiping her lips with the back of her hand. A disturbed expression ghosted over her face. Then she recovered. "So we're going for the 'raze to the ground' approach? Suits me. Let's tell my father."

At the same time that I said, "No," Nicha said, "Yes."

We looked at each other.

"Please, Cory." He only used my name when he was angry or wanted to beat me against the wall for stupidity. "I understand what you're objections are. Really, I do. OK, go back to Nations of

Earth. Give your presentation. Ask them to send troops. They may do it, or they may not, because are they going to understand the risk? But even if they send troops as soon as possible, there is an election on and armed action never looks good for the sitting candidate, or any of the candidates. So they'll wait. Someone will get elected. Danziger or anyone else, it doesn't matter, because half their supporters won't have been re-elected and they will have to start the process from the ground up. By the time something is finally done, what do you think will have happened to the settlements here? How much will they have grown? How many locals will have gone under *pahemin?*"

I thought bleakly, *In how many areas will these crops have been sown?*

Nicha continued, "We have everything here at the moment. None of the other settlements have gotten very far off the ground. The only crops that have been planted are around here. Tanaqan may be dead, but others would be keen to take over. For one, the Zhori clan would be in an excellent position to do so. They take over leadership, return freedom to all those who have sold their life savings to Mr Kray. Then those people will be loyal to Zhori forever. We have a chance, a short window to deal this movement a fatal blow and save everyone a lot of trouble. If we have to wait for permission, we'll miss it."

We met each other's eyes.

He said nothing. I said nothing. I wanted to say things about *act of war* and *sovereignty* and other noble concepts that, at the end of the day, meant nothing if one of the parties fought dirty. Indrahui were experts at fighting dirty.

Thayu held out her hand. "Give me the feeder. I'll do it."

I looked at Telaris. He nodded.

My mind went through all the scenarios. The constant news feed of battles won and lost as there had been from Kazakhstan. The assembly in uproar over how this could have been allowed to happen yet again. The whole of northern Africa in Coldi or Indrahui hands. Diseases coming in with illegal crops, destroying much of Earth's plant species, becoming poisonous weeds.

I blew out a breath. "I'll do it."

And another breath. This could potentially be the most stupid thing I'd ever do.

Thayu and Nicha and Evi and Telaris looked on, solemnly. We still stood in the room with that scene of blood and gore that served as a reminder: if we didn't do anything now, then there might be a lot more of this.

I willed the feeder to contact Asha. *I request that this building and surrounding fields be destroyed.*

We can look after that. We'll see to it that the dealing will be sufficient. I hoped I only imagined the glee in his voice. He thought I was *amusing.*

We're going to clear this area as much as we can. This building project needs to be utterly destroyed. I need your word that it will affect just this single locality. Only the areas of crops, this underground settlement and especially the storage where they keep the seeds. I will evacuate everyone.

From our point of view, I am only interested in eliminating the elements that we judge to be a threat: anything that points to Coldi involvement, or any offworld involvement that could be misinterpreted as representative of Asto.

He informed me that the ship would be ready for action within an equivalent of about an hour and a half. When he signed off, I felt numb. The team was right: it was the best way to deal with the plans set in motion by Tanaqan, but this was going to be very, very risky.

"Let's get the hell out of here."

27

W E LEFT THE SICKENING scene in the office for an equally sickening scene in the foyer. There was blood everywhere: in big dark puddles around the motionless bodies of guards, soaked into their uniforms, sprayed on the floor, and spread around as boot-shaped footprints.

"They attacked us with machetes," Nicha said by way of explanation, or apology, I didn't know which. He used the Isla word.

They *were* machetes, big, ugly blades that looked a lot blunter than they probably were, seeing the amount of damage my team had been able to do with them.

I wanted to ask, *Did you really have to make such a mess?* But they probably did, because I knew they did not attack easily, and I had never known Nicha to have killed anyone before he became my *zhayma*.

That was because we were never in situations of danger.

"Did any of you get injured?" I had to look away. My stomach still felt queasy. I found it comforting that at least Nicha also looked a bit pale. The unemotional expressions of Thayu, Evi and Telaris disturbed me.

"We fight Indrahui-style," Evi said, his voice dark.

And Indrahui-style fighting was dirty, rough and relentless. It was about breaking as many standards of common decency as possible when your enemy least expected it so that you could defeat a soft enemy in all sorts of sickening ways. I wouldn't have judged the krayfish soft, but Evi had judged differently. He was probably right. This was a rough place, but not half as rough as Indrahui.

Carrying that fearsome gun, with his sleeves rolled up, his clothes dusty and flecked with gore, he looked like the dirty fighter who had seen horrible deaths from a very young age. Not many places on Earth could compete with that.

I didn't know how many rules of security personnel protocol the two of them had broken, but someone was going to have to sit Evi, and Telaris to a lesser extent, down and give them a stern talk. That someone was probably going to have to be me.

Thayu took off across the foyer and back down the stairwell where we had come up. The guard at the bottom of the stairs didn't get to finish his question before he, too, was on the ground, courtesy of Thayu's excellent aim. She divested him of his weapons.

We ran through the passage. A lot of people were in the main thoroughfare. Most of them were guests carrying suitcases going in the direction of the car park.

A couple of krayfish guards tried to stop them, but they were too few, and they were arguing amongst themselves. The guests they had stopped, two tribal elders in long robes, were arguing with them in turn. I heard Mr Kray's name mentioned a few times.

"Mr Kray is dead!" I shouted at them. "There is . . . a counter-strike on this settlement about to happen. Help everyone get out, if you intend on staying alive."

People stopped and turned to me. Several faces displayed alarmed expressions. They were civilised, clean people, wearing suits or tribal wear, or dresses and pearl necklaces. We looked like we'd come from the abattoir. The guards glanced at each other, also alarmed.

The leader came towards us, while his mates held their hands on their guns.

The man lifted his chin in an attempt at a tough stance, but his dark eyes with blood-stained whites went from me to Thayu, to Nicha's sleeve which had a big blood stain, to Evi with the gun and back to me. "Eh, what's going on?"

"Tell everyone that they have an hour and a half," —a bit less by now— "to get out of here."

"Eh, man, it's not your job to tell people what to do."

"I'm telling you anyway, because we know what is about to happen. Everyone needs to leave this place now. Go outside, as far away as you can get."

A good number of people had gathered around us.

The krayfish were all surrounded, and kept looking over their shoulders, their hands on their weapons. One krayfish man at the back of the group was motioning people away from him with his gun. The guests stumbled back, but still more people were coming from the accommodation wing and pool hall and everyone was bunching up with nowhere to go. Panic could break out any moment, with disastrous results.

"Mista, you go over there with the others," the krayfish leader told us.

Evi and Telaris pushed in front of me. "You listen to the delegate," Telaris said. His clipped accent gave his words more punch. "You let people out, in the trucks. You don't want to die, no?"

I glanced at the time. One hour and fifteen minutes now. "We don't have time for this. Can you lift me up?" The latter to Evi and Telaris.

They looped their arms together and helped me climb to Telaris' shoulders.

Looking out over the people, I raised my voice. "Listen everyone. Be quiet. Listen to me."

They did, sinking into an expectant silence. Most of the people close to me were guests. Some further krayfish stood at the place where the corridor opened into the pool hall.

"We have one hour and twelve minutes before this whole bunker blows up. We need to get out now."

"Who are you?" a man asked. He was dressed in a business suit that would soon be far too hot and would get extremely dusty outside.

"I didn't see you at dinner last night," another man said, his voice doubtful.

"I'm not a guest of Mr Kray's, and how I got here is irrelevant. Mr Kray is not who you thought he is, or who he was rather, because he won't, ever, be making any more grand and illegal plans."

Talk rose again, voices alarmed.

"You received my message about Mr Kray's activities," I continued, "My name is Cory Wilson. I am a representative of *gamra* and I've been here because 'Mr Kray' is one of *gamra's* most wanted men. I have evidence for criminal activities, including slavery, smuggling and illegal production of arms—"

"That is just a rumour about the arms smuggling."

"It's true. He doesn't import, but he exports these guns. The factory is right here in this complex. I could show it to you, and there is much more I could say, but we really, really—" I checked the time, which was going much too fast for my liking. "We really need to get out of here. We're expecting action from outside and we need to clear this area before then. Urgently."

Everyone started shouting. Telaris set me down. "For your safety, delegate."

A man nearby yelled, "I've invested all this money. I want it back!"

"Yes, I agree." Another voice yelled.

And someone else. "Me, too."

"Come." Thayu pulled my arm.

"But these people . . ."

"I don't care if they don't want to listen. You can't save those who do not want to be saved. You told them. It's their problem if they don't want to listen. Now let's go. Whoever wants to follow can do so."

I didn't agree with her. Telling them was one thing, but making them comprehend was another. Was there any way of saying, *Look, there is a whopping great big alien ship out there that's going to fire at this place, and if you stay here, you might well be vaporised along with the rest of this building,* without actually saying that?

Thayu was already yelling, "Let us through!" in Coldi. Not that anyone would understand her. I thought the fact that she was waving a gun was more effective.

She led the way through the crowded corridor. Most people were now trying to follow us, but there was still a lot of confusion, a lot of shouting, all of it in languages I didn't understand.

"Hey, mister." A man pulled my sleeve. He was one of the tribe elders. "Mister, what's going on? They say Mr Kray, he is dead."

"Come with us," I said.

I'd just checked the time again. We'd lost another ten precious minutes. We seriously needed to hurry, because when that thing in orbit went off, I didn't merely want to be out of the building, I wanted to be as far out of the area as possible.

The old man protested. "No, mister. It's hot out there. You have no trucks, you die."

"You will die if you stay here."

We had managed to come within about ten metres of that door. I had no idea if the car park would hold enough vehicles to take us all out, or if they needed keys we didn't have, or if the vehicles could get out without security codes or cards.

Then a couple of men ran out of the parking area into the corridor. They shouted. They had guns. People at the front screamed and tried to run the other way. Some people fell, some were pushed into the wall.

We were swept up with the sheer mass of bodies. Nicha and Thayu positioned themselves on either side of me.

A bang went off that made my ears ring in that confined space. People screamed, pushing even harder away from the entrance. Others had dropped to the ground, covering their heads with their arms.

In a glimpse between two people, I saw a couple of krayfish guards, their backs to the door, guns raised. As I watched, another shot into the crowd.

Next to me, Nicha was looping his hands together. Thayu put one foot in them. As she hoisted herself up, she took the big gun from Evi.

I realised what she was going to do.

"No, Thay'!" She would be a target.

Nicha lifted her. Thayu rose over the crowd, raised the gun, pushed the release. A white flash went off, followed by another one, and another one.

A shot rang out. Thayu fell. She crashed into me and I fell sideways into the man next to me, and we all tumbled to the ground.

I yelled out, "Thayu!" My head was spinning. I'd lost her. "Thayu! Are you all right?"

A voice sounded behind me. "Calm down, I'm fine." She was helping up the man who had fallen down with us.

"That looked to me like you were hit. I told you—"

"Shh. Seriously. Calm down. This is my job. I'm not stupid enough to get hit."

Telaris had picked up the gun Thayu had dropped. He ran between the people, all of whom were by now cowering on the ground with their arms over their heads. He reached the door, raised the gun and fired three shots. Then he let the gun sink. He nodded. "It's safe now."

"I'm sorry," I said to the man who had taken most of our weight. He was wiping dust off his trousers.

People were already streaming out, sidestepping the bodies of the guards. Women streaming past raised their scarves over their noses.

We followed the stream of people through the door into a dark, low-ceilinged area, where sparse emergency lights cast ghostly light over rows of vehicles.

A couple of men in business suits were trying to break into the closest truck by climbing on the doorstep and pulling the handle as hard as they could. Another was trying to break the glass by bashing a travel bag into it.

"Excuse me." Nicha pushed between them, climbed up on the step, put his reader against the lock, and opened the door. He climbed in, slid back out, opened the back panel which held the engine, and did something inside. The truck's lights went on. He moved to the next vehicle, and the next one.

People climbed into the vehicle, into the back, or the cargo holds or trays. A lot of guests were still streaming out of the door. I hoped there were enough trucks. With all this messing about, we had lost another twenty minutes.

Thayu had gone to the car park's entrance and forced open the door. Bright midday light came in through the opening.

The first truck had been waiting and it went up the ramp into the sunlight.

Forty-five minutes, and so many people still to get out.

Maybe I should ask Asha to hold off.

Wait—why was it so quiet in my head?

I raked my hand through my hair.

"The feeder . . ." I couldn't feel it in the place where it was supposed to be. It must have fallen out, but I couldn't see it anywhere.

28

———

I RAN AFTER THAYU, who was trying to cram more passengers into a mini bus that Nicha managed to start. She was yelling, waving her hands. "Sit on the floor. No, you sit on his lap! Now you, get in." She was yelling in Coldi, but the people manage to get the gist of it anyway.

Nicha was working on one of the two remaining vehicles in the huge underground parking space. He had opened the hood and was using his reader to override the locking software. This sort of thing was handy, but it scared me at times. I preferred not to think about just how much of Earth's technology was rigged with little Coldi bugs.

It was a truck with a container on the back. Several people were already in the cabin, and a couple of men had opened the back door to the container. It was full of boxes and they were lifting these onto the ground so that people could get in. About twenty people were still waiting.

"Thay', hang on!" I ran up to her.

"What?" Thayu turned around.

"Are you in immediate contact with your father?"

"Only through the exchange."

And that meant you had to book a slot in advance. Damn it.

"Is there a problem?"

"I lost my feeder in the corridor back there. I have no idea where it went."

Her eyes widened. "Shit." And then again, "Shit."

"Can you try to contact him? Tell them that it's urgent."

"I'll try." She took out her reader. "I don't know if we'll be given anything like the priority we'd need."

The minibus drove past, groaning under the weight of passengers, throwing up a cloud of dust. My teeth were gritty with dust, my arms and face were covered in a sheen of sweat and goodness knew what else.

I went and helped the men unload the container, throwing the boxes on the ground. Some split open, spilling their contents over the concrete: little packets with plastic clips, bottles, plastic petri dishes. What the hell was all that for?

We hoisted up a number of passengers, mostly older men and women. I jumped out, a few younger men climbed in and the truck took off.

Now it was just us.

The last vehicle was a small truck with a cargo tray. It had once been red, but was now more pink than red. Judging by its position, it hadn't been used much for quite a while.

Nicha was at the front, pulling at various leads inside the engine.

Thayu called at him, "Hurry up!"

"I'm not sure how this one works!" he yelled back. "I can't find the computer."

I stared at the dusty inside of the engine. A distant memory came to me. When I was a young boy growing up in New Zealand on the Bay of Islands, an old man named Pete would drive up and down the beach each morning, dragging a rake to collect large items of plastic rubbish that had washed up overnight. He was a bit of an odd character. He didn't need to do this, and he wasn't paid for it, but he did it anyway.

He had an old, old tractor that sounded like a chainsaw and blew clouds of black smoke. Us kids used to run after it—it wasn't very fast—and sometimes he would let us drive it. He said it had belonged to his grandfather, and not until later had I realised that I'd been allowed to touch and learn to operate a precious piece of history that, anywhere else in the world, would have been displayed in a museum with big *Do Not Touch* signs all over it.

It had . . .

I opened the door and climbed into the cabin. Yes. I was right. There was a key. The krayfish had even left it in the car.

I pushed myself behind the wheel. "Nich!" I yelled through the window. He straightened and looked at me, mouthing, *what?*

I turned the key. The engine made a strangled sort of noise before falling quiet again. Nicha jumped back. "Whoa!"

Now. How did this work again?

Once again, I was a little boy, and I felt Pete's hands on mine. Make sure you have your foot on the brakes. Turn the key. Press the accelerator.

The engine started with an incredible racket. I balled my fist. "Get in!"

Nicha climbed into the cabin, followed by his sister, and Evi and Telaris went into the tray at the back.

I steered the truck up the driveway. It was making a lot of noise and smoke, and didn't go very fast. Out into the brightness of the day. I followed the tracks made by the other vehicles.

The truck crawled up a little hill. We were to the side of the underground settlement. To the right, the land sloped down to the water. Mr Kray's mansion lay halfway down. To the left was the building site, with sheds, stacks of materials and concrete foundations in trenches. Several concrete pillars had been built ready for the first floor to go on.

I looked at the clock. We had a mere fifteen minutes left and seriously needed to get out of here much faster than this. The road led past the length of the site.

The truck ploughed down the hill. It didn't have any trouble with the sand at the bottom, but it was so, so slow, no matter how hard I pressed the accelerator, it just seemed to make more noise.

I remembered something else. Pete had said, "This setting here is for driving on the beach. That one there, you don't touch. It's for when I go home on the road."

It had been a sliding stick set in the dashboard. This truck didn't have anything that looked like that.

"What are you looking for?" Nicha asked.

"There has to be some sort of gear control thing, a handle or lever to make it go faster."

Nicha bent and looked in places where I couldn't because I had to see where we were going.

"Did you know this thing was built in 2031?"

"Sheesh." It was probably even older than Pete's truck.

"What about this?" He moved one of the handles behind the steering wheel.

Nothing happened.

And another one. The windscreen wipers came on, spreading dust over the window.

"Hey! I'm supposed to see where we're going."

Thirteen minutes.

"And this one?"

I had no idea what he did, but we stopped dead. I pressed the accelerator, but the engine only made a lot of noise.

"Come on, Nich'. Put it back where it was."

He did something else.

The truck jumped forward.

"Whoa!" I took my foot off. Then slowly pushed down again.

The truck gathered speed. Come on, come on. We tore past the side of the building site, up another hill, down the hill and following the tracks that led away. I looked at Thayu's screen over her shoulder. The little dot moved away from the site.

Ten minutes.

Over bumpy and rocky ground, through a sand drift, up another hill.

Seven minutes.

Over another hill, and there we found the other trucks, in the company of a whole bunch of people on foot, all of them walking down the road. Some of Mr Kray's distinguished guests had exchanged their positions in the back of the trucks with women and old men, and weak and injured people. The gun factory workers.

There were a lot of people on foot. They were going too slow.

Evi yelled out the window. "Hurry up, hurry up!"

Five minutes.

We were not going to make it any further. I just had to hope it was far enough. I drove the truck off to the side and past the vehicle in front. I called out the window, "Stop, stop!"

The driver did.

"Get into the truck everyone. Shut the door!"

They didn't understand.

Four minutes.

Evi and Telaris had jumped out the back. They were physically lifting people up so that they could get into the back of the truck. It was the one with the container, and more boxes were thrown into the sand.

Three minutes.

Nicha found a folded-up tent cloth. He went out and helped people into the tray of our truck and covered them with the cloth.

Two minutes.

We tied the ropes of the cloth onto the tray. We shut the back door to the container. We pushed two very skinny kids onto the mini bus. Shut the door to that, too.

One minute.

We ran back to our truck. Scrambled in. Shut the door. Nicha had wound up the windows and it was hot in the cabin.

Thirty seconds.

I wiped sweat from my forehead. The smell of Coldi sweat was overwhelming. "We can open the window on the side away from the blast."

"There will be lots of dust."

Fifteen seconds.

"We'll die in here if we leave it shut."

Thayu opened the window. A head poked out of the back door of the truck.

Nine seconds.

I waved at the boy to go back inside.

29

He waved back to me.

Four . . . three . . . two . . . one . . .

I looked over my shoulder out the little window in the back of the cabin. Couldn't see anything except desert, blue sky and the khaki cloth. The little boy had ventured onto the bottom step of the ladder into the back of the truck.

Then: a blight flash.

The boy yelled out.

The blinding white light bloomed out over the sky. Grew stronger. Came down like a giant bolt of lightning.

I ducked.

A loud crack split the air, like thunder hitting really close. Thayu tensed against me.

A moment later, the shock wave hit. The truck wobbled. For a moment I feared it might tip over, but it landed back on its wheels. Clouds of dust rolled over us, reducing visibility to zero. Dust rained on the windscreen and slid down the glass to come to rest on the windscreen wipers. Thayu pushed the window shut again.

I didn't pay attention to how long we sat there, but gradually the dust settled, the wind stopped and visibility increased a bit. The truck next to us was fine, but the minibus had tipped over.

I opened the door, and stepped into knee-deep fine sand.

It was eerily silent.

People were stirring in the tray at the back.

Evi had already jumped off and was shaking sand out of his hair. He checked the gun, and put it back in the bracket at his belt. He went to help the people get out of the minibus.

Some people had started digging sand away from the wheels.

Telaris shook his head. "I don't think any of us are going anywhere with this sand. We'll need rescuing, I think."

Not much later, a whole bunch of messages arrived on my reader.

Amarru. *What just happened? I'm getting questions about an explosion where you are.*

It was a logged Exchange call, and I pressed reply. I was rewarded with a squeak in my ear. Ouch.

"What's going on over there?" Amarru asked. "What did you just do?"

"I got rid of some idiots." I was filthy, tired—how long since we'd last slept?—and not in the mood for apologies. "Danziger wanted Robert Kray gone. He's gone. The whole of his project, his illegal gun factory, his seed bank of illegally imported plants from Asto is gone, too. The reason why a lot of people in this region were reduced to slaves and were bound to *pahemin* style debts is gone. He's GONE, Amarru. No second Kazakhstan."

I didn't know Amarru as someone who was easily lost for words, but it took her a while to reply. "I thought that you would want to avoid this sort of action at all cost."

"Not *all* cost. Sometimes, the cost of doing nothing is higher than that of decisive action."

"Sometimes you scare the fuck out of me, Cory. You've been studying way too many proverbs. You're more Coldi than most of us. I hope to hell that nothing worse comes from this."

"It won't." I was a lot less sure about that than I sounded.

30

I ASKED AMARRU to get some people to come and rescue us as soon as possible. "There are hundreds of people here, many are weak, malnourished and ill, and we have no water."

She said she'd organise it. She sounded timid and subdued. I didn't know why, but I had the feeling that *something* had just changed in my relationship with her.

I had barely signed off when my reader lit up with another logged Exchange call.

Asha.

"I'm surprised," he said. "I didn't expect you to go through with this. I had expected to hear from you to call it off at the last moment."

I was going to, but there were fights and I lost the feeder. "Sometimes decisive action is needed."

"I'm glad you're smart enough to see that. I take it Romi Tanaqan is dead?"

"Very much so." I had almost forgotten about the mess in Mr Kray's office, but it would no doubt come to haunt me when I couldn't sleep at night. "We found no other Indrahui on site. No Zhori either. He appears to have been targeting his actions purely to the disadvantaged natives of this region, getting them to be dependent on him."

"Good. Then the dealing has been sufficient."

"I can't guarantee that the Zhori clan had nothing to do with it, nor that they won't try to continue the projects. I will raise the issue with Nations of Earth." Likely, Lucius Brown would lose his job, and maybe even Danziger, although there was no evidence that the photo I'd seen of Lucius Brown, Robert Kray and Danziger at a dinner was anything more than an opportunistic snap. It *would* create problems for Danziger, I was sure of that. "Thank you for your assistance, but at this point in time, we don't need it anymore. In fact, I think the situation would be helped if, when people went looking for your ship, they didn't find it."

He chuckled. "Don't worry, we're getting ready to leave."

Nicha laughed at me after I'd signed off. We were sitting in the sand on the shady side of the truck. "Did I hear that right? Did you just tell my father to bugger off?"

"I think I might have. I don't care if it upsets him. I'm not part of Coldi society."

"No." Nicha shook his head. He didn't sound convinced.

————

The afternoon dragged on. None of us were prepared for the desert. Some men started digging out the trucks, but I had to tell them to stop, because we had no water, and they'd only wear themselves out.

We sat in the lengthening shadow of the truck, leaning with our backs against the side in the sand that came up to the bottom of the door.

Thayu had been transfixed on her reader for a while.

"What are you looking at?"

She showed me the screen, and it was full of a giant block of random characters: capital letters, normal letters, numbers, other signs like currency signs, plus and minus, hyphens, underscores, quote marks, everything.

"What is it?"

"We found a whole bunch of these when we got the list of attendants and I'd been trying to figure out what it means. Then I noticed that the number of different characters used coincides with the number of characters in the Coldi alphabet. The top line of this block says, *We have dispatched your shipment. Payment will be due eight days from now. . . .* That's as far as I got."

"Who is it addressed to and who is it from?"

"To Mr Kray, from Deisha Zhori. There are a lot of these. Most are fairly short, but it's still going to take me a while to decipher them."

I stared at her. Here was our Zhori connection. They'd stepped back from Mr Kray's project so as not to receive the blame, but they were waiting in the shadows.

Well, they'd have to wait a lot longer now, hopefully forever, if I had anything to do with it.

It was late in the afternoon and we were dozing in the shade when we became aware of a droning noise in the distance.

"There," Thayu said, pointing at the horizon.

I saw them, too: gyrocopters, at least ten of them—heavy cargo machines coming for us at a high speed. Many of the local people got up and climbed back into the cabins or crawled underneath the vehicles.

A young man yelled at us, "You be careful, mista. They're PanAf soldiers. Never know what they will do."

Well, PanAf certainly had an image problem in this region, perhaps not unjustified.

As the gyrocopters came closer, Evi unclipped his gun and held it on his lap, just in case. The area of desert where the vehicles were stranded lay deserted, but millions of footprints in the sand gave away the presence of people.

The gyrocopters flew in a circle around the area, and then the first one came down on a patch of flat ground to our left.

The side doors of the cargo area were open, despite the dust thrown up by the blades.

While the engine shut down with a whine and the blades stopped rotating, a shrill voice yelled, "Mister, mister! In here, mister!"

I laughed. "It's Henri!"

I had no idea how he had made it so far out of the factory—I could only guess that he'd been able to take his plane to safety and had warned other people. I was glad. I'd feared that he'd be in serious trouble.

Within minutes, all twelve gyrocopters were on the ground. Soldiers in desert grey uniforms jumped out and unloaded crates that contained bottles of clear water. One soldier carried a crate to where the trucks stood. Within moment, she was swamped with people, mostly little boys, begging for some of the precious fluid.

Soldiers handed out bottles and food packs. Having come in the truck, we were not that desperate, so we waited.

Thayu tried to get into the news services, but our link to the Exchange had already been broken. Her father's ship must have left.

The PanAf soldiers rounded up everyone in need of transport and escorted groups of people to the vehicles. We went in the second-last one, treated no differently from all the other people.

In the gathering dusk, they took us to the nearest town, a small settlement that looked surprisingly modern from the air. The streets were lit, a giant solar power plant lay just outside the town and the buildings looked quite modern.

We emerged from sitting on the hard ground in the cargo hold of the gyrocopter into the mayhem of hundreds of people who had streamed onto the airfield. There was screaming and crying, and people falling into each other's arms. A group of young men had set up huge drums and many people were dancing.

There was no Exchange connectivity of course, but while we walked through the town in search of somewhere to stay, Thayu managed to get onto World Newspoint. Their top headline said, *Calls for Brown's Resignation Following Allegations of Corruption.* The article began,

Allegations have surfaced that PanAf president Lucius Brown may have had a hand in the smuggling of weapons that was recently discovered in Djibouti . . .

Hmm. It looked like Asha had done as I asked, and sent the material on to the news services. A message boy indeed.

————

We found a hotel in the middle of town. It was called "The Lucky Traveller", but that appeared to be the misnomer of the decade, since it lay right on the town's main square where most of the festivities took place.

The rooms were of a better standard than Tamu's hotel in Djibouti, but it was still too hot inside.

A man and his daughter operated a café in a small yard at the front of the hotel.

Thayu, Nicha and I sat in the dark while the people in the town celebrated the return of their fathers and sons. They cheered and sang and played music in the streets, hanging out of windows and from the backs and on the roofs of trucks. Bonfires cast an orange glow over the façade of the hotel.

"It's as if they won the cricket world cup," I said, but Thayu, who sat next to me, had yet to comprehend the concept of "cricket". The evening was warm, and after a quick shower and a change of clothes—that we needed to buy because all our stuff had been left at the research station and was probably fried—we felt much better.

"Delegate."

I turned around and there were Evi and Telaris. They wore dark clothing, but not their black security gear. There was a kind of heavy finality about their appearance that made me certain that they had decided to go back to Indrahui and were coming to hand in their resignation.

I gestured. "Sit down."

They did, perched at the very edge of their seats. A group of youths walked past laughing and talking.

"*Mashara* apologises," Evi began when they had passed.

"Apologies are not necessary. We seem to have achieved what we planned. Whatever went on that was slightly outside regulations will be forgotten." Or so I hoped. I hadn't yet seen mention of the strike on any of the news services, but I was sure it was only a temporary reprieve.

It was silent for a while, during which I could almost see the thoughts whirl behind his eyes.

Then he said, "Yes, apologies are necessary. It is *mashara's* task to protect the delegate. It seems I lost sight of that. I also exposed the delegate to unpleasant experiences. I apologise for that."

"I'm sure I'm tougher than that." I did suspect that the repercussions of seeing someone explode in front of my eyes would hit me later

"It was *mashara's* task to protect the delegate from things like this. The delegate was threatened. *Mashara* should have foreseen this."

"And how would you have done this? They had you restrained."

He shook his head. "There is no excuse. There is only one way forward from this."

"Don't you even think about it." I met his moss green eyes, and then Telaris'. "You're worth much more to me than that. You will go nowhere."

Evi looked down. "The delegate is much too kind."

I knew that putting their own interest ahead of their jobs was an unforgivable offence for security personnel.

"Just . . ." I hesitated. If they were Earth people, I would tell them to get counselling. I shrugged, and sighed. "Promise me never to do this again. I know and understand why this was important to you, but let's forget about it, and concentrate on the future."

Evi nodded. Telaris put his hand on his brother's shoulder. He nodded, too. "It won't happen again. Thank you, Delegate."

31

W E TRAVELLED TO Athens on a regular commercial suborbital flight the next day.

At the Exchange, we were told that Amarru was in damage control and had no time to see us. The press might not yet have understood what had happened—they still spoke of an explosion of an illegal weapons factory—but the military sure hadn't been fooled that way.

Amarru managed to free her schedule for half an hour to see me. She sat at her desk, looking extremely tired.

She said nothing while I took the seat opposite her.

"Two days until the elections," she began, and then she pushed her reader across the desk to me. On the screen was a giant headline: *Brown Resigns.*

I shrugged. "He allowed this to happen. He brought the Zhori to Africa. He allowed Tanaqan to settle. He even encouraged him and gave him grants. He should resign."

"It's far to close to Danziger. Africa is his support base. He's a friend of Brown's." She hit the corner of the screen and another article came up. *Connections Between Danziger and Brown likely.*

I nodded. "Dekker expected me to be able to fix it quietly, or maybe he expected me to stay away for much longer."

"I guess he *didn't* expect you to allow a strike from orbit."

"He probably didn't."

"Danziger wants to see you about it. He's been under a lot of pressure from the military. He didn't know anything about Brown's dealings. I believe him."

"I'm not saying that I don't believe him, but what else was I supposed to do? Let another Kazakhstan happen?"

"He'll close the Exchange down over this."

"If he wins. If he really wants to have a debate about how he allowed PanAf to support the Zhori, Tanaqan and goodness knows what other kinds of criminals. Because no one said anything, all in the name of maintaining support for Danziger's campaign. I don't think he'd survive that debate."

Amarru nodded, her expression grave. "I hope you're right."

———

The next day, I booked an expensive hoverjet trip to take me to Rotterdam and back in one day. I really did not want to stay any longer than necessary, and this close to the elections, I presumed Danziger had little time.

On the trip I read that he made some lame apologies that he didn't know what Lucius Brown was up to. One insignificant line in the article mentioned that he'd sacked his chief aide Simon Dekker.

He assured the news services that he would see to it that Lucius Brown was replaced with someone else as soon as possible.

I saw Danziger in his office while seated at the desk where Sirkonen had been shot.

He did not look healthy. His hair had gone completely white, lines on his face had deepened and his skin looked blotched.

He greeted me with a sharp, "Mr Wilson."

"You wanted to see me, Mr President?"

"With great reluctance."

Reluctance or not, I sat down anyway. As usual, Thayu and Nicha had remained outside.

He was playing with a document on his reader and let me wait for a while before he started, "It says EXO-NZ in your file. I could erase that with one press of a button. Certainly you have committed enough offences in the past few days to justify my doing that." His finger hovered over the keyboard.

"Maybe." My heart jumped. How much was I attached to that designation? New Zealand was no longer my home, but it would always be part of me. "I did solve the problem Dekker asked me to solve. He let me believe that he was acting with your knowledge."

Danziger chose to ignore that last statement. "You barged into a volatile part of Earth under an assumed name, you took offworlders, you implicated key government officials of virtually all Saharan countries in treachery and you sanctioned a hostile, peacetime attack on our soil from orbit by an alien army."

"It was the quickest way to destroy all the sites and to decontaminate the illegal crops. And to get rid of *gamra's* most wanted criminal. I solved the problem. Not just your problem, but *gamra's* problem, and a problem that would have led to something far worse than Kazakhstan. I solved the problem."

He sighed. Let his finger rest. "That, you did."

"They're not going to be back for long time. If any are still alive, the hardline krayfish may decide to keep going, but if you keep close tabs on them, they will never rebuild to the same strength."

"You are a rude, cocky bastard, but much as I hate to admit it, you're right." He heaved a sigh. "I've instructed my secretary to transfer payment to your account."

"Thank you."

"Don't expect any more jobs from this office. You can be a persona non grata without losing your designation."

"I understand."

"No, I don't think you do. You think you're above the law."

"What law would that be? Earth law that doesn't apply to offworlders or *gamra* law that Earth doesn't recognise?"

He glared at me, his tired eyes glowering. "Fuck off."

"With pleasure." I inclined my head, moving towards the door. "Good luck in the elections, Mr Acting President."

He glared at me.

I fled the room, meeting Thayu and Nicha in the corridor. We walked out of the building as fast as we could without running.

When we were safely out of the building and away from the guards, I said, "Did you hear what he said?"

"Yes." Nicha started laughing.

And I started laughing, too, because it seemed the best response to the situation. We'd been so goddamn lucky that the military had wanted to keep the strike quiet and nothing worse had come from this situation. I'd like to think that I could tell Thayu's father never to interfere in Earth matters again, but I knew I'd be speaking to a wall, because that was not how Coldi solved problems. Sovereignty be damned, if there was a problem, they solved it, no questions asked.

————

I voted in Athens the next day, just before returning to Barresh. Of course, we didn't vote for candidates directly, but we voted for candidates who would support one or the other for the presidency. I voted in the EXO section, where none of the available candidates supported Danziger. Once the full assembly was voted in, they elected a new president. Of course I was no longer on Earth when that happened.

I was sitting in my office in Barresh when I got a message from Melissa that consisted of just two words: "Margarethe Ollund".

So the tradition to elect a president of Scandinavian descent continued. More importantly, she was friendly to our cause. Even more importantly, she used to be a regular guest at my family home in Arcadia on Taurus when I was a teenager. If anyone could manoeuvre Earth into joining *gamra*, she could.

————

Thank you for reading The Sahara Conspiracy. The story is not finished here. In Ambassador 2: Raising Hell, the Exchange network goes down for a mysterious reason at an inopportune time. Cory goes on a hair-raising mission to help Ezhya.

Buy Ambassador 2: Raising Hell direct from the author.

ABOUT THE AUTHOR

Patty Jansen lives in Sydney, Australia, where she spends most of her time writing Science Fiction and Fantasy.

Her story *This Peaceful State of War* placed first in the second quarter of the Writers of the Future contest and was published in their 27th anthology. She has also sold fiction to genre magazines such as Analog Science Fiction and Fact, Redstone SF and Aurealis.

Patty has written over twenty novels in both Science Fiction and Fantasy, including the *Icefire Trilogy* and the *Ambassador* series.

pattyjansen.com

BOOKS BY PATTY JANSEN

For a complete list of books, scan the image below with your phone.